THE OTHER PLACE

The Other Place Series, Book 2

By Elizabeth Roderick

THE OTHER PLACE

Limitless Publishing, LLC
Kailua, HI 96734
www.limitlesspublishing.com

Formatting: Limitless Publishing

ISBN-13: 978-1-68058-703-6
ISBN-10: 1-68058-703-X

Dedication

For Phoenix

Chapter 1

Mom says I'm a screwed-up boy. I sleep backwards, from morning to afternoon, and talk backwards, always saying the wrong things. She tries to rearrange me, but I guess I'm like one of those rooms that's shaped wrong. The furniture never looks right, no matter which way you put it.

My clock says it's one thirty in the afternoon when I get out of bed, and my room is hot like an oven from the sun coming through the windows. I choose my light blue shirt, because it reminds me of ice. I feel cooler as I put it on, along with the pants and underwear that go with it.

I go out into the kitchen to look for my breakfast. Mom is there at the table, the glow from her laptop showing every mark in her tired face. She doesn't look at me as I head to the cupboards.

Before I got kicked out of school, I had a good teacher in health class. She told me how important proper nutrition is, especially for young men like me who are growing up as big and tall as cartoon

1

monsters. That's why I pass over the macaroni and ramen: that stuff's all sawdust and mealworms, probably.

Way in the back I find some oatmeal behind a package of food bank beans old enough to be a family heirloom. I take it out and read the nutrition information.

I get a visual in my head which makes me burst out in giggles as I pour oatmeal into a pot.

Mom quickly looks at me, then back to the screen. "What are *you* laughing at?"

I try to wrestle my giggles into order so I can talk. "I was just imagining my cells as little construction workers, with tiny hard hats on. They're stacking bricks made of amino acids and sugars in order to make me bigger. Then this girl cell swishes by in a mini skirt and they're all like, 'Hey, baby, nice nucleus!'"

My laugh snorts out my nose.

Mom rolls her eyes. "Act your age, Justin."

I stop my giggles and get very serious as I take the milk from the fridge. I speak in my Serious Adult voice. "Why are you on your computer so much, Mom?"

Her frown lines deepen, walls that imprison her mouth and keep it from ever smiling. "None of your business."

My hand stops before I can pour the milk in the pot, and my fingers clench tight around the jug handle. "What do you mean, none of my business? Some of your none-of-my-business business is really very much my business in a big way. Remember the bully llamas?"

2

"Justin—"

"Those llamas were an uncomfortable situation," I say, trying to catch my breath, "with the spitting and the long-necked staring contests. I didn't know if I'd survive it at all. You shouldn't have bought them. Craigslist llamas are definitely a bad investment."

"Justin!" Mom barks, and I close my eyes. I build a little bubble and push the angry thoughts on the other side of it. Mom's actions are a test, and I won't fail it by becoming angry.

I open my eyes again and take a deep breath. Mom stares at me tight-lipped a moment longer, then looks back at her computer.

I think about going into my bedroom to draw, since drawing usually calms the angry vibrations. But then I look out the kitchen window and see Miller and Cris slide by on their lowrider bikes. Their knees bend above their elbows as they pedal, and the bills of their hats are a little sideways.

I put the milk back in the fridge. I leave the oatmeal on the counter and grab a slice of bread from the box, instead. "I'm going to the park, Mom."

"Wear sunscreen," she says.

I go out, chewing on my bread. I don't put on sunscreen, because it has toxins.

It feels good to be outside. Big blotches of cool tree-shadow stretch out over the road, and I walk in them, out of the pounding-hot sunlight. I cross over into the park, where Miller and Cris are sitting on one of the picnic tables under the sycamores. Their feet are on the bench and their elbows rest on their knees, their bikes ditched in the grass beside them.

They see me coming. Miller turns and says something to Cris and they both laugh.

Cris is attempting his first moustache, and when he smiles it curves up lopsidedly, like a fuzzy caterpillar reaching for a leaf just above his nose. "What's up, pretty boy?" he says, and Miller giggles.

I grin. "You think I'm pretty? Thank you."

Cris' smile drops off his face and Miller cackles. I sit down and Cris scoots away, but Miller tries to push him back my direction.

"Don't try to get on *me* now, slut," Miller says.

"Fuck off, High Life. Nobody wants your greasy ass," Cris says.

"Eat shit, Crystal Ball," Miller responds.

High Life is what people call Miller because his mom drinks and probably named him after beer. Crystal Ball is Cris' nickname, because his name is Cristobal, but it's not as good a name as High Life, I don't think.

"Here comes Mina," Cris says, and they quit pushing each other. Miller takes off his hat and smoothes his dry-grass hair over his forehead, then puts it back on, still a little bit crooked.

I look up. She's coming toward us from the park entrance, eating a bag of Hot Cheetos. Her black, black hair is cropped on one side and left long on the other, dangling like a tattered witch's skirt over one side of her face.

"Hey, Meany," Miller calls.

Her brown-eyed gaze falls on me, and she smiles. "Hi," she says.

"Hello, Mina," I say.

She sits next to me, resting her feet on the bench. Her knees don't bend up like mine do because she's short. A little belly roll hangs over the top of her shorts, and she smells like strawberry shampoo.

She smiles at me again and offers me the bag of Cheetos, holding it out with fingers stained bright orange from the flavor powder. I take one just to make her happy.

We sit, and for a minute the only sounds are the ravens and the crunch of us eating Cheetos. I nibble mine like a rodent, taking tiny bites with my front teeth, making it last.

Mina speaks. "I got my driver's license," she says, deliberately not looking at us.

Cris and Miller jerk upright. "What?" "No way!"

Mina's lips curl up, and she looks at me from the corners of her eyes.

I grin. "That's a very nice thing. Congratulations, Mina."

"Man, I wish we had a car," Miller complains. "Maybe my cousin will let us borrow his."

"Maybe he'll buy us some beer too," Cris says. "We can go to Lake Nacimiento or something."

Miller pulls out his phone and starts texting his cousin.

Mina eats another Cheeto, chewing it thoroughly, ignoring the boys while they ramble into daydreamy speculation about our evening plans. When they fall silent, she swallows.

"I got a car too," she says.

The boys both go wide-eyed. Miller jumps on top of the picnic table and whoops so loud it startles the ravens. Mina grins at me, and I smile back.

"We should go adventuring," I say, and Mina laughs.

"We should. That's correct."

We head back toward Mina's house, Cris and Miller riding circles around us on their bikes. Cris waves his hat around in the air and sings lustily in Spanish, and Miller makes "vroom-vroom" noises.

"How did you procure your vehicle?" I ask Mina.

She shrugs, her hands in her pockets. "It was one of those shady, back-alley deals. I sold government secrets to the Sinaloa Cartel." Her eyes sparkle at me. Cris is now standing on his pedals, singing with his hands in the air as his bike drifts across the pavement.

"So they gave you a Bentley with Baja plates?" I say. "Can I ride in the secret compartment?"

She snickers. "Sorry, the secret compartment's full."

"Ah," I say, nodding wisely. "May your secret compartment always be full, and may it always be secret."

"Thanks, Justin." Her pretty lips twist into a smile as she glances up at me.

The car isn't a Bentley. It's a little silver Toyota Camry with a dent in the fender and a half scraped-off **'Coexist'** bumper sticker. Cris and Miller toss their bikes into the gravel and run up to it.

"Kickass," Cris says.

"Nice fuckin' car, Meany," Miller says.

"Shotgun," Cris says.

"Shotgun," Miller says a millisecond behind. He

stomps in disappointment. "Aw, man."

"Justin has shotgun," Mina says, unlocking the doors. The two boys scowl at her.

"But I called it," Miller says.

"My car, my rules." Mina climbs in, and the other two slouch dejectedly to the back as I prance up to the front, clapping and grinning.

The car is horribly hot inside, and I start to sweat. The upholstery is scuffed and ratty, but it's clean. It smells like Armor All and ancient spilled coffee and the Devil duck air freshener hanging from the rearview.

Mina starts it up and the stereo explodes with noise at the same time the air conditioning vents start to blast. For a second I think I've been hit by mortar fire, and I jump and bump my knees against the glove box. Mina's hand darts out to twist down the volume knob and the music settles into the background.

"Jesus shit, Meany," Cris says.

"That was very startling," I say.

She smirks. "Sorry, I like it loud."

We pull out onto Center Street, which stretches long and empty out to the Heights. I watch how she turns the wheel, presses the gas. "You drive quite well," I say. "You're a professional. If they give out a Nobel Prize for driving, I think you should win one. I think I'll contact them to nominate you."

Mina laughs. "Thanks," she says.

"What did you say?" Cris says. "Justin, you mumble all the time."

"Justin is THE MUMBLER," Miller says. "MUMBLE, MUMBLE, MUMBLE."

"He wasn't talking to you anyway, douchenozzles," Mina says.

"Sorry," I say, trying to talk louder. "Mumbling is my superpower, I think."

"When are *you* going to get your license, Justin?" Mina asks.

"Yeah, you're old, right?" Miller says. "You could buy us cigarettes and shit."

I look out the window at the water-starved fields. Mom says I can't get my license because they won't let people like me drive. I'm not sure what she means by that exactly, and I push that thought away. I don't want to think about Mom right now.

I realize that Mina is glancing at me, and I remember she asked me a question and I forgot to answer.

"I'll get my license when I can afford a Bentley," I say. "Then I'll mob around Piedras, busting loud music and smoking a Cuban cigar. I'll be king of the streets."

Mina laughs. Cris makes a "psh" noise.

"Where are we going, anyway?" Miller asks.

"Paso. I want some ice cream," Mina says.

"We should go to Vegas," Cris says.

"Shit yeah!" Miller agrees.

"We should go to the beach," I say. "They have ice cream there too, and it won't be so hot. We can see the elephant seals."

"Good idea, Justin," Mina says. "We'll go to Cambria."

In the back, Cris huffs. "Man, why does Cray Cray get to ride shotgun *and* decide where we go?"

Mina's burning glare pings off the rearview,

reflecting like a laser beam at Cris. "Shut up, asshole," she says.

I wiggle in my seat a bit. She doesn't have to get angry. People always say things like this as a test of the Dark Energy, but Mina doesn't know about the Dark Energy yet, so she can't see how it affects people.

"There's nothing crazy about ice cream and elephant seals," I say.

Mina's lips loosen into a smile, and she giggles.

"Ice CREAM and elephant SEALS," Miller bellows.

On the way, Mina explains that she didn't really get her car through shady dealings with the mafia. Actually, her mom bought it for her. "So I can come visit her in Fresno," she says. She picks at a crack in the steering wheel with her short, black-painted fingernails.

I know something Mina keeps secret from other people. The woman in Fresno is not her real mom. Her real mom is in a group home for the mentally ill, and has been since Mina was eight years old.

The road snakes along the narrow back of a ridge, and I stare out at the desert hills looming in the haze. Cris sings along with the music while Mina and Miller debate about what's going to happen next on some zombie show on TV. We pass by a field of cattle, and they look up to watch our car with their strange, alien eyes, their ears twitching. What would happen if the cattle suddenly realized they were being raised for slaughter? Would they jump the fences and run off? Would they fight back? I don't know.

One of the places I lived with my mom had a stockyard nearby. The smell was hot and dense; it slathered itself over you, making you feel like you always had to wash your hands just from touching the air.

One time, I pushed my way through the stink to go look at the cattle. They stood with their hooves squished into the goop, their eyes wild. The Dark Energy was warning them that something wasn't right. When I came up to the fence, they scattered and bucked away from me, jostling into each other.

I leaned there on the railing, breathing through my shirt and watching them. All those poor cows, forced out of their bodies just so that we can chop them into bloody, wet steaks. The poor cows, pulled down into the void. What happens to them there? Are they enlightened? Do they make it to the Other Place? Or do they just go from dimness to darkness, their pointless cow lives fading to nothing?

Mina's voice finds its way through my thoughts. "Justin, are you okay?"

I realize I have my forehead pressed hard into my knees. I straighten up. "I'm okay. Just thinking about the cows."

Her gaze holds mine a moment, a crease forming between her brows. She glances back at the road.

Cambria is a little town nestled in the folds of the oak-covered hills where they meet the ocean. We stop first to get ice cream. I order a cup of sugar-free chocolate, and Mina quirks her lips and pinches the skin at my waist, sending a shock through me.

"You should get the sugar kind, Justin," she says.

"Refined sugar is bad for you," I tell her. "It's pollution. The little sugar-monsters eat at your veins."

Her lips twitch and she shrugs, her pink tongue licking the drips from her cone.

We wander around the town. Mina takes a hat off a rack outside one of the tourist shops and stands high on her tippy-toes to put it on me. She smoothes the blond curls away from my forehead, which tickles in a nice way. "It looks good on you," she says. "It matches your eyes."

There's a tiny mirror on the hat rack, and my slightly distorted reflection looks back at me, the hazy blue sky behind. The hat is the color of that sky, and it has a bear on a surfboard on the front. *'California Republic,'* it says.

"I like it," I say, adjusting the bill to be perfectly straight. Next to us Cris and Miller are trying on all the most ridiculous sunglasses, the ones with the big, shiny lenses or the thick, neon frames, doing poses for each other.

Mina looks at me a moment, one dimple showing in her cheek. She reaches up and takes the hat from my head and goes with it into the store. I watch after her. I think I know what she's doing. "Mina, don't," I say, but she doesn't stop or look back.

She comes out after a minute and places the hat back on my head. "It's yours. I know how you like hats."

I touch the brim with my fingers. "Thank you, Mina. You're a very nice person."

She gets a little smile and looks away, shrugging.

11

We go to the beach after that, but not the one with the elephant seals. Miller says they smell sour like homeless people and all they do is lie there sneezing. He's right, of course, but those things don't bother me. The smell isn't too strong and I like watching their peaceful faces. But I'm not going to argue, because the regular beach is good, and because arguing makes angry Dark Energy vibrate into the cracks of our souls.

The sun is in our faces and soaks blindingly into the water. Mina and I take off our shoes and walk along the shore, letting the foam slide over our toes. Cris and Miller chase each other down the beach with long strands of kelp.

The breeze flutters Mina's hair across her face until she tucks it behind her ear. "How's your mom?" she asks.

I think of her, sitting there all day in front of her computer. "Still burdened by her frailties, I think."

Mina presses her lips back against a smile. "What do you mean?"

I stare down at the sand. "She's lonely, and sometimes she does crazy things when she's lonely."

Mina's hidden smile disappears. I can see her pity for me, and also that she's worried. "Wasn't that why you ended up with your grandma before? Because your mom took off with some dude?"

I nod. "His name was Steve. He lived in Idaho. But there was drama and complications when I went up there. There was an instability in the framework of our relationship which disengaged the lodestone of the whole edifice. I don't like to talk about it, actually."

Mina blinks and scowls and looks like she wants to ask something else about Steve, but she doesn't. I'm glad. "Then your grandma bought you the house in Piedras, right?" she asks instead.

"Yes." I look over at the waves crashing roughly, then calming into smooth foamy sheets. "I hope we can stay there this time. I like it in Piedras. It's a good house, right by the park."

"I hope you can stay too. Are you going to school in the fall?"

The Dark Energy vibrates a low note of warning. I realize Mina is looking at me and I've stopped walking. I shove my fists in my pockets and start off down the beach again.

"I don't know about school," I say. "Those places can be complicated."

There was a teacher at the Paso high school with very bad sickness in her, and she contaminated me with it. I blow out a puff of air, trying to push those thoughts back.

"School in Piedras isn't so bad, Justin. I can take you to meet the teachers first. The time before, they were just ignorant, I think. They didn't know you."

I don't say anything.

"Justin, slow down. I can't walk that fast," Mina says.

"I have to run," I say, and I take off down the beach.

The sickness makes you vibrate the wrong way so that the Dark Energy sucks you down, but it doesn't give you enlightenment. It doesn't want to forgive. It's the scariest thing ever. I've only caught

13

the sickness once, but that was enough. It was a long, long time before the Dark Energy let me go.

I breathe deeply, the ocean air pulling the death stink from my lungs, the heat in my muscles spreading out into the Energy to soothe its agitation. Pretty soon the bad thoughts retreat behind the wall. It doesn't take long, because the Dark Energy is happy. It likes the ocean, and Mina. They harmonize with it.

I run to the end of the beach and then back to Mina, who watches me with her brow furrowed. I stop when I get to her. The breeze curls around my neck, cooling my sweat.

"I'm sorry," I say.

"No, Justin. I'm sorry. I shouldn't have said…"

"It's not you," I say. "It's never you."

Mina's forehead smoothes out. She gives me an uncertain look. She reaches out slowly and takes my hand. When she interlaces her fingers with mine the Dark Energy sings, and everything is gentle.

We turn around and walk back toward Cris and Miller, who are trying to catch seagulls, but they're going about it all wrong. "Mina," I say, "You have magic in you. Your aura is like a rainbow gas nebula."

She smiles, but her brow is furrowed. "What? I can't hear you."

I don't know when I'm mumbling sometimes. "Nothing. Mina, you're very beautiful."

I can tell she heard me that time because her cheeks go pink.

Chapter 2

When I wake up the next day, the first thing I notice is the smell of Lemon Blast floor cleaner and Spray Away.

I come into the kitchen, and Mom is hunched over on the floor like an armadillo, her mousy hair tangled up into a bun. She's cleaning the grout with a toothbrush. The stacks of bills and religious pamphlets are gone from the table, which has a light green cloth on it. The faucet drips into an empty sink, the stainless steel gleaming, just a trace of scouring powder left in the corners.

I get a nervous feeling. "Why are you cleaning, Mom?"

She doesn't look up. "We're going to have guests."

"Who's coming over?"

"His name is David. And he's bringing his daughter, Rebekah."

I clutch my elbows, my stomach going as sour as tamarind candy. I can suddenly see the trap the Dark Energy has been building, and why mom has been on her computer so much. "Who are they? Who are these people, Mom? Why are they coming?"

The toothbrush goes still. Her head snaps up. "David is a very nice religious man, and he understands about you. Justin, *stop pacing*. You're getting footprints all over my floor!"

I realize I'm walking back and forth across the kitchen. I stop and stare at her, even though holding my legs still is pulling against the magnetic force of their desire to keep walking.

Mom looks up at me from her hands and knees, and her lips move rhythmically as she chews on her cheek.

"I don't want these people to come," I say. "Your men are always trouble, and we're fine on our own."

"My *men* are trouble, Justin? It's *you* that's trouble."

It's getting harder and harder to hold my feet still. "This isn't the way for me to reach enlightenment, Mom. Sometimes I think you don't want me to reach enlightenment."

She clutches tight around the handle of the toothbrush and smashes it against the floor. "You think it's easy, taking care of a son like you?" Tears pool in her eyes and spill over as she pounds the floor again and again and again. My ears ring. I can feel the anger seeping into the cracks all around us, and the fear starts in me.

"You get yourself kicked out of school," she says, "and you chased off Steve, calling him a demon and all that bullcrap, even though you knew there were no goddamn demons in him. Now I finally find a man who understands, who wants to help me, and you think you can call the shots and tell me he can't come here. No, Justin, I'm not going to let you mess it up this time!"

I dart out of the kitchen, grabbing my shoes from the mudroom shelf and some dirty socks from the basket.

"Don't you run off again!" Mom yells. "Goddammit, Justin."

But I hardly hear her. My thoughts are loud about my need to be gone. I dodge out the door and through the streets, running past the school and into the vineyards.

I breathe in, breathe out, trying to cleanse the bad vibrations from my lungs, but the air is too hot and thick. The rising heat makes it like rippling water, and I have to be a fish to breathe it.

Sweat pours stinging into my eyes. Underneath my hat, my head itches, and I wonder, do fish itch?

It would be hard to scratch your back with those little fins. They'd never reach.

I feel what's coming right before it happens, because the Dark Energy sings a discordant note. I twitch and have a sudden pang and I know what it's like to be an itchy fish.

I twist my arms around, stumbling as I grope for a prickling spot on my back, but my fingers graze the sweaty skin just below or above when I twist the other way. I shouldn't try to scratch it, but it itches, it sears.

I force myself to run faster, until my legs ache and my lungs burn. Faster, my sneakers crunch,

17

crunch, crunching on the gravel shoulder. The heat bugs sizzle in the ditches. Lizards dart out of my path, skittering over the burning pavement. I grab onto the noise. I focus on the lizards. I feel the horrible itch, my muscles moving and hurting. I cling to my body and to this world.

I shouldn't resist, but my guts tangle up when I think about what's going to happen. I don't want it to. I don't want it.

"I'm a coward!" I yell. My voice cuts through the wavery air and startles up a hawk from a power pole, his wings black against the light blue sky. He screeches at me, and I know he's transmitting the angry retort of the Dark Energy. But still I beg, as if it will do any good. "I'm a coward and I can't!"

The words squeeze the last air from my lungs, and I gasp. My legs are a fish tail now, and I flop onto the pavement. It hurts, but not enough to keep me here.

It's no use. I can feel the Other Place closing in, the Dark Energy wrapping me in its strangling dream-arms. I twist and wriggle off the road, through the chemical dust and into the vineyards to let it have me.

The Dark Energy has angry fangs and a tongue rougher than the evilest cat's. I can see the barb on the end of each pulsating, Pepto-Bismol pink taste bud as it licks me, scrapes my flesh away. I think I'm screaming but I don't have ears to hear with anymore. It chews me up, and I can hear my bones crunching, can feel them snap. I can feel my intestines swelling up full of rot gas and exploding. I smell the stench of my rotten body and see it pressing around me, oily and green-yellow. I am nothing but pain, my whole existence a solid vibration of hot, grotesque agony.

Then the last molecule of me is torn apart, and the pain stops. There's nothingness, and I'm so grateful.

Is it the end this time? Will the Dark Energy take me for good now, and never send me back? It might be better that way, but then I think of how the sun shines through the windy leaves outside my bedroom window, the shadows moving over the paper as I draw. And that girl from the park who I met back when I lived with Grandma, her brown eyes dreaming in their sad depths.

And Mina.

So I don't want to stay here in the void, because of those things that are sweet and peaceful.

I know that there is movement around me. There always has been movement, just like it's always been nothing. I feel the caress of the water, the vibration of the rocks rolling across the riverbed. I hover over mossy stones caressed by ripples of sunlight, the muted colors bright with immediacy. There is only now, and only what is.

I swim around the undulations of the current into a place that is cool and still, where I can rest. There are good bugs there. There are other fish, their big, round eyes looming up out of the murk to stare into mine, transmitting thought: *Bugs. Bugs. Still water.*

A shadow passes over, and we startle and scatter to the safe darkness under the roots. I can feel the fins of the others brushing against my scales.

And I realize, I don't itch. Fish don't itch,

because they can't scratch. They can't scratch, because they don't itch. The world is set up this way, giving us all what we need so that we can survive. It is my lesson.

I find my heart again. The Dark Energy isn't angry at me anymore. It forgives. It gives me back to the Physical World, and I rise up out of the Other Place.

I wake up in the shady mud under the vines, an irrigation hose dripping onto my neck.

Chapter 3

Mom isn't in the kitchen when I get home. The place is unnaturally clean, the late afternoon sun gleaming on the polished appliances. I get myself a glass of water, then another, until my belly is full of it. I wiggle around to make it slosh. I laugh. But I stop, because I don't know if Mom is around, and I don't want to prod her into action by not acting my age.

I don't want to even think about Mom and her men right now. It's too much, and those thoughts need to leave me alone, *leave me alone* right now, because the Dark Energy is happy and needs to stay that way.

The air conditioner is on, and I give it a wide berth on the way to the bathroom. It hums and rattles like an angry thing, and I think if it weren't stuck in the window it would lunge after me, snarling and dragging its cord like a tail.

The whole house has odd odors because Mom has gone snooping into all the ancient, secret crevices of it with her cleaning rag. She has polished the bathroom faucets and scrubbed the grime from the window. When I go into it for a new razor, I see the medicine cabinet has been arranged neatly.

The bathroom door chirps against its frame when I shut it. I smear dirt on the clawfoot tub as I climb in, which makes the place look more normal. I pull the curtain around, twist the squeaky faucet handles.

The cool water brings peace. I curl up with my knees under me and let the shower hit my back. I like these times, when the Dark Energy is happy.

I lie there singing a song from *Blazing Saddles*, which is an old movie I like but Mom doesn't. Then I stop singing. It's made me think of Mom again. I take a deep breath and let it out. I turn over and let the cold water run into my mouth and over my stinging-burnt skin, letting it draw out the body poisons. I use my special no-toxin soap and shave my face carefully because of my sunburn. Then I get out and wrap the clean towel around me.

I still don't see Mom anywhere as I go into my room, but she's been in here too. The dirty laundry is gone from the floor. The clean laundry sack is empty and hanging from my closet door.

The cleanliness makes me dizzy. There's too much space around me. It's inorganic.

I open my dresser and find my clothes folded neatly there, and I toss some of them out, just to relax the atmosphere a bit. I find the right shirt for today, my Bugs Bunny one, at the very bottom. Bugs Bunny was a true hero. Everyone was always trying to attack him, but he never fought back. He just let his enemies destroy themselves through their own ridiculousness. I get dressed in the shirt, and in the pants and underwear that go with it, and I feel a little bit better.

Mom has stacked my drawing pads on the shelf along with my portfolios, and put all my pencils back in the pencil box, but I get them out.

My bed squeaks as I lie on my belly to draw. Drawing can get you to the Other Place without getting dragged down by the angry Dark Energy, or being asleep. It can smooth out the vibrations and make things right again, just like running. I draw the fish, their eyes peering at me through the gloom, their bellows-lips sucking, their gills working their intricate magic, taking the oxygen from the water. Their fins wave like delicate silk, and their scales flash bright silver where they catch the filtered light. I feel the peace of their presence. I share their uncomplicated knowledge.

I blink. I can't see them anymore. I float up to the surface and realize it's getting dark, so I turn on my lamp. The silent house creaks as it settles in the cool night air. I sink back down into the cool depths, swimming with my peaceful fish.

My spine jolts like a fist has punched it. My heart beats fast as the Physical World wavers suddenly back into existence around me. Someone is tapping at my window.

I look over my shoulder and see a pale face peering through the glass, black hair falling over one of her big, beautiful eyes. My anger and confusion turn to warm happiness, though my heart is still racing.

The window groans against the frame as I pull it

up. "Mina," I say.

She doesn't quite look at me, one of her sneakers tapping against the dry dirt. "Hi, Justin."

"Climb up." I stick a hand out to her. "I was just drawing the fish."

She looks at me now and smiles, and she takes my hand. I help her scramble up onto the windowsill, then into my room.

She's very close, looking up at me with her pupils big in the dim light. I'm still holding her hand, and I want to brush the hair out of her face. I want to kiss her. I can see her breasts rise and fall under her tight shirt as she breathes, and I wonder what they would feel like if she let me touch them. But she might not like that at all, and it would leave a very bad emptiness in me if I made Mina angry, if she wouldn't be my friend anymore.

I drop her hand and clutch at my t-shirt instead. "I'm glad you're here," I say.

She breaks into a lopsided grin, with the smiling part of her mouth under the curtain of her hair.

"Sit down," I say. I turn to clear away my drawing stuff from the bed.

She looks around my room as she sits, and her gaze falls on my sketchpad. "Is that your drawing of the fish? I want to see it."

I sit down next to her. I hand her the drawing, and she tucks her hair behind her ear as she examines it, scooting a little closer. She gently traces the curve of one of the fish's backs with her fingertip.

"You're so good at this stuff," she says. "You should frame them, get them up in a gallery so other people can see."

"That would be nice," I say, but I'm not really listening to myself, because her knee is touching mine. Mina is sweet and beautiful and peaceful, but she also makes me a little bit nervous.

"You didn't come to the park today," she says.

"No. My mom told me that she's having a new man come to stay with us, and I had to go running."

Her hand comes up to brush her hair out of her face, even though it's already tucked behind her ear. Her brow furrows, changing the topography of her freckles.

"Do you want to go driving with me?" she asks. "We could go out to where the road ends, out there at the ranch, and look at the stars."

I know the place, and it's a good one. "I would like that," I say.

We both hesitate a moment before getting up and going to the window. I follow her out of it, both of us dropping to the ground in the dry grass.

Our footsteps crunch on the gravel as we walk to her house, where her car is parked. The crickets chirp. A neighbor sits on his porch with his shirt off, listening to Tejano music. I can only see his silhouette in the light through his screen door, but I can feel him watching us as we go by.

"Who's this man that's coming to stay with you?" Mina asks.

"His name is David. Mom says he's a religious man. And also he has a daughter."

Mina sucks back a corner of her lips. "What kind of religious is he?"

"I'm not sure. With Mom, you never know. It

could be Jesus, or one of the gods with all the arms, or maybe even Jesus with a bunch of arms."

She presses her fist to her lips to cover up her giggles. We're at her car, and we get in. She's quicker to turn down the stereo this time after she cranks the ignition, and we only get a millisecond blast of pure noise.

"You shouldn't listen to music so loud, Mina," I say. "You'll make your ears go deaf. Then you'll have to use TTY when you call up your contact in Sinaloa."

She grins. "That's okay. They run the TTY network too."

I nod. "Of course. The deaf are in on the deal. No one ever suspects them, even though they run in packs and are always flipping each other hand signs."

She laughs, shaking her head.

We head past the school, which is dark and shut up for the summer. I watch it slide by.

"Why is your mom hooking up with some religious guy, though?" she asks.

"Mom often makes forays into religious life. It's not always so bad. I really enjoyed the Catholics. They have very nice churches with pipe organs, and those little nooks with the dolorous-faced saints."

She grins. "And eye-rolling hipster Jesus front-and-center on the crucifix."

I think about it. "Yes. He wore a loincloth before it was cool."

She snorts and giggles. "He's like, 'Can we get this crucifixion over with, you guys? This band called the Brides of Obscurity is playing in downtown Santa Monica. I can't believe more people haven't heard of them.'"

I laugh. "Aren't you Catholic?"

She shrugs. "My family is."

"You don't believe in Hipster Jesus?"

She rubs her nose, the little tip of it wagging back and forth under her fist. "No," she says. "You?"

My eyebrows pull together as I consider it. "I've never seen Hipster Jesus, only statues of him. I think I would have seen him if he were real, but he could be hiding in the cracks, waiting to step out after I reach enlightenment. Or maybe he doesn't live in the Other Place. Maybe he lives someplace I haven't even been to yet."

Mina squints at me, and I pick at the callous the drawing pencils have left on my finger. I think I've violated the social dance by almost talking about the Dark Energy, so I don't say anything else and just stare out the window.

We drive out through the vineyards until the road turns to dirt, then park at the cattle gate. She turns off the car, extinguishing the headlights. Everything goes black. There's no moon and no lights, and the stars are spread out above us like glittering mist.

We get out of the car. Mina climbs up on the hood, the metal thumping as it dimples under her knees. She leans back against the windshield, crossing her ankles.

I stand watching her, shifting on my feet. "I'm afraid I would dent your new car permanently if I sat next to you," I say.

"Oh well. It already has dents."

I shift on my feet a moment longer. Then, carefully, I climb up. I'm a cat that steps lightly. I uncurl my cat back and stretch against the windshield next to her.

It is very peaceful here. The only sound is the crickets and night rattle-bugs, the hiss of the warm breeze through the stunted oaks. I try to flick my ears, the way cats do when wind hits them. I don't know if I'm doing it correctly, but I think I am.

Mina scoots closer against me, and I forget all about being a feline. I hesitate just a moment, and I put my arm around her shoulders. She cuddles in with her head nestled on my chest. I can smell the good smells of her shampoo and laundry detergent.

My heart is beating very fast. We lie there looking up at the stars, but I'm not really seeing them because all I know about right then is the feeling of her there. Her warmth flowing into me is something I've been missing all my life but didn't know it.

She rolls over and looks at me, and suddenly her lips are on mine, and my arm is around her waist, pulling her closer. The windshield wiper is poking me but I don't notice, because her lips and her body send sweet pain through me. And I want her in a way that's overpowering, her lips and breasts and hips, her hand sliding up the bare skin of my back.

She pulls away and looks at me. Her breath is warm against my face, and her eyes glint in the starlight. The Dark Energy and breeze are beautiful and gentle, and somewhere close by a pack of coyotes takes up yelping. I start to kiss her again, but I make myself stop, because I won't be able to ever stop if I don't now.

"Mina," I say, and I brush the hair away from her face so I can see her better. "Will you be my girlfriend?"

She breaks into a smile and giggles. I can feel the giggle in her body. "Yes, Justin," she says.

She kisses me again.

Chapter 4

I don't know for sure that my mom has been gone until she comes back early the next morning. I'm drawing, and I'm thinking about Mina. I can't think about anything else. Mina is like one of those songs that gets stuck in your head, except she never wears out with repetition. She just gets better and better.

But then I hear the door open and close, and I hear voices—Mom's voice, and a man's voice—and my pencil goes still. I get chills of fear and burns of anger.

"Justin?" Mom says from outside my door.

My stomach cramps up. I think about going out my window, but that would be cowardly, and the Dark Energy might not like it.

I twitch in surprise as my pencil snaps apart in my hand. I stare at it, my ears ringing, then throw the splintered pieces down on my bed, pounding the mattress. "Dammit, Mom, you made me break my pencil!"

"Don't you use that language!" she says.

I clutch my hair in my hands for a moment, then snatch up the halves of the pencil again and examine them. Charcoal pencils are expensive, and Mom doesn't like to buy them for me, even though I have my own money.

"Mom and her angry vibrations," I say. "It's like she wants me to fail the test. She wants to keep all the enlightenment for herself." I take a deep breath and let it out slowly. "Calm down. Calm down. Calm down."

"David and Rebekah are here," Mom says through the door. "Come out and meet them."

I squeeze my eyes shut, pushing my anger behind the wall. "Go away," I whisper, and I don't know if I'm talking to the angry thoughts or to Mom and her strange new man, whoever he is. I force the thoughts back with my hands. "Go away. Go away."

"Justin, open the door." She jiggles the knob, but I ignore her, the splintered pencil-ends poking my palm as I push and push.

"Go away. Go away."

"Justin, don't do this! Not now!"

"I can't come out," I say through my tight throat. "I don't have the right clothes for this situation."

I sit there, breathing.

"What goddamn clothes are the right ones today?" she asks.

"I need my aqua blue shirt." Thinking about the color of it is like putting a shield around me. "And the jeans with the double pockets that go with it. But they're dirty."

"They are not. I washed them. They're in your

31

drawer."

I take a deep breath. The Dark Energy smoothes out a little, though it's still wobbly. I put down the broken pencil and get up, pawing through the clean clothes in my dresser until I see my aqua blue shirt. Some of the tension goes out of me as I finger the fabric.

"Hurry up!" Mom hisses through the door.

Her words are like a buzzing fly, and I flick at them with my hand. I find the right pants in the wrong place, in a separate drawer from the shirt, though I don't know how that made sense to Mom when she put them away. I change my clothes, then open the door.

Mom is there, her eyes round and shiny, watching me closely. She has on a brown dress with cream polka-dots that I haven't seen before, and pink lipstick. She looks very nice, but her muscles are tight and she's squeezing her hands together.

"Come have some coffee with us," she says.

"You made me break my pencil," I say.

Her eyes flash and her lips twist, and when she speaks her voice is a low growl. "I'll get you another damn pencil. Just come have some coffee."

I nod, my neck rigid. The things we are saying to each other are not really the things we are communicating, but I agree to play along.

We go out into the kitchen. Two people are staring out the window silently, side by side. It is a very short man in a tan suit and a teenage girl with a ponytail hanging down her back. They both turn when we come in.

The man is older than Mom by at least fifteen

years. He has hair almost the same dark brown as his daughter's, but it looks dyed with too much fake orangyness. It's slicked back from his pale forehead, which has a permanent crease in it, a canyon carved by a constant flood of worry or confusion, I'm not sure which yet.

It deepens as he looks at me now. He holds out his hand.

"You must be Justin. My name is David Esau."

His hand is small and dry in mine. He squeezes firmly, as if to say, "We are both men."

It doesn't make me squeamish to touch him. I don't see the sickness in him, but sometimes it can hide.

"It is nice to meet you, David," I say. "I like your suit."

He glances down at his clothes and his lips curve into a strange smile. "Thank you." He lets go of my hand and gestures toward the girl. "And this is my daughter, Rebekah."

Rebekah smiles at me, and her eyes are blue, but they don't smile along with her mouth. They are full of anger and hurt. I shake her hand also, trying to shift around her sharp emotions.

"Nice to meet you, Rebekah," I say.

"Sit down. I'll bring you some coffee," Mom says.

David and I sit facing each other across the kitchen table. He folds his hands on the green cloth. They have lots of freckles and long reddish hair on the backs of them. Rebekah sits down next to him, and now there are three of us watching each other. I pick at the callous on my finger.

Mom brings us coffee in the good cups, deep blue porcelain with matching saucers. There is a round-bellied pitcher with cream and a sugar dish that's always reminded me of a blue Easter egg. When I see it I taste chocolate, and the sweet tang of melting jelly beans stuck to those long strands of plastic grass. Thinking about candy makes me feel better.

"Do we have any jelly beans, Mom?" I ask, but then I remember all that sugar and how it makes my veins burn. "Never mind, actually. I don't want any jelly beans."

"We don't have any jelly beans," Mom says with a smile that isn't normal on her. "There's cake, though. Poppy seed, your favorite kind."

She shoots me a stern look as she lays out the plates. *Don't mess this up,* that look says. But it is just a test of the Dark Energy, because she knows that if this man or his daughter have the sickness, I will have to keep it out. She may be strong enough to tolerate people with the sickness, but I'm not. Not yet.

Mom sits down on David's other side, crossing her legs and holding her cup close to her chest. David serves us all cake. Mom's right. It's my favorite kind, so I'll do a water detoxification later in order to have some. I take a big bite.

David gives me a squinty-eyed smile. "I think we'll dispense with the prayer this time, since it's just a snack."

Mom glares at me, and I realize I have done something wrong. I cover my mouth and stop chewing.

"It's okay, Justin," David says. "Go ahead and eat." He takes a tiny bite of his slice and smiles at my mother. "This is excellent cake, Jane."

My mother's scowl softens. "Thank you."

"Yes, Mrs. Flaherty, it's really good," Rebekah says. She takes a nibble and gets some crumbs on her t-shirt, which says *'New Eden Bible Camp.'* She brushes them off, smoothing the fabric over her small breasts.

David's grey eyes lock on me. "So, Justin, you're eighteen?"

I swallow my mouthful. "Yes." I put my cake down, because I'm squishing it between my fingers.

"Rebekah here will turn seventeen on September first," he says.

She ducks her head in acknowledgment, her mouth full. She has round, rosy cheeks and doesn't look old enough to be almost seventeen.

"Your mother has told me a lot about you," David says.

All three of them are looking at me very intensely, and my ears ring.

"That's good you know some things about me," I say. "I would like to know more things about you." I cross my ankles tightly so that my foot will stop tapping.

David unbuttons his jacket, which falls open, revealing his blue tie. His vibrations are strange. They leave a space around him that is almost blank.

"Well, Justin," he says, "I have been a minister with the Baptist church for almost thirty years now. For the last fifteen of those years, I've been in charge of a flock in a small town called Zillah, in

35

Eastern Washington State. But my dear wife, Rebekah's mother, died a year and a half ago, and I feel God has called me to move on to a new place. That's why I'm here to start a new church in Piedras."

Rebekah pokes her fingers into her cake and frowns, and I think I know about her emotions now.

"I'm very sorry about your wife," I say.

David nods sadly. "It was very hard, but Rebekah and I are enduring it through the grace of God."

I want to ask him how she died, but Rebekah is looking very fragile and I don't want to break her. "Where are you going to build your new church?" I ask instead.

"We've already bought a house here on Second Street, and we'll have services there once it's fixed up."

I squint at him, at the strange silence in the Dark Energy around him. "What things do you believe about God?"

Mom twitches and takes a quick sip of her coffee.

David smiles at Mom, then leans forward over the table. "I'm glad you asked that, Justin, because there's no greater joy to me than to bring the Good News to young people such as yourself. I believe in our Lord Jesus Christ, that he died on the cross for our sins so that we could all have eternal life. And I am grateful each day for that sacrifice, because I'm a humble sinner that needs all the Grace he can get." He turns a smile on Mom, who quickly smiles back. But when he turns to me again, her smile goes away and she glares at me.

"Your mother tells me that you haven't yet accepted Jesus into your life," David says.

I don't bother looking at Mom, even though I can feel her eyes pull at me like suction cups. Our thoughts shimmer between us, flowing around the blank space created by David, and through Rebekah's turbulence. People say they believe so many things about God, and Mom seems to somehow believe them all, fitting those ideas together like a puzzle in her head. She gets mad when I get confused.

"I have never met Jesus," I say cautiously. "I've heard lots of people talk about him, and they often seem very happy with him."

"Yes," David says. "Having Jesus in your life and being saved is a joyful thing, Justin. I hope you will open your heart and let that joy into your life as well."

"I will keep an eye out for him," I say.

David freezes for a second, looking at me closely. Mom's knuckles are white as she clutches the handle of her cup. David smiles again. "Do you not believe in God, Justin?"

I twirl my cup on the table. When people talk about God, sometimes it seems like they are talking about the Dark Energy. Since it's a violation of the social dance when you talk about the Dark Energy, God could be a code word for it.

I don't know yet if David knows about the Dark Energy, though, so I don't know how much I can say. I clear my throat. "I'm not sure."

David and I watch each other. We're like a cat

and a dog staring each other down, our tails held high and frizzy, each waiting for the other to make a move.

The crease between his brows becomes more pronounced. "I've never understood how people have enough faith to not believe in God. He's all around us, in everything. It's impossible not to see him."

The Dark Energy hums, because it sounds for sure like he is talking about it now, and this may be a test. My fingers tangle together on the tabletop. "I may believe in the same things you do, but maybe not. When we're absorbed by death, I guess we'll see."

He puts his coffee down and scoots forward in his chair, leaning his elbows on the table. I back up a little. "Death is the enemy, Justin. Jesus defeated death when He died on the cross for our sins and was resurrected. Through Jesus Christ, we have eternal life. You don't have to walk in darkness any longer, because He is the light in the darkness."

A jolt runs through me, because this is a test for sure. How can you defeat death and the Dark Energy? "I think we must be talking about different things," I say.

David stares at me with a thoughtful expression. I wonder if I have passed the test. Mom has a sour look, but she usually does. Rebekah looks at her plate, her mouth twisted. My heart pounds in my chest.

After a moment, David sits up straight. "Will you pray with me, Justin?"

I unclench my hands. "Sure, I'll pray with you."

David smiles, gazing around at Mom and Rebekah. "Let's all pray together."

He takes my sweaty hand. My body feels jittery, but it still doesn't hurt to touch him. We all close our eyes, because God is like Santa Claus. He will not come if you're peeking.

"Heavenly father," David says, "Thank you for bringing Jane Flaherty and her son Justin into our lives, and thank you for this beautiful new day that is dawning, with the opportunities for joy that it brings. Thank you for giving us the privilege of bringing your Word here to the little town of Piedras. I pray that the hearts of the citizens be opened to your love, and that your Kingdom find fertile ground here for expansion."

"I would like to pray right now that you come into the life of this young man, Justin Flaherty. Dear Jesus, he is lost, but we know you love him and have not forsaken him. We know that through you he can be found. Help him to see your light, Jesus, so that you can lead him out of the darkness. Clear away the shadows from his eyes, the false images put there by the Devil, who runs so rampant in the society of young people these days. Help him to open his eyes and find his way to you, so your light can shine within him for others to see."

"We know through you that all things are possible, Lord, and know that you can and do answer our prayers. We are grateful for your love and Grace, which you show us each and every day of our lives."

"In Jesus' name we pray, amen."

"Amen," Mom and Rebekah say.

39

I open my eyes, blinking. "Amen," I say.

David looks at me. He is still holding my hand, and he pats it with his other one. I shrug to loosen up my tight shoulders.

"Can I continue to pray for you, Justin?" David asks.

"Yes, that's fine with me," I say, still shrugging.

David smiles. "Good," he says. "Good." He pats my hand one last time. "I'll pray for you every day."

Chapter 5

I don't say much as we finish our cake and coffee, but mostly I sit there thinking about Mina while David and Mom do most of the talking. Rebekah seems like she's thinking about something too, and every so often I catch her glancing at me.

David announces he wants to go see his new church. "Will you come with us, Justin?" he asks.

I fidget with the hem of my t-shirt. I'd like to get away from this man. He has drained all my energy out. But Mom is looking at me tight-lipped, and I don't want any trouble from her. "Sure," I say. "Let me get my hat."

I go into my room and get the hat Mina got me. I think of Mina again as I put it on, and I feel better, very warm and good. Then I realize I've been standing and staring at the wall for a long time.

They are waiting for me in the kitchen, and we go out.

We stroll down the road and David smiles at the houses and the trees, seeming pleased, as if he'd ordered up the whole town from an online catalog and it arrived just right, with no parts broken and exactly the color it had been in the picture. "What a beautiful place," he says.

I look around at the crispy dry lawns and the broken down cars and twisted chain link fences. I'm not sure what to think of Mom's new man yet, but at least he seems to have a positive outlook.

Mom eyes me. "Where did you get that hat, Justin?"

I reach up and touch the brim. "Mina got it for me." I like saying her name, and I smile.

"Mina? Is she that Mexican girl with the funny haircut?" she asks.

"Mina isn't Mexican," I say. "She's Mexican American. She was born in Sacramento. And her haircut isn't funny."

Mom stares at me with glassy eyes. David has a little smile. "It sounds like you like this girl," he says.

"I do. Very much. She's my girlfriend."

I shouldn't say it, but I do because it makes me happy. But Mom narrows her eyes, David raises his eyebrows, and Rebekah looks at me sidelong.

"Oh, you have a girlfriend," David says. He glances at my mother.

"I don't think he means in that way," she says.

Anger burns up inside me, and I try to fight it back. "I do mean it in that way. I asked her if she would be my girlfriend, and she said yes."

We cross Center Street on the crosswalk, not bothering to look for cars on the silent road. "Justin," Mom says, "sometimes when people say things, they don't really mean them. Like when they're telling jokes."

"I know what a joke is, Mom, and Mina wasn't joking." I say it louder than I mean to. We quit walking, and they all stare at me. My heart pounds. I take a deep breath.

"Justin, you're a very good-looking boy," Mom says, "but you have to realize that..." She cuts off, because we hear footsteps running up behind us.

All the muscles in my chest that have tightened suddenly loosen up again, and my heart aches in a very good way. I smile. "Mina."

She runs to me, her breasts bouncing under her dark blue t-shirt. "Hey, Justin. I was at the store and saw you."

I take both of her hands, running my thumb over her fingers, remembering how it felt when she touched me last night. I want Mom, David, and David's nervous-emotion daughter to go away. One corner of Mina's mouth curls up and I can tell she wants that too, but she turns and smiles at them very politely.

"Hello, Mrs. Flaherty," she says. She tugs one of her hands out of mine and holds it out to David. "I'm Saramina Aceves."

David shakes her hand, smiling and puffing his chest out. He's only a few inches taller than she is. "Very nice to meet you, young lady. I'm David Esau. This is Rebekah, my daughter."

Mina shakes Rebekah's hand too. Mom watches my girlfriend like a cat with its ears back, ready to hiss.

Mina turns to me and takes my other hand again. I notice how the morning sun slants through her long black lashes and leaves shadows on her freckled cheeks, and how perfect creamy pink her lips are, even without lipstick. "Mina," I say. I brush her hair away from her face and tuck it behind her ear.

"Will you come to the park later?" she asks.

"Yes. After I sleep for a little while."

She scrunches her eyebrows together. "You didn't sleep yet?"

"No. I don't like to sleep at nighttime because I like the nighttime and don't want to miss it."

"We should all get together for dinner. Don't you think, Jane?" David says, and it startles me. I've forgotten entirely about the other people.

Mom has a look like she's caught in a net. She does a weird nod. "Yes, that's a good idea. Can you come tonight, Mina?"

Mina and I glance at one another and then she looks over at them, all bright, smiling politeness again. "I would love to."

"Six thirty?" Mom asks.

"I'll be there," Mina says. She turns back to me.

"I'll see you in the park later," I say. I want to bend down and kiss her, but I know that would be a bad idea in front of the serious-faced Adults. Mina gives me a smile very different from the one she gave Mom and David. She lets go of my hands and turns and runs back toward the store, where I can see her little twin brothers waiting, each eating a bag of Hot Cheetos. I feel lonely already.

"She seems like a nice girl," David says.

"Yes," Mom says, frowning.

Rebekah stares at me very carefully now,

looking for something in me, like I'm a closet full of objects. I stare back at her for a moment, and she smiles and looks away.

We start walking again, and Mom straightens her shoulders. "Mina's mother left her and her brothers and went to Fresno, right?"

I think this is a very odd thing for her to get judgmental about considering past events. "Her mom and dad broke up, and her mom got a job in Fresno," I say. "Mina wanted to finish her high school program here, and they didn't want to split up the siblings, so they're staying with their dad for now."

"How old is Mina?" David asks.

"She's sixteen," I say.

"So she's going to be a junior? Or a sophomore?" he asks.

"A senior," I say. "She's in an accelerated program. She takes classes at the community college in Paso, and she'll graduate this year with about twenty college credits."

David raises his eyebrows. "That's quite impressive."

"Yes," I say. "Mina is very wonderful."

Mom shoots me a look that makes my mouth taste sour. Her thoughts leave patterns around her, so I know what she is thinking. She is thinking that there is something wrong with Mina liking me. Mom thinks since I'm "too much" for *her*, that no other woman should ever like me, especially a good one like Mina.

Mom won't love me until I reach enlightenment. She is a test of the Dark Energy for me, and I won't fail it by becoming angry.

"And what about you, Justin?" David asks. "What are your plans in regards to school?"

My feet stumble as I get a sharp pain in my head. Mom gives David a confused look. "Justin got kicked out of school."

"Yes, I know," David says, "but there are special programs. In fact, I know of a good one. Some friends of mine in Wyoming have a school for young men like Justin, to help them finish with their education and get on the right path. It's Bible-based, and they do lots of amazing things there."

My arms ache because they are clamped so stiffly to my sides. My thoughts are starting to race out in front of me, and I feel like I need to run in order to catch up with them, but I can't. That would make mom angry. Very angry and too much trouble.

"I don't want to go to Wyoming," I say. "I don't know about school, and I don't want to go to Wyoming."

Mom stares at me with pursed lips, and her gaze darts to David. "We don't have to discuss this right now," she says.

"Okay," he says. "I didn't mean to upset you, Justin."

I try to breathe in some calm vibrations from the Dark Energy, then breathe them out again. "Not upset. I'm not upset," I say.

David studies me with that crease between his brows, and I look away from him. His face makes me ill. I am not so sure about David. I can't think about him. I try to concentrate on a long crack in the asphalt, try to align it with the directional component of my bad feelings and funnel them away, but it won't. It's not working. All of a sudden I realize something, and the world goes white like an overexposed photograph. My body tenses like an arrow poised to be shot.

"I have to go," I say.

"Justin—" Mom says.

I take off running. The Dark Energy has told me I'll die if I stay there, that it will drown me and dissolve me like acid. I'm not sure how that would manifest in the Physical World—maybe I'd get hit by a car or crushed by a falling airplane part. Maybe David would kill me for some reason. I don't know. But I would die for sure. I know Mom is angry about me leaving, because her anger is a scorching heat on my back. I don't know why she would want me to die, and that makes me even more scared.

I run up past the school, then over through the neighborhoods. The color starts to come back into the world as I get away from the danger. I go over the bridge, past the chicken farm, then out to where the cows live in the fields by the sandstone hills.

I stop. My breath burns me with clean, good oxygen. I watch the cows watching me as they chew dry grass, their eyes like billiard balls, their mouths and noses wet with mucus. They radiate calm, and I breathe it in. They are big, warm creatures, and their thick skins and hard skulls make it difficult for them to get the sickness. I wish I were a cow sometimes.

After a while it is safe again, so I turn around and run back toward town. When I get home no one is there, and I crawl into bed, thinking about Mina.

I dream about Mina too. We're driving in her car, bringing paperwork to the elephant seals so they can enroll in school. But the dream changes; it's not really a dream anymore, and Mina is no longer Mina. She's the girl I met in the park in Paso, with long, dark hair and dark eyes, extremely pretty but very sad, her death wrapped around her like a blanket.

She sits in the passenger seat of a creamy blue convertible, and I'm in the driver's seat. We're parked in a swamp. A parrot sits in the branches of a banyan tree draped in writhing vines, peering at us, a cell phone clutched in its clawed hand. Every so often it raises it to its beak and mutters something I can't hear.

Other shapes lurk in the shadowy centers of the trees, and some of them inch out along the branches: businessmen in suits, hunched around their bent knees, gazing at us with dull eyes.

The girl from the park has her arms crossed. She stares at the dashboard.

"Love isn't the most important thing, if it isn't love," I say. "Sometimes what people call love is really just a test of the Dark Energy."

She blinks and puts her head on my shoulder, tears sliding over her cheeks. "But it's the only thing I have."

I put my arm around her and hold her as she cries. The businessmen watch us silently and the parrot reports it all to his correspondent, but the girl from the park needs me. So I stay.

She looks up at me and smiles, big tears shining on her eyelashes. "I'm so glad you're here."

I wake up with the afternoon sun shining in my eyes, wondering why I keep seeing the girl from the park in the Other Place.

Chapter 6

My house smells like cooking meat when Mina and I come in from the park. I like it when Mom gets in these moods because she buys actual food and does a lot of good cooking. She also tends to forget that I don't eat meat, but I see a salad on the counter, and she is mashing potatoes.

David sits at the kitchen table working on a laptop computer. Rebekah is beside him, reading what looks like a textbook. They both look up, and David flips his computer closed.

"There you are," he says. He stands up and shakes Mina's hand as if he were running for office.

My mother looks over at my girlfriend, but goes back to mashing her potatoes, her arms jiggling as she pounds them.

"What's this you have in your hand?" David asks Mina.

She hands it to him. "Justin drew this for me this morning," she says.

It is a drawing of her face reflected in a pool of water. Her fingers touch the surface of the pool, ripples spreading out from them and distorting the reflection.

David looks at it. He glances up with a different sort of look than he's given me before. "This is very good. Jane, you didn't tell me that Justin was an artist. And a spectacular one at that."

"Yeah, he draws," Mom says. "Does it so much he doesn't finish his chores."

Rebekah comes over to peer at it as well, and looks up at me as if she's startled, twisting her ponytail. I shift on my feet.

David gives the sketch back to Mina. He stands, studying me instead of the drawing. "God has given you a great gift."

"He forgot to wrap it," I say because I am not really sure what else to say. Mina coughs and covers her mouth.

David breaks into a grin. "God often forgets to wrap his gifts, but they're wonderful all the same."

Mom rinses off the potato masher in the sink and dries her hands, frowning at me. "Dinner's ready."

Mina and Rebekah help her carry the food out to the dining room table, which is set with the silver-rimmed plates and the blue tablecloth and linen napkins in the beaded napkin-holders. I am not used to eating in here, because it is usually stacked with boxes and spread out with whatever Mom's current project is. But it is clean and pleasant now. A window looks out over the porch through the climbing wisteria and grapes, which are drooping because I've forgotten to turn the water on.

We all sit down. Mina sits next to me and takes my hand under the table. I almost reach over to serve myself potatoes, but I remember about the religion happening in our house right now.

David looks around at us, and we bow our heads. Mina squeezes my hand, and we peek at each other.

"Heavenly Father," David says. "Thank you for this wonderful meal that Jane has prepared for us, and for all the other gifts that you give us. Even though they may not come wrapped in pretty paper, Lord, please help us to recognize them, and to be thankful. Please help us to find joy in being your instrument, and to accept your guidance in our lives."

"In Jesus' name we pray. Amen."

"Amen," the rest of us say.

Mom and Mina pass their plates to David so that he can serve them prime rib, but I just spoon myself up a big, creamy heap of mashed potatoes and a lot of salad, which Mom has made with romaine lettuce and sliced black olives, grated mozzarella cheese and croutons. There are also warm rolls. I'm very hungry.

"You don't want any meat, Justin?" David asks.

"Justin is *vegetarian*," Mom says, giving him a look which says, *Look at all the complicated ways he finds to annoy me*.

"You are?" he asks. "Why is that?"

"I don't like the way it tastes," I say. "It absorbs the death-thoughts and sadness of the animals, and that tastes bad." I put a square of butter onto my potatoes and spread some onto my roll.

David gazes at me. "Fair enough, though God did give us dominion over all the creatures of the Earth, Justin. It's His way of providing us

52

nourishment, and taking care of us." He takes a bite of his beef and smiles at Mom. "I *do* like the way it tastes, Jane. This is wonderful."

"Thank you," Mom says.

David presides over the small-talk as if he were mayor of the dinner table. He asks Mina all sorts of questions about her school program, and what she wants to do after she graduates.

"I'd like to study software engineering," she says.

"Oh," he says. "Where would you like to study?"

"Well, Cal Tech, if I can get in, but I don't think I can. It's really, extremely hard. I'll be sending out applications soon."

"I wouldn't be so sure you won't get in, young lady," David says. "You seem very smart to me."

Mina shifts in her chair and gives him a jerky sort of smile. "Thank you."

"Rebekah here is planning a mission trip to Brazil after she graduates," David says.

Rebekah pushes her meat around her plate, her cheeks going pinker. "And then I think I'll go to college to be a social worker." She says it very quietly, not looking at any of us. Rebekah doesn't want to make any waves at all in the Dark Energy, I think. She doesn't want to let the howling-wind hurricane of her emotions free, because we all might get blown away.

"That's awesome, Rebekah," Mina says. Rebekah glances up at her and smiles, but her eyes bite and sting like a salty gale.

David turns on me now, the canyon between his eyebrows deepening. "Education is very important.

It can help us see the path that God has laid out for us more clearly, and help us realize our potential." He takes a bite of his meat and chews it, his jaw muscles rolling around under his skin. "I wish you would at least consider the program in Wyoming, Justin. I think you'd be happy there. I can show you their website, if you like, just to see how it strikes you."

The food I've eaten eats my stomach in return, and I curl around my middle to protect it. Mina looks at me with her eyebrows together, and then at David. "What program in Wyoming?"

"It's an alternative education program for young men like Justin who have had trouble in public school," he says. "He could complete his high school studies there."

I scrape my fork through my mashed potatoes. I cannot look at David. The Dark Energy presses against my chest. It is making my stomach very sick.

Mina speaks up. "I'm going to help him get his GED. He doesn't need to go all the way to Wyoming."

I look over at her. This is the first I've heard of this, but the Dark Energy likes it a lot and stops squeezing. I smile, and Mina smiles back.

"I think you should go study art," she says, taking a bite of her salad.

"Yes," I say. "That would be ideal."

David exchanges a glance with Mom. "Well, that could work," he says, "but the program in Wyoming is something to think about, Justin. Don't rule it out. The self-directed approach isn't for everyone."

He takes another bite of meat, and Mom stares out the window as if she thinks the wilting grape vines will commiserate with her.

Chapter 7

We sit at the dining room table while Mina reminds me about algebra. It's been a long time since I learned it. I've never been good at math, but she is. It makes sense when she explains it to me, even though she is sitting close and that's distracting.

Mom, David, and Rebekah are at the church house, praying for God to buy them some better carpet I think. I'm glad to be away from them. David and Rebekah live in the church house, not with us, because David believes God gets in a smiting mood about unmarried people living together, but they are always here, and their presence is like a rock in my shoe.

"There's something I wanted to talk to you about," Mina says, and I look up from my word problem. "My uncle has a friend, Stewart, who owns an art gallery in San Francisco."

I put my pencil down, and my hand slowly creeps up her leg. "Is this about making me into Andy Warhol?"

She grins and pinches me. "Yes…sorta. I sent my uncle a picture of the drawing you gave me. He showed it to his friend, and he wants to see more. He likes your style. I hope you don't mind I sent it. It was just so awesome."

"I don't mind. What do I need to do?"

She taps her pencil against the open math book. "How many other drawings do you have?"

"Hundreds of thousands," I say, and she cocks an eyebrow. "Okay, I'm lying. It's one hundred thousand times x minus y."

"That, I believe," she says. "Will you show me?"

"Of course."

We get up and go into my room, and I get the notebooks full of my drawings off of the bookshelf. "I had more," I say, "but Mom threw a lot of them away when she took me up to Idaho. She said there wasn't room."

Mina gives me a look to show me she's not happy about this, but doesn't say anything.

We sit on my bed and she flips through the notebooks. She takes a picture of the one of the squid in a business suit smoking a cigarette, and of the one where the kitten is angry at the hand mixer. She also likes the coyote in the grape field, and the crow's face reflected in the back of a spoon. She gets to another one and stops.

"Who is this?" she asks.

I pick at a hole in the leg of my shorts. "That's the girl I met in the park when I lived with my grandma."

"Oh." She looks at me closely. "She's super pretty. What's her name?"

"I don't know. I never asked her." The hole in my shorts is fraying down to strings. "She was very sad."

Mina flips past that drawing without taking a picture.

We are still looking at drawings when we hear the door open, and voices. Mom says, "Justin?"

"In here, Mom," I say.

She appears in the doorway with David next to her. Rebekah peeks between them. David is wearing a Hawaiian shirt and shorts today, and has paint splotches on his clothes and hands. His grey eyes slip back and forth between Mina and me, very serious and stern. "Hello, Saramina. It's nice to see you again."

"Nice to see you too, Mr. Esau," she says.

David's seriousness pours out of him, filling up the Dark Energy and creeping up my spine. I straighten, puffing my chest out. We are both serious Men now, taking care of Man business. Mina shoots me a look, and we try not to laugh.

"What are you two doing in here?" David asks.

"I was showing her my drawings," I say very gravely. "Before, we were studying algebra."

"Hmmm," he says. "I don't think it's right for two young people to be alone together in the house, do you, Jane?"

"No, I don't think that's right at all," Mom says. "We all know what trouble teenagers can get up to."

She and David exchange a smirky look with raised eyebrows, as if to show each other they are enlightened about teenagers. Mom is doing a social dance, because this is not her normal personality, but I don't say anything about it, because the Dark Energy is uncomfortable enough as it is right now.

"I think, from now on, someone should be with you at all times, as a chaperone," David says.

My manly posture wilts a little. "A chaperone." The word is like foreign food, the flavors strange and slightly sickening on my tongue.

"I have to go now, anyway," Mina says. "I said I'd take my brothers to the pool." She looks at me, and she is so beautiful. "Will you come to the park later?" she asks.

"Of course," I say, and I let my finger graze over her knee, not because I have forgotten they are watching us, but *because* they are watching us; because I am a legal adult and David is just my mom's flavor of the month and can't tell me what to do. Mina gives me a little smile. She knows this is our own little social dance.

She hands me back my drawings and gets up. David, Mom, and Rebekah stand aside so she can leave. "I'll see you later, Mr. Esau, Mrs. Flaherty, Rebekah," Mina says. Then she is gone, and I already miss her.

"I'll go start lunch," Mom says. Rebekah goes with her to help, but David remains standing in the doorway, his hands in the pockets of his khaki shorts.

"Mina is a nice girl," he says.

"Yes, she is extraordinary." We squint at each other. David is much different than my mom's normal men. He has a lot less color and vibration, and it is hard for me to see him correctly.

"Do you know what it means to be a man,

59

Justin?" he asks.

I think about it. "That is a very strange question."

He glances down the hallway toward the kitchen, where we can hear Mom and Rebekah talking to each other. He looks back at me and smiles as if we are sharing a secret. "Being a man isn't an easy job. Sometimes it means not following our desires, because as men, we always have to do what's best. So we always have to look not to ourselves, but to God for guidance."

"It is not always easy to do the right thing, Justin, because the Devil whispers in our ear, telling us to do the wrong thing. But we can ignore him, because we are Men. The women look to us for protection, and to lead them on God's chosen path, and we can't let them down."

I pick at the hole in my shorts some more. It almost goes through to my skin now.

"Do you understand what I mean?" he asks.

His words have tangled up in my brain like a long string of Christmas lights, and every way I try to pull the knots out it just gets worse. David is a puzzle, the hardest test of the Dark Energy yet.

"I don't know if I understand what you mean," I say. "I don't think anyone looks to me for leadership or protection, because those things are meaningless in the face of death. But I do always try to do the right thing because if I don't, the punishment will be horrible."

His smile goes away, and he looks down his nose at me thoughtfully. "Yes, that's true. The punishment for doing the wrong thing *will* be horrible. But we Men *can* offer leadership and protection, Justin. Protection from other people, and from the Devil. Leadership on God's path. That's why I'm putting the chaperone rule in place, because I want to help you do the right thing, help you become a real Man as opposed to just a male. The Devil speaks very loudly to people your age, and I want to keep you, and Mina, safe."

I don't say anything, because it seems like there isn't anywhere for me to grab hold of this conversation.

David comes into the room, laying a hand on my shoulder, which is very tense. "Let's go have lunch," he says.

I stand, shrugging off his hand, and we go out to the table.

Mom and Rebekah have made us all sandwiches with potato salad. Mom puts a plate down in front of me as I sit, and gives me a challenging look.

I pull back the top slice of bread. It is yet another test of the Dark Energy, because it is a tuna fish sandwich. I was one of them, and so eating fish would be especially cruel and evil and would make the Dark Energy furious.

"I'm not hungry," I say. I get up from the table and go back into my room.

I shut my door and sit on my bed. The Dark Energy is angry and dangerous. I close my eyes and see the fish around me, staring at me with their big silver eyes. They are frightened. Being eaten hurts them. I hear their mind-thoughts about death and smell its heavy stench. They press around me in a frantic mass, their fins and scales brushing against me with a sick feeling.

But the actions of the others are just a test for me. They are part of my enlightenment. I take a deep breath and tell the fish I'm sorry, but I can't control the actions of others. I have not killed any fish myself. I say it over and over again, until they finally start to listen.

Slowly, the fish calm down. I let the anger drain out and clear itself from the air around me. I realize I am rocking back and forth and clutching my arms very hard.

I stop. I take a couple of deep breaths, snatch up my drawing pad, and start to draw.

After a while, the bad vibrations settle down because I have captured and organized them on the paper, drawing them out of the Physical World and into the Other Place where they are happier. I think about sneaking out the window to meet Mina at the pool. I don't know if David would impose his chaperone rule in a public place, but I'm not going to ask him anyway.

There is a soft tapping at the door. It is not the way that Mom or David would knock. I get up to answer it. It's Rebekah, standing there, tugging at the fold of her shirt where it is tucked into her shorts.

"Hi, Justin," she says. "Can I come in?"

"Sure," I say, standing aside so she can walk past me.

I wonder if this is about the sandwiches, and I hope it is not. I don't know if I can think about the sandwiches right now.

She sits on my bed, staring at her knees with her

forehead scrunched up. I sit down next to her. She looks up at me, and the Dark Energy jolts through me because of her strong emotions.

"I wanted to talk to you," she says, her eyes fixed on mine.

"Okay," I say.

But she doesn't talk for several moments. She breaks her eye-lock with me and looks at her lap, her foot tapping on the floor, the corners of her lips curling down and burying themselves in her round cheeks.

Finally she looks back at me again. "You're very special, Justin. Do you know that God has chosen you for special work?"

"Oh," I say. "No, I didn't know that." I think about it for a moment. "If I end up doing God's work, will I lose my Social Security? Mom wouldn't like that."

Rebekah shifts in her seat, making my bed creak. She doesn't smile at all. "No, you wouldn't lose your Social Security. It's not that kind of work."

I tap my pencil on the paper, wishing Rebekah would go away so I could draw. But she sits there twirling her hair around her finger, staring at me with her mouth slightly open. "What work do you think God has chosen me for?" I ask.

"I don't know. But I can see God in you. I can see his hand on you."

I look around, but I don't see God's hand anywhere and I can't feel it touching me. Rebekah's big, blue eyes shine. They are so full of emotion she can't blink, and it is making me a little bit nervous.

"You draw so beautifully," she says. "Can I

see?"

She leans over my lap to look at my drawing. It is of a big fish in a Cadillac convertible, wearing sunglasses and holding a gun. Another fish is sprawled out on the sidewalk next to him, shot dead. I'm not entirely sure what the Dark Energy is trying to say with this one.

Rebekah's eyes are wide as she gazes at it. "It's very interesting. Can I see your other ones?"

"Sure."

I get the notebooks off my shelf. Rebekah flips through them, looking at each one carefully. When she gets to the drawing of the swarm of ants pulling the pouting girl in the rickshaw, she stops and stares at it for a long time.

"This is amazing," she says. "The perspective..."

I pick at the hole in my shorts again. I don't know if Rebekah knows about the Dark Energy. It is hard to tell with her.

"It's how I saw it," I say. "I was one of the ants."

She finally blinks. "What do you mean?"

"I was taught a lesson about the ants. I was an ant, and we all had a great desire to work together to pull the rickshaw. We didn't know we were pulling the rickshaw, or what our goal was at all. It was just the need that was put in us, and so we did it and found joy in it. We were doing what we needed to do. But the girl didn't find any joy in being pulled, I don't think."

"You had a vision?" she asks, and she's leaning close to me.

I lean away a little. "I don't know."

A smile passes briefly across her lips. "I think

sometimes people are cruel and don't understand that when others are different. It doesn't mean they're..."

I know what she was going to say, because people say it a lot about me, but she doesn't say it. Instead she takes a little breath and lets it out. I can feel it, warm and damp on my neck. We are sharing the same breathing space, competing for oxygen.

"I think you're very special, Justin," she says again.

"Thank you." My voice is a little choked because I'm trying to conserve air.

She smiles, and resumes flipping through the drawings, her hair falling over her face in a thick, shining curtain. I scoot away from her a little, to make it more comfortable in here.

I'm not quite sure about Rebekah. She's like a slightly untuned guitar string. Her intonation is off, and she buzzes against the fretboard.

She stops again at a drawing of a bunch of men in business suits sitting up in a tree like vultures. "Was this another vision you had?"

I have to think about it, because I don't know for sure what she thinks a vision is. "No," I finally say. "I saw those guys in a dream. They lurk. They're lurkers. I'm not sure what they're up to, up in those trees. I think it might be capitalism, or espionage, or they're just parasitically feasting on our vibrational signatures."

She gazes at me for a moment. She flips to the next drawing.

"You need to get your drawings somewhere where people can see them," she says.

"That's what Mina says. She took pictures of them with her phone because she knows someone with an art gallery in the City."

Rebekah's chin comes up so quickly that I jump a little. "I worry about your relationship with Mina. She doesn't let God guide her, and I'm afraid she'll lure you down the wrong path."

It is not the sickness I see in Rebekah now, but the Dark Energy is definitely doing something angry and painful in her.

"You don't need to worry," I say very soothingly. "Mina is extremely good."

But this just stirs her up worse. I can see all those emotions swirling in currents behind her eyes, and her lips tremble. I don't know what's going on with Rebekah, but it seems to be pushing me out of the room, and I have to clutch my mattress in order to stay put.

"Justin," she says, "I'm worried your wonderful gifts will go to waste. You need to be around people who appreciate you for who you are, and who will help you to hear God's voice more clearly."

I clear my dry throat, clutching at my mattress harder. "What does God's voice sound like?"

Her wide eyes shine. "You hear it in your heart." She presses her fingers between her small breasts, where her heart is. "It fills up your whole soul, and helps you to see your way."

I imagine her red, pulsating heart, with tiny little ears sticking out on either side of it. I see a man with a long, white beard speaking loudly into one of those ears. I don't say anything.

"Justin," she says, "may I pray for you now?

Will you pray with me?"

"Certainly," I say, though I think God must be tired of hearing about me at this point. I make my shoulders relax and pry my hands off the bed. Maybe if I pray with her, then she'll go away.

Rebekah sets my drawings aside and takes my hand very gently in both of hers, pressing her thumbs into my sweaty palm. She bows her head to her chest and closes her eyes. I'm so busy trying to interpret her strangeness that she has already begun to pray before I remember I'm not supposed to peek, and close my eyes.

"Heavenly Father," Rebekah says, "I lift up to you your special child, Justin. He is so talented and has been touched by you in so many ways. Please help him feel your presence and your guidance. Sometimes those with special gifts are misunderstood. Others scorn them and try to exploit or mislead them. But we know you are with him, and that you will protect him. We know you will give him people in his life who will support him and help to lead him on the right path. Help him to feel their friendship, and to see your light in his life. Help us all to know what your will is."

"In Jesus' name we pray, Amen."

"Amen," I say, opening my eyes.

Rebekah is staring at me and is still holding my hand.

"Thank you for praying for me, Rebekah," I say, because I want to be polite and hope it will help calm the bad vibrations in her.

She smiles and squeezes my hand. "I'll keep praying for you, Justin."

Chapter 8

I'm trying to concentrate on my math, but it's hard because Mina's cousin, Angelica, keeps coming up behind me, putting her little, grubby hands over my eyes and giggling. "Peek buh, Yustin," she says.

I reach over the back of the couch, find her armpit with my finger, and tickle her. She squeals and twists around, and I have to grab her arm so she doesn't fall off her stepstool.

"Do 'gin, Yustin!" she demands.

"Angelica, leave us to study," Mina says. She turns and yells down the hall. "'Nulfo! Get your sister! She's bugging us!"

A door down the hall opens and Arnulfo ambles in with his hands in his pockets. He grabs Angelica, then lifts her up and pretends to eat her ear while she giggles hysterically. He throws her over his shoulder and takes her back down the hall as she screams and reaches for me, her sticky fingers splayed.

"No! Yustin! I want Yustin!" She starts crying

and kicking, but Arnulfo ignores her, and her wails diminish as he shuts the door to his bedroom.

Mina looks at me and sighs. "I'm sorry."

"Don't apologize," I say.

We are studying at Mina's house because of David's chaperone rule. Apparently Arnulfo and Angelica are good enough chaperones for David, since he and Mom are having one of their romantic lunch dates today.

"Maybe we should've just taken Rebekah up on her offer to stay with us at your house," Mina says, scowling.

"I believe she decided to go out driving in her new car, anyway," I say.

David bought Rebekah a used Audi. She'd invited me to go with her to the beach today, which was very confusing because of the chaperone rule. I'd told her I needed to study and couldn't go.

The front door opens. It is Eugenio, Mina's dad, home from work with a big paper sack in his arms. He grins. "How's the studying going?"

"Very well," I say. "Mina does magic things that insert knowledge into my brain, and I believe I'm ready for the test."

Mina's two brothers come tumbling in behind their father, pushing and shooting invisible guns at each other.

"That's great," Eugenio says, wading through his pandemonium of sons to set the sack down on the breakfast bar. "I know that Mina knows lots of magic brain tricks. That's why she's so smart. Wish she would share some of them with me."

He turns to yell down the hall. "Hey! There's

69

chicken for dinner!" He turns to his sons. "Knock it off, you two. You're too rowdy."

Mina's brothers simmer down slightly and grab plates, hovering around the food as Eugenio takes it out of the bag. The door to Arnulfo's bedroom opens, and there are thundering footsteps as Angelica comes running, Arnulfo following her more sedately.

"Po-yo!" Angelica yelps. "Po-yo, po-yo, poeeeeeeeee-yo!"

"Chicken, chicken," Arnulfo says, scooping the wiggling toddler up in his arms.

Mina's family is a lot of noise and commotion, but their vibrations are calm. I very much enjoy her house.

"Come have some *pollo*, you lovey-doveys," Eugenio says to us.

"Justin is vegetarian, Dad," Mina says.

"Well come have some potatoes and salad, then," he says.

Mina and I wait for everyone else to get food. The kids all go back in Arnulfo's bedroom so they can play videogames while they eat, and we get up to get some for ourselves.

"Thank you for dinner, Mr. Aceves," I say.

"No problem, Justin."

Just as we are sitting down on the couch, Mina's phone dings, and she fishes it out of her back pocket.

She gasps, then smiles at me, bouncing in her seat. "It's Uncle Julio. His friend, Stewart with the art gallery, loves your drawings and wants to see them in person, and meet you. Stewart's in Europe for another week or so, but he'll call me to set up a time when he gets back."

Eugenio sits down in a recliner opposite us. "That's awesome," he says, raising his eyebrows at me.

"It is," I say. The Dark Energy does a strange dance around me, and my nerves sing. It is nice to think other people enjoy my drawings. "But I don't know how I'm going to get to San Francisco," I say. "My current domestic climate is not conducive to me getting a ride, and I don't think Grandma would have time."

"I can take you," Mina says. She stares at her dad, pressing her pretty lips together.

He runs his hand over his graying hair, shooting me a look. Mina huffs.

"Come on, Dad, we could stay the night at Julio's house. He'd let us. It would be fine."

"I don't know." His gaze rests on me. "What would your mom say, Justin?"

"It's not Mom I'm worried about," I say. "It's the man in whose sphere of influence she is currently caught."

Mina spears a chunk of her shredded cabbage, her eyebrows scrunched together. I notice something. "Mina, you're not eating any chicken."

She shoots me a little, lopsided grin. "I'm caught in your sphere of influence."

"Mina," I say, "that's not necessary."

She pokes me in the ribs and looks back at her dad expectantly.

Eugenio sighs. "I guess if you can clear it with your mom and her boyfriend, Justin, then you two can go."

Mina and I grin at each other because we are excited.

"BUT," her father continues, "you need to go right there and right back, no dawdling in between. I'm going to time you, and have Julio tell me when you get there and when you leave."

"Okay, Dad, but there's always traffic."

"I'm gonna check the traffic cameras and make sure I see you on them," he says.

Mina blows a raspberry. "Whatever."

"I'll whatever you, Saramina." His smile fades slightly, and he looks at me hesitantly, twiddling his fork. "Speaking of your mom's boyfriend, I wanted to ask you…" He laughs nervously. "I mean, what's up with that guy, anyway?"

"Do you mean to say, what's up with him being such a gigantically strange person?" I ask.

Mina snorts into her salad, and Eugenio laughs loudly. He's not hesitating with his emotions any longer now that he sees we share a similar opinion of David. "He was over here yesterday, inviting me to his new church." He squints over the top of a chicken leg as he takes a bite. "I told him I was Catholic but the guy, like, tried to argue with me about it."

"Yes," I say. "David thinks your Jesus is just some guy in a Jesus costume, but that he knows the real one."

Both Eugenio and Mina choke a little, and Eugenio shakes his head. "Man, that heavy religious stuff's too complicated for me." He looks at me sadly. "I hope you can get that guy to let you go to the City. Your drawings are really great, and you need to get them out there for people to see. I'll bet you could even make a career at it."

"Thank you," I say.

But I think it will not be easy to convince David to let me go. I look over at Mina, who is frowning at her potatoes. I know she's thinking that too.

***

Mina walks me home after dinner, and kisses me under the dangling grape vines on the porch.

"I'll see you tonight," she whispers in my ear, which makes the back of my head tingle. I watch her as she walks back through the gate to the street. I enjoy watching her walk, and she is almost around the corner before I remember to go into the house.

I pause at the door, my shoulders tense. The thought of facing David makes my stomach pucker. But when I open the door, David isn't there; Mom is alone in the kitchen, scrubbing furiously at a spot on the refrigerator.

"Hello, Mom," I say. "Where's David?"

"He's out talking to people about the first service this Sunday," she says. "The pews came today. We need you to help us put them in tomorrow."

"Okay." I stand there, shifting my weight from foot to foot, wondering if Mom will even make this decision without consulting David.

"Mom," I say, and she stops scrubbing and turns her head to look at me. "Mina sent some photos of my drawings to a guy in San Francisco with an art gallery. He wants me to come there so he can see the real drawings and meet me."

She turns completely away from the fridge, staring at me and twisting the rag in her hands. "That's great, Justin. It really is. But don't you think it might be too much for you to go to the City?"

I clutch my arms over my sour stomach. "I'd be fine, Mom. Mina will drive me, and we'll be staying the night with Mina's uncle. He lives there."

"That's not what I mean." She sighs, and her eyelids flutter closed for a moment before they snap back open. "I think it's great that you draw. Your artwork is very pretty sometimes, when you're not drawing nonsense. But you're just setting yourself up for trouble by getting involved with art galleries and those people. It's very nice of them to show interest, but..." She puts her hands on her hips and squints at me. "Justin, this Mina girl, I just don't think she's good for you. She may or may not have good intentions. I don't know, but you're just going to end up getting hurt with all these *plans* she has. She doesn't know how you are yet."

My teeth feel like they're stuck together with Jolly Ranchers, and I have to pry them open. "Mina is a wonderful person, and it's a very good opportunity to have my pictures up in a gallery." I close my eyes and huff a breath out my nose, but the anger pours in before I can stop it. I open my eyes and glare at her. "You're just farting bad smells out of your mouth, Mom. You're just cluttering up the airwaves with your stupidity. This isn't a good way to help me reach enlightenment."

"Don't start on this enlightenment crap with me, Justin. It's not even biblical."

"I don't like your tests, Mom. Your tests are the worst."

"Just *shut up,* Justin." Mom's nostrils flare and she flings her hands jerkily up in the air, the rag flapping. "I've worked my ass off my whole life to take care of you. Look at the bullshit I went through when you were just trying to go to school. How do you think it's going to go with this? You'll crumble under the pressure sooner or later and end up back in the hospital. I spent months fighting to get you Social Security so that you'd be taken care of. You're just going to end up losing that money if you try to sell your art, and it will be a fight all over again when you flip out and the money dries up."

I take a breath to say something, but Mom has already taken all the breaths out of the room to use for her own words.

"Mina just doesn't understand she's going to make you worse," she persists. "She doesn't stop to think about what a pain in the ass it is for the rest of us to deal with you. Do you think she's going to stick around and help deal with it when you freak out, when she sees what kind of person you really are? No, that will all be left up to me, and she'll be off at her little college learning how to tinker with computers or whatever. So cut me a break once in your life, Justin, and just be happy with what you have, which is a good home and regular meals, even if you won't eat them because of your silly ideas."

The Dark Energy squeezes around my heart. I'm floating in a bubble of it, detached from the earth. I dig my fingers into my palms, clinging to my body. "Mom," I choke out, but she presses her lips together and stomps.

"*Don't argue with me, Justin*. Just forget about this bullcrap and get on with your life."

The Physical World is barely visible. Mom's angry face is grey and hazy behind the veil which surrounds me and separates me from her. I want to run, but my feet hesitate, trying to take me in two directions at once. I think I'm going to be torn in two or disintegrate completely into a pile of chunks on the floor. But I don't. I turn and go into my room instead, slamming the door and flopping on my bed.

I realize I am crying. This is new for me. I don't feel like this is a test of the Dark Energy. I don't believe there is any lesson in what I am feeling. I'm just sad. I'm worried Mom is right, and Mina doesn't feel the same way about me that I feel about her. I'm worried sooner or later she'll get tired of dealing with me, like Mom has.

I curl up tight on the mattress and ask the Energy to not let that happen. I beg for it to let Mina and me stay together. I need her, because she makes me happy and makes the vibrations smooth out.

The Dark Energy tells me our physical bodies are temporary, and what I'm asking for is meaningless. We will both be absorbed in the end. We are both part of the same energy, and when we reach enlightenment the concept of love will lose definition as our individuality does. But I don't care about that, because I love Mina, and that is important to me and my physical body right now.

My thoughts are pulling out in a long string, like a leash tugging me forward. My feet and fingers twitch and my legs writhe. I jump up. I pace around my room. I still feel like I need to run, but I decide to draw instead, because I think that maybe if I draw more, it will keep Mina with me. Maybe if I get famous like Andy Warhol, she will love me.

I force my body into stillness and lie down on my bed, picking up my art things. My pencil scratches on the paper with a soothing whisper as the sun goes down and the pink evening light comes through my window.

The Dark Energy stops pressing, though I'm still sad. I turn on my light and keep drawing, the picture coming into focus. It is very calming to watch it form, to let my pencil bring that image out of the Energy and onto the paper. I'm drawing a picture of a lemur peeling an orange, except instead of fruit inside there are algebraic equations. I want to give it to Mina because she has done a very good job teaching me math.

I hear my mom go to bed. The house creaks around me as it cools.

I enjoy the nighttime. It's like a quiet cocoon. It's like a hug.

I am still drawing when I hear the back door open. The person opening it is trying to be very quiet, but it makes a certain little squeak that is very easy to identify. It closes again, and there are slow, careful footsteps heading down the hallway toward my mom's room, the old hardwood floors cracking and popping.

It's just David. He has been sneaking in the past few nights. His chaperone rule does not apply to himself, apparently.

A few minutes later there is a light tapping on

my window, and my chest aches with happiness. I open the window and climb out, then put my arms around Mina. We all have our secret love lives here in Piedras, I think.

"Mina," I say. I kiss her. When she is there, when she is kissing me, everything is all right. It doesn't feel like a trick. It feels like Mina cares for me. It is wonderful.

But until I am enlightened, I can still be tricked. This may be a very hard lesson. This may be the Dark Energy's way of undoing me completely, so that I can be shown how truly meaningless the physical world is.

Mina takes her lips from mine, and I can see her worried eyes in the light from the streetlamp. "Are you all right, Justin?"

"Mina," I say, "you are very important to me." That is not quite what I want to say, and I think Mina might know that, because she is silent for a moment. She gives me a funny smile.

"You're very important to me too." We both look at each other quietly for a little while, then she takes my hand. "Come on, let's go," she says.

We drive out of Piedras. I stare out the dark windows, digging my fingers into the skin of my upper arms.

"What's wrong, Justin?"

I glance at her worried, beautiful face, lit by the glow of the dashboard lights. I pry one of my hands away from my arm and run my fingers through my hair. They tangle up in the curls, since it's getting long. "I talked to my mom about San Francisco."

"Oh. It didn't go well, I take it?"

I look at her. I want to tell her everything that Mom said. I want her to say Mom is wrong, and I'm not too much to deal with. But what if she doesn't say that? And even if she does, how do I know it's not a trick?

She's glancing between me and the road, her face full of concern. Then her brow furrows as she looks in the rearview. "Who else is out here at this hour?"

I look back and see headlights behind us, two little circles of light bursting forth out of the blackness. "It's only ten," I say. "Maybe some farmer is coming home after a night on the town, doing farmer things, like hoedowns and trading chickens for medical services."

She snorts. "There aren't many houses out here. I don't know why anyone would be out here after dark." She wrinkles her nose. "I'm just being paranoid. Tell me what your mom said about San Francisco."

I look out the side window at the grape fields skimming by in the moonlight. "She thinks it's a waste of time."

It is a while before Mina speaks. "We're going to go anyway. You're eighteen, and they can't stop you."

She's clutching the wheel, and she looks very angry. We come to the stop sign at the T intersection with San Pedro Road, and she turns right. She glances in the rearview again, and her shoulders relax slightly. "Good. The person behind us is going the other way."

"Good," I agree.

We park in front of the cattle gate. Mina has brought a blanket so we don't have to sit on her car, and she spreads it out under the live oak tree. She lies back on it, and I stretch out next to her, brushing the hair back from her face. "You are so beautiful," I say.

She smiles. "So are you." She scoots closer, kicking off her flip-flops and intertwining her legs with mine. It makes electricity buzz through me when she does that. I can feel the warmth of her skin, sweet and perfect.

"Will you go to San Francisco with me?" she asks. "You can't listen to your mom, Justin. She's just trying to keep you from ever being successful. She has problems."

It is hard for me to pay attention to what she is saying because she is so close to me, and I'm so full of emotions my heart hurts. I can't stand to think about Mina leaving me. I don't remember how I survived before I had her, before she touched me and let me touch her like this. "I'll go wherever you take me," I say. "I'll go to San Francisco. I'll go to Duluth. I'll go to the worst part of Jupiter."

She giggles and squirms even closer, brushing my lips with hers, and my desire starts to push out my coherent thoughts. "Be careful what you say," she murmurs. "I hear Jupiter has some pretty bad neighborhoods."

I kiss her, and suddenly I need her so badly I can hardly breathe. I want every part of her. I want her forever. Her fingers slip under the waistband of my boxer shorts. I pull her closer, my hands moving along all her curves.

I pull my lips from hers. I'm breathing fast. "Mina," I say. "I love you."

She lets out a little sigh, and her body presses against mine. "I love you too, Justin."

Mina takes her shirt off, and her bra, and her shorts. She helps me off with my clothes too, and I feel her bare skin against mine, warm and smooth.

I know it is the first time for both of us, because we have had a conversation about it before. I am worried about hurting her. I have heard it hurts for girls on their first time. And I think that it does hurt her a bit, but I feel her wanting me and loving me until the truth of that is all I know, and the pleasure of her body. Everything bad is gone from the Dark Energy, and it is just the two of us together.

Afterwards, we lie there in each other's arms, and she kisses me and tells me she loves me again. The breeze is cool, but her skin is warm, and I never want this to end. I have never felt so good. There is peace all around me. I almost wonder if I am enlightened now.

But then we hear a frightening sound. It is a car engine, approaching us on the dead-end road.

We jump up and start pulling our clothes on. We are both still pulling on our shirts when the headlights find us and leave us helpless, blinded and caught.

I take Mina's hand and tug her out of the beams so we can see, and not be so starkly seen. I wonder who it is. I wonder if it is David, or the cops, or perhaps one of those axe murderers. I put my arm around Mina and feel her trembling.

The car pulls up behind Mina's, and I see it in

the dim light reflected from its own headlights.

"That's Rebekah's car," I say. The Dark Energy throbs with deep, sickening notes. I can suddenly see the trap it has laid for me with Mom and David and Rebekah. I can see it, but it's too late now.

The engine shuts off, and those horrible x-raying lights extinguish. The door opens as I blink the spots out of my eyes.

Footsteps crunch on the gravel, and a dim shape approaches us. Rebekah's voice speaks, its fury ripping through the Dark Energy.

"I knew it!" I flinch as her words hit me. "I knew you were sneaking out together so that you could..." She makes a noise like the last part of her sentence is dammed up against the inside of her mouth.

Mina and I slide closer together. "Why are you here, Rebekah?" I ask. "Are you here to stop my enlightenment?"

"I'm here to stop you from being led into Hell! To try to save you from this...from..." The gravel crunches as she stomps. The moonlight glints ghostly off her contorted features. I'm holding Mina's hand, and I can feel her tense up.

"I'm not leading him into Hell, Rebekah," Mina says. "Are you fucking serious? This is none of your business."

"It *is* my business," Rebekah says.

My ears ring as the Dark Energy sings a bad note. I want to run, but I can't leave Mina, and I think it's too late to run away from the trap anyway. I squeeze my eyes shut. "Please don't trap me," I plead. "Please let me go, let me go."

"Justin is innocent and has been chosen by God, and you're corrupting him and causing him to sin!" Rebekah says. She steps forward so that she's very close to Mina, who clutches my hand.

The Dark Energy is pulling hard at me now, and I'm having difficulty breathing. I keep begging, but the Dark Energy is hissing about Hell and sin and doesn't listen. Its slimy dead fingers caress me very horribly and the smell of decay oozes all around.

"Did you know he has visions?" Rebekah says. "Do you know God sends him messages and teaches him lessons? He probably hasn't told you that, because you'd laugh at him. You'd call him crazy like his mother does, and wouldn't understand what it means. You don't know how special he is. You're just some whore who wants to sleep with him because he's hot!"

Mina lets go of my hand now, but I hardly notice. The Dark Energy is covering my eyes. It's pulling me in, away from this, but into something much worse. I hear Mina scream something in Rebekah's face, and I see Rebekah hit her, and then I don't see or hear them anymore because I'm gone. The Dark Energy has me, and it's burning me up.

Chapter 9

I'm lying on gravel, sharp rocks poking into my shoulder and hip. I feel arms around me. I'm very cold, and my legs are stiff because I'm curled tightly around my knees. I let go of them, and open my eyes.

"*Justin*," Mina says. It's her arms that are around me, and they pull tighter now. She's wide-eyed and crying, lying next to me on the ground. I straighten my legs out so that I can get closer to her.

"Mina," I say. "Don't cry."

She cuddles against me and presses her face into my chest. The stars are cold points of light in the black sky, and in their dim glow I can see Mina's car, but Rebekah's car is not there anymore. The blanket is over us, but I'm still freezing.

"Justin, what happened? You passed out or something. I couldn't wake you up or move you and my phone didn't have any signal out here. I was so scared. I was going to go for help, but I didn't want to leave you..."

"It's okay, Mina. I was just in the Other Place.

The Dark Energy took me there."

I don't know why I say it, but I feel like it's okay to talk about this with Mina now. We are important to each other.

She squints up at me, tears covering her cheeks. She sniffs and wipes her nose. "The Dark Energy?"

"Yes. It may pull you in someday too. But you don't know about it yet."

She frowns and wipes her nose again. I am very calm. The Energy has given me a lesson, and I feel better now.

"Justin," she says, "What's the Dark Energy and the Other Place? What happened to you?"

I can see the ghosts of her freckles in the starlight. They're like the stars in negative, dark in her creamy skin.

"The Dark Energy is the energy that makes up everything that isn't solid, physical matter," I say. "It shapes and is shaped by people's thoughts. It's like how some people describe God."

"So, it's like...a being?"

"I wouldn't call the Dark Energy a being. It's the vibrations that make up part of this world, and all of the Other Place."

"Is it dark? Like, blackness?"

"No. I call it that because that's what it seemed like at first. But I didn't understand, at first." I press closer to her. I remember what it felt like to be with her, and my cold hands make their way up her shirt, against her warm skin.

"I don't understand, either," Mina says. "What is it like? And, I mean...when did you start seeing it?"

"I felt it around me when I was a kid, and knew

when it was angry or sad. When I was very little I thought it lived in closets and under the bathroom sink, so I was afraid to open them." I press my face into her good-smelling hair. "It was silly, and my mom got angry because when she cleaned my room and hung my clothes up I never wanted to get them out. Later I understood better that the Energy didn't like to be talked about until you reach enlightenment, and that's why Mom got mad. It's something not everybody sees, and so it's a violation of the social dance to talk about it."

She rests her chin on my chest, chewing on her lip. "What about the Other Place?" she asks. "What is that like?"

"That's where I was just now, when I was gone." I squirm.

"What's it like there?"

"It's like here, but different. It's just…it can be all sorts of things. I can go there in dreams, sometimes, or when I draw, when the vibrations are just right and resonate with mine. It's like, you know, it's sort of transportation. Like probably in Star Trek when they would beam people places. A little like that, except only with your soul instead of your body. It's nice when that happens, but it's not nice when the angry Energy takes me there and I get a lesson, like it did just now."

"What was your lesson about?"

I squirm again, and the rocks dig into my skin. "I had a lesson about Hell."

She runs her fingers up and down my spine and is quiet for a long while. "Will you tell me about your lesson?" she asks.

I fidget some more. "I saw Hell. It's a very bad place. It's the sickness. It's being caught in the transition between the Physical World and the Other Place, and having to die and be torn apart forever, over and over again. It's extremely horrible."

"It's okay, Justin. You don't have to talk about this if you don't want."

"No, no, it's okay." I try to stop moving around, but my body is in squirm mode and it's difficult to stop it. "It's important that I learn this lesson and sometimes voice vibrations can calm the Dark Energy down too, because I'm showing that I've learned the lesson. It can hear me talking about it and the vibrations combine and it's good."

Mina keeps running her hand up and down my back and I finally get myself to lie still. Mina is looking at me, and my brow furrows.

"Are you sad?" I ask. "You look sad."

She blinks and tries to smile. "No, it's just…you know other people don't see this stuff, right? You know that the Dark Energy and the Other Place aren't real?"

"They are real," I say. "Some people know about them, but the Dark Energy doesn't like to be talked about, so they only say little things, or look at me in a certain way, to test me and see how much I know, and to see if I'll do the right thing. They have to keep it a secret from people who don't know, like you, but I'll tell you, because I love you and because you're wonderful, and because I don't understand that social dance."

She frowns, and I can feel her foot wiggling. "No one is testing you, Justin."

"That's not true," I say. "I can tell because of the way they act. They get nervous and angry when I talk about the Dark Energy, and they act like they know something I don't. But when I'm enlightened I'll know everything, so they won't have to test me anymore. I'll be able to tell exactly who knows about the Dark Energy and who doesn't, and we'll be able to speak freely without the social dance. It will be nice because I'll be strong enough that I won't be able to get the sickness, but it's also really scary because you have to give up so much. You have to let go of your physical existence and all the things that are important to you. And enlightened people sometimes seem bad to me, because of how much they have given up. The Dark Energy uses them to test people in ways that scare me sometimes, or make me angry." I shudder. "I don't understand yet, I think. But sometimes I wonder if there might be something else going on. Something I don't know about yet. Some other force at work. And that's even scarier to think about."

Mina stares at me. I think that this is a lot of information about the Energy for someone who doesn't know about it.

I smile at her. "You're extraordinarily beautiful, Mina," I say.

All of the sudden her eyes fill with tears and she curls up against me. "I love you, Justin," she says.

I stroke her hair. No one has ever cried because I talked about the Dark Energy before, and I get a sudden fear Mom was right, that I'm too much trouble for Mina because I don't know the social dance. "Don't cry, Mina. Why are you crying?"

She is shaking and sobbing and it takes her a long time to answer. "Because I don't want this to be happening to you. I knew you were different but I didn't know you were like this. You're so funny and smart and talented. It's *not fair*."

I don't feel well at all now. "What do you mean, Mina, that I'm like this?"

She doesn't answer. She just shakes her head back and forth, sobbing hard, and I want to get up and run away from her. I don't. My love for her keeps me there, because I need to know how she feels.

"Am I too much for you?" I ask. "Are you going to leave me? Are you not going to love me anymore?" I'm colder than ever, and I'm shivering. I don't want to lose Mina. I don't want the Dark Energy to do this to me.

Mina looks at me, wiping her nose. Her eyes are very red. "What would you do if I left you?"

Fear comes in me. It's hard for me to answer, because I don't know. I don't want to think about it. "I would be empty," I choke out.

"You wouldn't be angry?" She has fear in her too. I can see it in her, and in the Energy around her. "You wouldn't hurt me?"

It's like Mina has squeezed my heart in her fist, and her face blurs because I have tears in my eyes. "No, Mina. No. I would never. What do you mean would I hurt you?"

The psychiatrists asked me that question a lot, if was going to hurt myself or others. It was some game they were playing, some hint they were trying to give me on the path to enlightenment, but I don't want to learn that lesson. Sometimes the Dark Energy makes people hurt or kill each other and I don't even want to know why it would do that. I don't want to think about it, and I struggle to put those thoughts behind the wall before they destroy me. I'm not strong enough for them yet.

A breeze is blowing and I concentrate on that, letting it pick up the bad thoughts and carry them away. I close my eyes and whisper along with it. "Peace is blissful business. Less hard darkness. Coalesce the listening visions."

"My mom put herself in an institution," Mina says. I jump a little, my eyes popping open. "After she had my little brothers, she was afraid she was going to hurt them and me."

"No, no, I said I don't want to think about that," I say. Mina looks confused and I remember I didn't actually say that out loud. She doesn't know about the Dark Energy yet so she can't know. "I can't talk about it," I say. "I can't talk about the Dark Energy making people hurt people."

"She didn't hurt us, Justin. She wouldn't have ever hurt us. She's a very sweet woman. But she stays in the halfway house because she's scared. She says God wants her there." Mina nestles up against me and holds me very tight. "I'm afraid what happened to her will happen to me too, when I get older. Sometimes it runs in families."

It's hard to breathe because my heart hurts so badly. "And you're worried I'll want to hurt you someday too? You think I'm like your mom?"

She looks up at me and grimaces a little. "It's different with her than it is with you. She hears voices yelling at her. And she sees people who aren't there. She sees a woman who she says is the Virgin Mary."

"Those things don't happen to me. It's just the Dark Energy. It's just the lessons." Tears start running down my face. "I just don't like to do the social dance, and I don't understand why people think I'm crazy. If it's a test, I don't understand how to pass it."

Mina slides her warm hand up under my shirt. "Don't cry, Justin," she says. "I'm sorry."

"Are you going to leave me because you think I'm crazy and I'm going to hurt you?"

"No," she says. "No. I love you, Justin. I want to be with you. And I can help you. You don't have to let the Dark Energy pull you in like that. You can take medication."

Fear squeezes my breath out, and my heart pounds sickness into my stomach. Mina's face blurs in front of mine, and I struggle to keep the Dark Energy from taking me away again.

What if I've been wrong about Mina all along? What if she does know about the Dark Energy and is testing me too? I shake my head, forcing that thought away from me. "I can't take medication. I don't think the Dark Energy would like that, because it needs to be able to teach me lessons."

"It's okay, Justin." She holds me very tightly, and I can feel her breath against my chest. "Please don't be upset with me. I'm trying to help you."

I take a deep breath, but my rib bones are squeezing my lungs like skeleton fingers. I want to run, but my muscles are so stiff I don't think I could get up. "I don't like it, Mina. I can't."

"Have you ever tried it?" she asks.

"No. After I got kicked out of school, they tried to give me some pills, but I didn't take them because the doctor said they might make the lessons stop. And the Dark Energy…the sickness was so close still and the echoes…" I put my arms over my head. "I don't want you to be one of the testing people because some people shouldn't be like that, especially when they're important to me and so irresistible to touch."

"No, Justin—"

"Some things should be real. The Dark Energy should leave me some real things and pure things that don't taste like death or bad chemicals and that don't leave a heavy grease on your spirit. I can't do it yet. I can't."

"Justin, stop," Mina says. She's crying again. "Justin, please, I'm not trying to test you. I'm real. I love you, and I'm trying to help."

I take a deep breath, but it squeezes out again. "It's a hard road to enlightenment. I don't like it."

"Shhh, Justin."

I take another deep breath, and this one comes easier. "I thought I was happy for the first time in my life with you, but what if I don't know what happiness is?"

"I want you to be happy," she says. "Please believe me."

My next breath is almost calm. I take my arms from over my head and look at her.

I look at her for a long time. Her eyes are shiny in the early dawn light, tears in them. She looks worried and frightened and upset, but I don't see the Dark Energy working in her. I remember what she looked like the night before, and how it was, feeling like she loved me.

"You're not testing me, Mina?"

"No, Justin, I'm not."

I want to believe. She's so beautiful. My heart perks up and tells me she's not lying. "Pinky promise?"

"Pinky promise." She holds out her pinky, and I wrap mine around it. I smile hesitantly, and she smiles back.

The weight begins to evaporate from me. "I'm glad you're not a test, Mina. I'm so glad."

She wipes her eyes and squints at me. "Will you just try it?" she asks. Her hand is stroking my back again, and I take another deep breath. "The medication? Will you please? For me?"

"But, Mina—"

"Maybe it won't make the lessons go away, Justin. You won't know until you try it, and I just want you to try."

She's looking at me and I'm looking at her. I feel like the Dark Energy is a slippery octopus I'm wrestling with, and I can't even get a hold of it to understand its shape, so I don't know what to do. "I'm scared to take the medication," I say. "I'm afraid the Dark Energy will be angry and there will be bad consequences."

"If the Dark Energy is angry, then we can deal with that," she says. "I just want you to try it. If it doesn't work, you can stop taking it and we'll figure out something else."

I swallow the bile in my throat. "You'll stay with me? If I take the pills, you won't leave me?"

She blinks, the dawn glowing bright in her wide, brown eyes. "I'm not going to leave you, Justin. I just want you to try taking medication. I think you'll be happier that way."

I press my lips together. My heart is pounding and I'm holding my breath. But I nod, and I let my breath out. "Okay, Mina. Okay, I'll try it." I flinch a little, expecting punishment, but none comes. My shoulders relax slightly.

Mina smiles and snuggles up against me so that I can feel every curve of her body. "Good," she says. "I love you, Justin."

"I love you too."

I huddle in her arms. It can't hurt to try medication, as long as the Energy knows I'll stop if it's not what it wants. *I'll stop taking it if you tell me to,* I say in my head over and over. I think it hears me, or at least it isn't angry.

"Thank you for not leaving me, Mina," I say out loud.

She lets out a little sigh. "Justin, I..." she says, but then doesn't say anything else.

I look up at her. "What, Mina?"

She is gazing at me like she's upset, and like she's going to say something, but then she kisses me instead. Her lips are warm, and my tears are drying cold on my cheeks in the dawn air. She keeps kissing me and crawls on top of me. I forget all about the Dark Energy.

We hear the meadow larks and white crowned sparrows singing. We realize the sun is almost up, and the punishment may be horrible for us in the Physical World if we don't get home.

We get up and get dressed, though I wish I could stay in her arms forever.

It's strange to be in the cabin of the car, with the engine noise and the stereo playing quietly, warm air blasting on my legs. It feels almost spaceship-like and foreign, as if I haven't been in a car in ages. It has been a very long night.

Mina has a grim look as she speeds over the back roads toward home. "That little Rebekah better not go running to her dad about what happened."

"I'm not certain what she'll do," I say, staring out the window at the grazing cattle. "What happened with her anyway, after the Dark Energy took me?"

Mina scowls and slams her foot on the gas, pushing the car to a horrible speed around the curves. "That little bitch hit me, so I decked her." She shows me her knuckles, which are swollen and bruised.

I clutch my knees. "That is unfortunate."

"She started screaming some bullshit at me about Jesus and drove off. I didn't even notice what had happened to you until she was gone." She rakes her fingers roughly through her hair, making the short part stick out in all directions. "I told you she likes you."

"I don't know if whatever it is she feels qualifies as liking me," I say. "I think she's just worried about religious issues."

"Nobody is that worried about religious issues. She likes you." Her eyes linger on my face. "And you told her already what you just told me. She already knew you...have visions, or whatever."

Her lips are thin, and I shuffle my feet on the floorboards. "I think Rebekah knows about the Dark Energy," I say. "That's why I talked about it. But I think it was a mistake. The Dark Energy seems to be using her in strange ways."

"She's strange, all right." Mina chews on her lip and doesn't say anything else.

We pull into town, which is still quiet except for a few white farm trucks heading out to the vineyards. The dashboard clock says it's five thirty in the morning.

Mina parks in front of her house, and we get out. She comes over and puts her arms around me, lays her head against my chest. "My dad will be up in half an hour. I'll be fine, as long as Rebekah keeps her mouth shut."

"I doubt Rebekah will talk to your father," I say. I'm shifting from foot to foot, because I'm nervous about what Rebekah will say to David and Mom, and how those two will react.

Mina looks up at me. "I'll be over later to check on you."

I smile. "Mina, I love you."

"I love you too, Justin." She smiles back, but her eyes have hurt in them. I wonder if I have hurt her somehow. This is some part of the social dance, I think, and I don't know the steps. I cause so much trouble to people sometimes by not knowing.

We kiss goodbye. I go around the block to my house, my head still full of Mina.

The sky is rosy, and the dry hills around the

valley are catching the first sunlight. The air is cool and smells good. No one is out in their yards yet, but the scruffy little dog at the corner house trots up to the chain link fence to growl a greeting at me.

When I come around to my street, I stop. My chest clamps around my heart and my body explodes with a sudden, dizzy, sick wave of adrenaline.

There are two cop cars in front of my house.

My feet hesitate. They don't call the cops when an eighteen year old has sex with his girlfriend, do they? And the cops can't be involved if said eighteen year old's mom's boyfriend's weird daughter gets in a fistfight with his girlfriend?

I don't know. I don't know much about the law. But what if they are there because something happened to Mom?

My heart pounds. I can feel it all through my body, and I have a very bad feeling. But I walk forward.

Suddenly there are cops coming toward me, four of them in their uniforms, walking tall and straight and purposeful with frowns etched in their hard, wooden faces.

I freeze. Two of them have their guns drawn. The Dark Energy does a strange thing around me, like I'm suspended in it, like it's the only thing holding me up.

The policemen stop about ten feet away and stand watching me like hungry coyotes.

"Justin Flaherty?" one of them asks. He has a round face and a little mustache, which I see through a veil because the world has gone white. He doesn't have his gun drawn, but he's holding his hands stiffly out from his sides with his fingers splayed. I wonder if he's a wizard about to cast a spell on me.

One of the cops with a gun out starts moving again, circling me, coming around behind. I can feel the presence of his pistol at my back like a hot poker.

"I'm Justin Flaherty," I say, and the Dark Energy keeps my voice steady. "What's wrong?"

"Do you have any weapons, Mr. Flaherty?" Mustache Cop asks.

"No," I say.

"None at all? No knives or guns or brass knuckles?"

"No," I say again.

"Put your hands up," he says.

I do it.

"I need you to lie face-down on the ground," he says.

The world is very immediate. All my thoughts are about what is happening right now. It is like being a fish. The cop's command is ridiculous, and very hard to comply with when my hands are up. But the Dark Energy is telling me to do it, and do it quickly.

I get down carefully on my knees. I almost fall onto my face, but I don't. The gravel cuts into my skin. I hesitate a moment, because I don't see how to get face-down onto the ground with my hands up, other than by falling.

"Face down on the ground!" Mustache Cop yells, and it is very frightening.

I put my hands down on the ground and lower myself onto my face. The gravel bites into my nose and forehead. Each footstep crunching on the crumbly pavement as they run toward me is a bright explosion in my mind.

I twitch as they grab my wrists and twist my arms behind my back. This motion scrapes my palms and my forehead hard against the pavement, but I don't yell, because the Energy is telling me to be very quiet right now. The cold metal of the handcuffs makes me taste vinegar. Arms under my armpits haul me up. I get to my knees and stand, feeling strange and dizzy. I have one cop on each side holding my arms, and they pull me toward one of the cars.

The Dark Energy is like liquid flowing around and through me, and the whole world is shining white and beautiful. The neighbor across the street is on his porch, watching. His round, bare belly hangs over his sweatpants, and he has a can of beer in his hand.

The cops push me against the side of their car and pat me down roughly, but I have nothing at all in my pockets.

I hear Rebekah's voice screaming from the porch. "I had to do it!"

I look up at her. Her face is blotchy and covered in tears. Her left eye is purple and swollen, and I feel sick. Mina did that.

"I'm sorry, Justin! I had to tell them! I had to help you! I had to save you!"

David comes out onto the porch and hauls her back in. "Rebekah, be quiet," he says. "You're upset, sweetheart." He says something else I don't hear as he leads her back inside.

The cops watch her go back in, exchanging glances. Mustache Cop looks at me. "Justin Flaherty," he says, "You are under arrest for the crime of sexual battery as defined by California Penal Code 243.4 (a)."

"What?" I say. "But I…but she…"

The cop doesn't listen to me. "You have the right to remain silent."

He tells me the rest of my Miranda rights, just like on television. I am trembling, but the Dark Energy is wrapped around me soothingly. My pain and fear dissolve into it. It's a little like being in a dream. The cops put me in the back of the car.

The door shuts. It is very quiet. It is only now I realize I'm probably not being arrested for having sex with Mina. I'm being arrested because Rebekah told them I tried to rape her. It is a strange trick of the Dark Energy. There is a message in this. I wonder if it is about the medication Mina wants me to take, if this is the punishment for agreeing to take it. I curl around my knees, which is uncomfortable because of the handcuffs.

Mustache Cop and one of the others get into the front of the car, which is separated from the back by an iron grille and a thick panel of plastic. My forehead and the palms of my hands sting from where the gravel scraped them.

The engine hums to life and we drive away from my house, up past the Heights, and out of Piedras.

Chapter 10

They take me to the sheriff's station a few towns away. There they handcuff me to a chair in a room with sickly beige walls and concrete floors.

I wait like that for a long time. My shoulders and hips ache and my scrapes are stinging and itching, but I barely notice. I don't have very many thoughts right now. I am just here. I am just waiting.

I don't know how long it is before two police detectives come in and sit across a table from me. The older one with brown hair frowns, watching me in silence for a moment. I don't see anger in him. He is dry of all feelings except a little bit of sadness. The other man, young with blonde hair, shuffles through a folder of paperwork.

The brown-haired man tells me his name is Detective Bickman. He introduces the other man as Detective Clabber. Detective Clabber finishes flipping the papers around and sits back in his chair, crossing his thick arms.

"Mr. Flaherty," Detective Bickman says. "Tell us what happened last night."

101

The Energy makes me warm and calm, and tells me it is very important I stay this way.

I tell them how Mina and I were out in the desert, but I leave out the sex part. I tell them about Rebekah showing up, and what she said. I tell them I saw her hit Mina, then about how I lost consciousness.

"You lost consciousness?" Detective Bickman says, his black eyebrows pushing together.

"Yes," I say. I hesitate a moment, but I tell him because I'm supposed to. "The Dark Energy took me," I say.

His eyes cloud over, and he folds his hands in his lap. Detective Clabber leans forward and looks at the paperwork. The muscles in his meaty arms twitch. He looks up at me with eyes the pale blue color of robin's eggs, his pupils sharp like pinpricks.

"You've been diagnosed with schizophrenia. Is that correct?"

I nod slowly. "Yes. A doctor told me that a few months ago."

"Are you on medication?" Detective Clabber asks.

"No. Mina says she is going to help me get on medication." My throat gets hot with tears, but I swallow them down. This must be the test. But it isn't Mina who is the test of the Dark Energy. It's Rebekah. I miss Mina very badly. The Dark Energy tells me to forget about that right now.

"Who is this Mina you keep talking about?" Detective Bickman asks.

"My girlfriend, Saramia Aceves."

They ask me for her phone number and address, and I give it to them. Detective Clabber writes it down.

"What's your relationship with Rebekah Esau?" Detective Bickman asks.

"She's Mom's boyfriend's daughter," I say. "She's a very strange girl."

The cops exchange a brief glance. "Rebekah isn't your girlfriend?" Detective Clabber asks.

"No," I say. "Mina is my girlfriend. I don't like Rebekah that way."

"Sometimes a guy likes more than one girl at a time," Detective Bickman says. "It's okay to tell us, Justin. We won't tell Mina and get you in trouble." He smiles, but not with his eyes.

"I don't like Rebekah romantically at all, Detective Bickman."

Both the detectives look at me. Detective Bickman squints and tugs at his mustache.

"Where'd the scrape on your forehead come from?" Detective Clabber asks. He gets a half-smile which makes his face very ugly.

"From when they arrested me," I say. "They had me lie face-down, and when they handcuffed me I got scraped."

He blinks.

"You say you lost consciousness," Detective Bickman says. "What happened when you regained consciousness? When you woke up?"

"I was on the ground. Mina had her arms around me. She stayed with me while I was gone in the Other Place. She was very scared. We went home again, and that's when I was arrested." I leave out

103

the sex part again.

"Did Mina tell you what you did while you were unconscious?" Detective Clabber asks.

I am confused for a moment. "What do you mean?" The two cops stare at me with expressions like they know every bad thing I've ever done. "I...Do you mean what my body did?"

"Yes, what your body did," Detective Bickman says.

"It lay there on the ground," I say. "It didn't do anything." I look back and forth between the two of them, and I realize what they mean. They think my body hurt Rebekah while my mind was gone, and I just don't know it.

My nerves sizzle and my stomach goes hollow. "When the Dark Energy takes me, my body just goes to sleep. It doesn't keep doing things here in the Physical World while I'm gone. I saw Rebekah hit Mina, and that was the last thing I saw. After that, I only know from what Mina told me. But I know I didn't do anything else because that's not the way it works."

They should know that, because they know about the Dark Energy, I think, but this is a very hard and strange test. My ears ring, and I squeeze my eyes shut.

"If you want to pass it, you have to relax," I whisper to myself. "Relax, relax, relax."

"What did Mina tell you happened while you were unconscious?" Detective Clabber asks, and I pry my eyes open again. I squirm, and the handcuffs pull at my wrists.

"Relax," I tell myself again.

"Answer the question, Mr. Flaherty," Detective Bickman says.

I squeeze the hem of my t-shirt in my sweaty palm. "Mina was only protecting herself," I say. "Mina is a wonderful person."

The detectives look at one another before focusing on me again. Detective Bickman smiles. "Don't worry, Mr. Flaherty. Mina isn't going to get in trouble for anything she did."

I squeeze my shirt harder. My shoulders are so tight I think they must rise up higher than my head. "Mina says she hit Rebekah, but that was only because Rebekah hit her first. She said Rebekah yelled some religious things at her and drove away. That's when Mina realized I was on the ground unconscious, and she stayed with me."

The two of them sit staring at me a long time, and a drop of sweat trickles down my chest.

"Mr. Flaherty, do you ever get the urge to hurt people?" Detective Clabber says.

My teeth press together, but I unstick them. I let out a breath. "No, Detective Clabber. It's wrong to hurt people."

"You don't hear voices telling you to punish other people, or anything like that?" he persists. "You don't feel like others deserve to be hurt?"

"No. I don't hear voices at all. It's not like that. The doctor said I have schizophrenia, but that's just because he was giving me a test. I'm not crazy. I don't hear voices or see things that aren't there, and I really don't want to think about things like that. It's too hard."

Detective Bickman rubs his chin, squinting at

me. "Justin, Rebekah Esau is saying you did some pretty violent things to her."

"I know. I have figured that out from the things you are saying. But I didn't do anything to her. I've never..."

"It's okay, Justin, calm down," Detective Bickman says.

I realize that the handcuffs are cutting into my wrists because I'm hugging my knees. I put my feet back on the ground. "I'm calming down," I say. I let the soothing Dark Energy take my agitation. I take a deep breath. "I'm calm. I'm calming down."

"That's good," Detective Bickman says. "We're not going to hurt you, okay? We're just asking questions."

I nod.

"How does that make you feel, that Rebekah is saying those things about you?" Detective Bickman asks. "Why do you think she's saying them?"

I think about it. "I don't know why she's saying those things. Mina says she acts strangely because she likes me, but I just believe she's a nervous girl who is confused about God."

The two detectives glance at each other again. "And how does it make you feel, that she's lying about you?" Detective Clabber asks.

"Scared," I say. "I'm scared right now, but I'm trying not to think about it."

"But how does it make you feel about her, about Rebekah?" he asks.

"I don't know how to feel about Rebekah," I say. "She is very sad and the Energy does strange things with her, which is why I'm here. I know it's not her fault. And it must be horrible for the Dark Energy to make you do things like what she did."

Both detectives are squinting at me now. Detective Bickman runs his thumb over his chin stubble, and I can hear the raspy sound it makes.

"Are you attracted to Rebekah Esau?" Detective Clabber asks. "She's a pretty girl, and she likes you. I wouldn't blame you for being attracted to her, even though you have a girlfriend already."

My stomach flops over. They keep asking the same questions. It is a strange game they are playing. "No," I say. "I don't like her like that at all. Just…just Mina."

They are silent again, watching me.

"Mr. Flaherty, will you show us your hands, please?" Detective Bickman says.

I'm confused, but I hold up my palms for them to see. My left hand only comes up part way, because of the handcuffs.

"Where did the scrapes come from?" Detective Clabber says.

"From when they arrested me and made me lie on the ground," I say.

"Show us your knuckles," he says.

Then I understand what they are looking for, and I turn my hands around so they can see the other side. They both lean forward and examine them to see if they have bruises like the ones that were on Mina's knuckles this morning.

"What are those black marks?" Detective Clabber asks. He is talking about the black stains on my left-hand fingers.

"It's from the charcoal pencils," I say. "From

when I draw."

Detective Bickman raises his eyebrows. "Are you an artist?"

"Yes, that's what they say."

The two cops look at each other again. Detective Clabber gets up and goes out of the room with his paperwork without saying anything else. Detective Bickman leans back in his chair and crosses his arms. They are not as beefy as the other man's. They look like they might hug you instead of crushing you.

"What kind of drawings do you do?" he asks.

I realize some of the bad feelings have gone out of the Dark Energy now Detective Clabber has gone. I take a deep breath, let it out. "I draw lots of things. Animals and people and whatever the Dark Energy gives me to draw."

Detective Bickman has a tiny smile, and it is in his eyes this time. "It's good to have a hobby."

I don't know drawing is a hobby. It is something I have to do to make the Energy happy, like running. I nod slowly. "Yes. And Mina showed some of my drawings to a guy with an art gallery in San Francisco. He wants to meet with me."

Detective Bickman's eyebrows go way up, and he smiles wide. "That's good. That's really good." His smile fades. He uncrosses his arms and taps his fingers on his knee. "I know a lady with schizophrenia. She's a really nice person. Life's hard for her sometimes, but she has a job as a librarian, and as long as she stays on her medication, she does pretty well."

"A librarian is a good job," I say to be polite.

"Yeah, she likes it." He looks at me, and leans forward a little. "You should get on that medication, Mr. Flaherty."

I stare at him, my heart thumping and head buzzing. I'm confused as to what the Dark Energy is trying to tell me now. Is this arrest and everything all a punishment for agreeing to try medication? Or is it to try to convince me it's the right thing, because of what the detective is saying now? Is it possible the Dark Energy wants me to take medication?

"I'm going to try it, like Mina says," I respond uncertainly.

"That's good. You live with your mom, right?"

"Yes."

"Doesn't she take you to the doctor?"

I try to wrap my arms around myself, but the handcuff clanks against the bar and jerks my left arm back, so I just clutch my left forearm with my right hand. I know what Detective Bickman is saying. He's saying I'm dangerous and I should be going to the doctor already. My thoughts try to jumble up in my head, arguing about whether this is a test, but the Dark Energy puts its fingers on each those thoughts and they dissolve, one by one. It still wants me to be fully present in this situation.

"No," I say. "It's hard to find a doctor that takes our Medi-Cal, and that's a lot for Mom to deal with. But Mina will help me. Mina is wonderful."

He smiles, and it is a complicated smile with lots of emotions. "Stick with this Mina girl." He stands up. "I'm going to have to ask you to wait here for a little while, Mr. Flaherty. Can I get you anything?

Water, or something to eat?"

"No, thank you."

He leaves, shutting the door. The sunlight streams through the bars over the window, leaving grey and golden stripes over the polished concrete floor. There is a crack through the middle of it. It looks like a river gorge viewed from space.

I wait a long time. I trace the stinging scrapes on my hands and forehead. I tap my foot. A fly buzzes against the window. Every so often, a muffled voice speaks outside the room or a car pulls through the parking lot.

My brain isn't working exactly correctly. The Dark Energy has cleared my thoughts away, and my mind is quiet and blank. I know I should be worried I'm going to go to prison, because Rebekah is an underage preacher's daughter with a black eye and I am a legal adult who has been diagnosed with a mind-disease which certain people think is dangerous. But I can't do anything about it. I'm stuck here, handcuffed to a bar. I can only hope they believe me, even though they think I'm crazy. I can only hope they talk to Mina, and that they believe her. But if this is a test, if the Dark Energy wants me in jail, then there's nothing I can do. It will tell people to put me there.

If they take me to prison, I will never see Mina again. This thought makes me dissolve into the Dark Energy for a little while, but not for very long. I belong in the Physical World right now. So it brings me back into my body, which is curled up tight in the hard plastic chair, hugging my knees, the handcuffs digging into my wrist.

110

The sun has moved further up the sky, and is no longer shining through the window by the time the door opens again. It is Detective Bickman, and he smiles at me. He has keys in his hands, and a slip of paper.

"I'm going to unlock your handcuffs for you, Mr. Flaherty," he says, and he does this, the key clicking in them and the cold metal falling away. I sit there rubbing my wrist as he sits down across the table from me again.

"You're no longer under arrest," he says, and I take a deep breath, feeling a sudden lightness in my soul. "We talked to your girlfriend and her story matched yours. She has bruises on her knuckles which backs up your version of the story." He looks at me with a slight smirk, tugging at his mustache. "I wish the girls would fight over me like that."

I laugh, because I am so relieved. "It's not so great to have girls fight over you, Detective Bickman. It didn't turn out very well for me this time."

His smirk fades. "We have a problem in that your mom says she won't let you back in the house. She doesn't technically have a right to do that since that's your home, but if you have someplace else to go, I'd recommend clearing out at least until she calms down."

I am not surprised, but this information still makes my insides solidify. "I could maybe go to Grandma's," I mutter.

The shadow of tension in his features clears away, and he smiles. "Good. That will save lots of trouble." He hands me the slip of paper he's holding. "I wanted to give you this. It's a list of psychiatrists who take Medi-Cal. You should call one of them and get an appointment."

I stare down at the paper, which is a handwritten list of names and telephone numbers. "Thank you," I say.

He stands up. "Let's get you out of here, then."

My legs are a little wobbly as I follow him into the offices outside, where he has me sign a bunch of paperwork. Detective Bickman tells me it says that there are no charges against me at this time. I don't read it. I just want to be out of there. It is a long run to Grandma's, but a long run is better than being handcuffed to a chair in a sheriff's office.

"I'm really sorry about all this," he says. "Try to stay out of woman trouble."

"I will certainly try to do that," I say. "Thank you for your kindnesses."

He gives me a smile as he opens the door to the lobby for me.

Mina is there in one of the chairs. She jumps up and runs over into my arms.

"Justin," she breathes.

"You're here." I hold her. Her body is warm and lovely, and draws the rest of the bad feelings out of mine. I remember what it felt like when she was naked under me, and I laugh, because I shouldn't be having that thought at the police station.

She pulls away from me and raises an eyebrow. I stop laughing, clamping my hand over my mouth.

Mina turns to glower at Detective Bickman. "He could sue you for false arrest. You had no evidence at all other than the crappy story of that..." She winces and huffs.

"Mina," I say.

"It's bullshit," she says. "And what happened to your forehead, Justin? Did they beat you or something?"

"Mina, stop it," I say. "Don't be angry."

"Listen to your boyfriend, Miss Aceves," the detective says. "We were just doing our jobs."

She huffs again. "*Badly.*"

My legs feel like they're turning into strings and it's hard to keep them steady. I grab both her hands, the paper Detective Bickman gave me crinkling in my grasp. "Mina, let's just go. There's no point in angry feelings right now."

She glares at the detective for a few moments longer, then whirls and stalks off toward the exit, pulling me with her.

It is hot outside, and it's hotter in Mina's car. She turns it on and cranks up the air conditioning to full blast so it blows its bad, damp breath in my face. She pulls out of the parking lot and heads toward the 101 as the air begins to cool down.

My body is weak and achy. My thoughts are back now, and they are shouting very loudly at me, but I can't hear what they're saying because there's too many of them at once. I'm extremely tired.

"What happened to your forehead, Justin?"

"From when they arrested me," I say.

"Did they *beat* you?"

"No, just scrapes. I was on the ground." It's hard to talk. "Mina, I can't go home. My mom…"

"I know."

Mina is shaking me and saying my name. I open

my eyes and realize they are pressed into my knees. I uncurl and look up to find Mina looking at me with tears streaming down her cheeks.

My jaw is so tight it hurts and it's hard for me to open my mouth to speak. "What's wrong?" I manage to ask. I lift my head up and look out the windows. We're parked in front of Mina's house.

"You were gone again," she says. She pounds her fist against her dashboard, which rattles. I flinch. "Goddammit, that *bitch* and her *fucking lies* are doing this to you. Doesn't she understand what's she's doing? And it's not just to you. She makes up fucking bullshit like that, and then when a woman really does get raped, people don't believe her. Because of *fucking shitass lying bitches like Rebekah.*"

I feel very strange. I wasn't in the Other Place just now. I don't even remember where I was. The Dark Energy grapples at me and mutters in an agitated voice, and I curl around my knees again.

"I'm sorry," Mina says. The anger is gone from her. She puts her arms around me. "I'm sorry, Justin, please."

"I don't feel well," I say.

She hushes me and strokes my back, but it's not helping very much.

"I need to run," I say.

I open the door, and dive out of the car into the heat.

I run up Center Street. When I pass the park, I hear someone yelling at me, and their anger hits me like a fist, but I keep going.

I run through the vineyards and out past the

114

empty fields. Vultures circle in the hot blue sky. They are the only ones here. They are not angry, so I don't mind their company. The sun burns me, making my skin feel tight and thick.

Gradually, slowly, the Energy calms down. By the time I'm back in Piedras, it is smoothed out again. I still feel heavy and strange, though.

A woman comes out of the store as I jog by. She glares at me and backs quickly out of my way. As I pass the post office, a truck passes me and revs his engine, a beer can sailing out the window, clanking across my path.

They all know. They all believe Rebekah's story. I do not feel good about that.

I go to Mina's house. I don't know where else to go, and I want to go. As I jog up to her gate, I see her face disappearing from the front window. The door opens and she comes out. She throws her arms around me, even though I'm very sweaty.

"I'm sorry, Justin," she says. "Are you okay?"

"I feel better, but the people of Piedras are not happy with me. They all believe Rebekah's story. I think this test isn't over yet."

She frowns, resting her chin in the notch in my ribcage. "Why do you think that?"

I tell her about the woman at the store, and the beer can, and she keeps frowning. "I don't think that means anything," she says. "That's just life in Piedras. Bitchy-faced ladies and people throwing beer cans."

I don't believe her. She didn't see them.

"Come on, Justin, let's go inside."

She leads me in, and it is cooler in here. I go to

the kitchen and get some water. I drink it, and I stare at the floor, which has an orange and green pattern in the linoleum with a diamond and curling arabesques.

"Justin," Mina says, and I look up. "I called my dad at work. You can stay here for a while."

"Thank you," I say. I look back at the linoleum. Its pattern is soothing.

"I didn't tell him about…about sneaking out, of course. I said that everything happened in the morning, after he left for work."

"That was probably a wise decision," I say.

She sighs. "I went to your house to get some of your stuff." I look up again. She is hugging herself and biting her bottom lip. "Your mom…she flipped out. She tore up a lot of your drawings when I was trying to take them. I was only able to save some of them."

"That is unfortunate," I say.

"Your mom is a fucking cunt," she mutters.

"Yes," I say.

She comes and takes my hand, then leads me into the bathroom and runs the shower. She takes off her clothes, and I see her big, round breasts. I take off my clothes too, which are very dirty. We get into the shower together.

We sit in the bottom of the tub with the cool water running over us. She rubs me all over with soap, and I have to tell her to stop, because it's the kind of soap with toxins. She puts it aside and rinses me off, then curls into my arms and we hold each other, the water raining down and seeping between our bodies. Feeling starts to flow back into the Dark

116

Energy, and it is sadness, thick and dark blue.

"Mina, I'm too much trouble for you," I say.

"No, Justin, you're not. You're an amazing person."

"But you think I'm crazy, like you said. You think I'm dangerous."

"You're not dangerous," she says, smoothing the wet curls from my forehead. "You're one of the kindest people I've ever met. And your drawings are amazing, and you're smart, and funny and super handsome."

She smiles, and I try to smile back. "You're not worried I'm going to hurt you, like even on accident? That's what people think, or what they say they think about people with schizophrenia, that we get ideas we should murder people."

"Shhh, no, Justin. I don't believe that about you. And if you get medication, I think you'll be a lot happier."

She kisses me then, and I want her, but I feel too numb, too tired. She says we need to get out before her cousin or her dad get home.

Mina was able to get a lot of my clothes from my house, which are in a pile on her bed. My Bugs Bunny shirt is there, and I put it on. It makes me feel better, a little. It is a shield against the bad thoughts of people in Piedras. I imagine Bugs Bunny tricking Mom into climbing into the mouth of a cannon, then shooting her far away over the desert. I see Mom land hard on a cactus and jump up howling, her butt full of thorns and her face covered in soot. I laugh, but then I stop. I feel a little bit bad.

117

When we are dressed, we go through the drawings Mina was able to save. Mom tore up the one of the giraffe-neck Mobius strip and the vulture businessmen. She also destroyed the one of the girl from the park in Paso, and that makes me very upset. But the ants pulling the rickshaw is okay, and the fish, and many others.

"When I went, it was just your mom there," Mina says. "She screamed at me and said she was going to call the cops, but I told her to go ahead, that I was just getting your stuff. When I tried to take your drawings and art things, she got…really bad. It was frightening, to tell you the truth. She said I'm ruining your life by telling you your drawings are good, that you're going to end up dead or in jail if I encourage you. She tried to tell me what you did to Rebekah was just proof of it." She smashes her face into her hands, her fingers clutching her hair. "I was fucking *there*, but she wouldn't even listen."

"Mom is just testing me," I say. "You're definitely not ruining my life."

She takes her hands from her face and gazes at me. Her lips are scrunched up and moving like she's chewing on the inside of her cheek. "That paper, in the car, that you brought from the Sheriff's Office. Are those psychiatrists?"

"Yes. Detective Bickman wrote them down for me."

Mina scoots closer and puts her head on my shoulder. "It's okay, Justin," she says. I'm getting tense again and twisting my Bugs Bunny shirt in my hands. I let go of it and smooth it over my chest.

"We don't have to talk about this," she says.

"I don't know what the Dark Energy thinks about medication," I say. "It's making me nervous. I don't know if I was arrested as a punishment for saying I'd take it or if it was a way to get me to take it, because Detective Bickman gave me the list. I don't know if it's a trick or not."

Mina is very quiet for a little while. She pulls her fingers through my wet hair, and I can feel her chest rise and fall with her breathing.

"That cop gave you the list of doctors, and that means you're supposed to go see them," she finally says.

Mina doesn't know about the Dark Energy yet, so she can't be certain. But she is trying to be helpful. "I said I would try it, and I will."

She smiles. "Good. I'll call them for you tomorrow."

"You're a very nice person, Mina," I say.

Chapter 11

I'm having a dream about the girl in the park. She's caught high up in a tree like a kitten, and she's crying for me to get her down, but I can't reach her. Businessmen crouch in the lower branches. They open the breasts of their suit jackets and flap at me like bats if I try to climb up.

A noise wakes me. I smell coffee. It takes me a moment to realize I'm sleeping on Mina's couch, and even longer to realize that it's morning. I remember I'd fallen asleep here yesterday afternoon, before her father had even gotten home, and now he's up making coffee and the light through the windows is pink. I never sleep all night, and I just slept all night plus half the day. My thoughts are strange, flowing like shining liquid.

I sit up, rubbing my eyes. My brain feels clean, and there is a peacefulness in the Dark Energy.

Mina's dad comes in with his cup of coffee and sits in the recliner. He smiles, but his eyes are worried and dull. "Did you sleep okay?" he asks.

"I slept extremely well. Thank you very much

120

for letting me stay, Mr. Aceves."

"No problem." His foot bounces up and down. "It wasn't right for your mom to kick you out. It's bullcrap what that religious guy and his daughter did to you and Mina. My daughter was a goddamn witness, and if the police believe her, your mom should too."

I twist the blanket in my hands. I hope he doesn't find out I had sex with his daughter. That would not go well at all. "It doesn't have anything to do with Mom not believing Mina," I say. "She just wants me out."

Eugenio's eyebrows creep together. "Why does she want you out?"

"Because I'm too much for her. Because I run and I draw and I got kicked out of school. I also don't like to sleep at night, and that bugs her. I'm different than other people, I think."

Now it's like my head pokes out through a little window into the cold air of another world, and I remember what it felt like when I used to sleep at night, and when I didn't know about the Dark Energy. And my thoughts rush in, bumping into one another trying to find their places.

"I don't want to upset you, Justin," Eugenio says. I realize I have my head in my hands, and I look back up at him. My ears are ringing and I'm dizzy.

"That's okay, Mr. Aceves." My voice echoes in my ears.

"You're a good kid, and your mom should realize that." He squints at me with his brow furrowed. "Mina's mom is different than other people too."

I stare at him, wondering if this is a test, him calling me crazy. I don't know if Eugenio knows about the Dark Energy, and my thoughts jostle harder. "I know," I say, watching him carefully. "Mina told me."

But then all of a sudden I think, am I actually crazy? Is that what they call people who talk about the Dark Energy? Do they want to shut them all up in institutions just because they speak up about the Other Place? Is that what crazy means?

"I wish I could have kept her out of that halfway house," Eugenio says, his voice pushing in through my thoughts. "Sometimes she still wants out, but it's complicated to get her somewhere safe."

"She's too much for people to deal with, I think," I say.

I realize I'm crying. I hide my face in my hands, trying to stop, but I can't.

"Shhh, it's okay, Justin." I feel the couch sag as Eugenio sits down next to me, putting his arm around my shoulders. I hear a door open, and then Mina's voice.

"*What did you do to him?*" She sits down on my other side and her arms go around my waist.

"We were just talking about your mom," he says.

"*Dad,*" she hisses.

Eugenio squeezes my shoulder. "We're going to do whatever we can to help you."

I'm not sure what he means by that, because I don't think that there is any way to make me a normal person, to make me want to do the social dance or stop knowing about the Dark Energy. But right now I wish I could. I wipe my eyes. "Thank you."

He squeezes my shoulder again and gets up. "I've gotta go to work."

Mina scoots closer to me and holds me as he leaves. I'm not crying anymore. It feels very good to have Mina there.

I'm peaceful as Mina and I make breakfast together. She shows me how to make pancakes with powdered mix, but she's not very good at it.

"Your pancakes are all shaped like countries carved out by political disputes," I say. "The borders are winding and complicated."

She bumps my hip with hers. "Shut up. Yours look like diseased lungs."

"Be careful, or you'll burn the face of Jesus into one of them. We won't be able to eat it," I say.

She pinches my waist and snorts.

The smell of food brings Mina's brothers and cousins thundering out of their rooms, and we serve them up plates of pancakes with butter and syrup.

Angelica insists on sitting next to me at the table while we eat. She talks to me with her mouth full about the kitten next door, and she pokes me with her sticky fingers and laughs.

After we eat, Mina and I go into her bedroom and she starts calling the psychiatrists on Detective Bickman's list. I sit with my back against her headboard and draw. The thing I am drawing is very detailed. The top part is the world that my head poked out in this morning, the place where I could see what it is like for people who don't know about the Dark Energy. The bottom part is the Physical

World, with the Other Place boiling up into it from below. I am trying to see how they all fit together.

Mina calls name after name on the list. The first three are not taking new patients. The fourth is, but when they find out my diagnosis they will not take me. She goes through more of the same with the others, until she finally finds a doctor all the way in San Luis Obispo who will see me, but not for another nine weeks. She makes the appointment anyway, and throws her phone down on the bed.

"Why is this so fucking hard?" she says, clutching her hair in her fists.

I put my drawing down. "You are a very kind and amazing person. Thank you for doing this for me."

She scoots back next to me and we put our arms around each other. "You're a kind and amazing person too, Justin. You deserve to be happy."

"You make me happy," I say.

I start to kiss her, but someone knocks on her front door and we freeze.

"*Toquen la pwerta!*" Angelica squeals. "'Nulfo! *Toquen la pwerta.*"

Mina stiffens. "Who the hell is that?"

I have fear in me. It could be the police again. We stare at each other, but we get up together and go out.

We get into the living room just as Arnulfo opens the door. The fear wraps tight around me now, because it is worse than the police. Standing on the front step are David and Mom. Mina takes my hand very tightly.

"Hello, good morning," Arnulfo says to them.

He looks back at us looking confused, because he doesn't know who they are. Angelica clings to his leg, staring up at David, and Mina's brothers come out of their room into the hallway to peer around us.

David fixes me with a look, and it is ugly; it makes the air taste like bad cheese, like the time I ate enchiladas which had been in the fridge too long. Mom stands behind him, staring at her feet and fidgeting with the buttons on her blouse.

David snatches his eyes away from me and smiles at Arnulfo. "Good morning," David says. "We're here to speak with your father."

"My father's in Afghanistan," Arnulfo says, looking back at us again in confusion.

"My dad's at work," Mina says angrily. "What do you want?"

David's gaze flicks over me like I am something very horrible and bad he would like to crush with his bare hands. I stand very still so that my anger can't make me move.

David looks at Mina now, his lips pressing together. "I'd rather not discuss this with you. I'll wait for your father to get home."

"He doesn't want to talk to you," Mina says.

Mom winces, still frowning at her feet, and David smiles very condescendingly. "I think you should let *him* decide that, young lady. We'll come back this evening when he's home." He nods at Arnulfo and smiles at Angelica, who clings tighter to her brother's leg. He and Mom turn and leave, and Arnulfo shuts the door, pursing his lips at us.

"Who were those *cabrónes*?"

"Justin's mom and her boyfriend," Mina says.

125

"That guy is weird," he says.

"He's a fucking cockhead," Mina growls.

"I wonder what he wants," I say. "Nothing wholesome, I don't think. David creates bad landscapes and farty smells."

Arnulfo laughs. "You're tripped out, Justin."

Mina and I look at each other; her lips twist in a slight grin, but it fades. I believe we are both worried Rebekah has told David she caught us having sex, and this is what he is going to tell Eugenio.

"Whatever he has to say, my dad won't believe him," she says, but she doesn't look so certain.

Mina and I watch the others play videogames for a little while, and I try to work on my drawing. But I can't stop thinking about David, and Mina is tapping her foot and frowning, so I think she is having the same problem.

After a while, she sighs. "Let's go to the park."

I put on my hat and we head out. It's starting to get hot already, so we decide to go to the store and get something cold. There's a group of field workers lounging on a shady bench by the entrance, and I can feel them watching us, their conversation stalling as we walk by. The Dark Energy is tense around me. I know they're thinking about what Rebekah said I did.

Mina gets a popsicle and a Dr. Pepper, and I get a water and some peanuts. The woman looks at me for a moment as she takes my money, and she starts talking to Mina in Spanish.

Mina smiles at first, and I hear the words *novio* and *guapo*, but then Mina's forehead bunches up

126

and I hear *chiflado* and *policía*, as the clerk glances at me curiously.

Mina rambles out a long string of words, and the woman nods and smiles at me and says some things back to her. Mina says goodbye and takes my hand and we go out, the men on the bench still watching us as we cross the street to the park.

"You were gossiping about me, I think."

Mina's lips press together. "Piedras is a small town and that David guy has a big mouth."

"Yes. You have to have a big mouth to be God's boyfriend," I say.

Her lips slowly curl sideways, and she snorts, smacking me lightly on the arm. "Shut up."

"So David is going around telling everyone I attacked Rebekah."

Her smile turns to a grimace. "Yes. And he says the only reason you were released is because I have some uncle or something in the Sheriff's Office, which isn't even true. So I told her that I was there when this supposed incident happened, and I told her exactly how it went down, and I don't have an uncle who's a cop. They just figured out Rebekah was lying and let you go. I think she believed me."

We sit down on a bench in the shade of a sycamore. There is no breeze at all, and the woodpeckers are carrying on like grouchy old ladies with smokers' voices up in the branches. Mina scoots close to me and I put my arm around her, even though it's hot.

"Do you think that David is going to tell your dad...about us?" I ask. I can't find a word to say out loud that seems right for us having sex with each other, but she looks up at me and I see she knows what I mean.

"I don't care," she says, although I don't think that's true. "I love you, Justin."

"I love you too," I say, but I am nervous. "I think your dad will kick me out if he finds out, Mina. And I think you'll be in bad trouble."

She snuggles closer and looks out across the park, crunching the last of her popsicle in her teeth. Her eyes study the distant, dusty ridges. "We'll lie, then. He already knows Rebekah's a liar, so he'll believe us."

I hope this is a correct assessment.

Across the soccer field, two people on bikes cruise down the dirt path from Center Street. "Here come High Life and Crystal Ball," I say.

They ride up to us, but they are subdued, and they look at me nervously. "Hey, Meany. Hey, Killer," Cris says.

The Dark Energy creeps up through my nerves, making them buzz with anger. "Yes, now I kill people," I say. "I especially kill people who wear their hats just slightly sideways."

Cris stares at me. Miller straightens his hat.

"Thank you," I say. "You've cut my to-do list down by half today."

Mina smirks at me, then turns a scowl on them. "I suppose you've been listening to the God Squad telling their lies about Justin."

Cris rocks back and forth on his bike while Miller tries to draw himself up tall and tough, glaring at me. "Rebekah told me exactly what happened," Miller says.

I know Miller has been hanging out with Rebekah lately, and my stomach plunks. Miller is not incredibly smart, but I thought he was my friend enough to not believe things like that about me.

"She told you a bucket of shit," Mina says, her eyes flashing fire. "I was there, High Life, and I saw what happened. She stalked us down way out in the middle of nowhere and started ranting about us going to Hell. She attacked me, so I punched her. Justin never did anything."

Cris laughs. "You punched her? That's kickass."

Miller focuses on my girlfriend. "That's not what Rebekah said," he says, but he sounds uncertain.

Mina grips the front of the bench seat, her knuckles going bloodless. "You've known me for eight years, High Life. How long have you known that little cunt?"

Miller's gaze drops, and he picks at the rubber on his handlebar. Cris looks back and forth between us, bouncing the front tire of his bike thoughtfully.

"Yeah, exactly," Mina says. "She's not going to fuck you, anyway, Miller. She's a prissy little church girl and she'll only put out for Jesus."

Cris grins and snickers. Miller shoots him a dirty look.

"She seems nice," Miller says, "and you have to admit that Justin is a little, you know…" He twirls his finger around his ear.

Mina's back stiffens. "Fuck you, you douchenozzle. You're the crazy one."

"Mina, it's okay," I say, putting a hand on her shoulder. "I'm what you would call crazy."

She looks at me, blinking. Her shoulders relax

slightly. "Justin…"

"That's the word people have for people like me who don't know the social dance. But I've never hurt anyone or tried to rape them. That's not the kind of crazy I am."

They are all looking at me. Mina's pretty mouth hangs slightly open as she studies me closely. She turns to the others, her eyebrows raised, silently daring them to challenge us. Cris takes off his hat and rubs the back of his neck. Miller fidgets with the gears on his bike.

Cris puts his hat back on and smiles at me. "Can I have some peanuts?"

I smile back, and hold out my bag of peanuts. He scoots forward on his bike and takes some. He adjusts his hat so that it is even more sideways. "My hat's the shit, Cray Cray, so kill me for it if you want." He pops some peanuts in his mouth.

"If I killed you for it, they would just bury you in it anyway, with it a little bit sideways, so it wouldn't actually solve the problem," I say. "Instead, I will just try to educate you about the correct way to wear hats, in order to improve your life and the lives of those around you."

Cris' forehead scrunches up, and he laughs.

Miller watches me. "You really didn't do what Rebekah said, Justin?"

"I really did not," I say.

"He *didn't*," Mina says.

Miller sighs, looking at the ground. Cris laughs.

"You always pick the spooky bitches, High Life. Better luck next time."

"Yeah," Miller says. "I don't want to risk her

saying the same shit about me. That's fucked up."
He shoots me a glance, and I can see the apology in
it. I smile at him.

We hang out for a little while. Cris and Miller
ask to know the whole story about what happened
with Rebekah, so Mina tells them. She doesn't tell
about the sex part but they guess at it and do a lot of
hooting and giggling and acting juvenile. But when
Mina tells about how Rebekah yelled about Jesus,
they go silent. Cris scowls.

"That's crazy," he says.

Mina rolls her eyes. "Exactly. *That* bitch is the
crazy one."

She tells about how we went home, and I notice
she's left out the part about me getting pulled into
the Dark Energy. I tell about getting arrested, and
their mouths drop open.

"Holy shit, those cops pulled *guns* on you?" Cris
asks. "But you're *white*."

"Cops don't like white people, either, unless
they're rich," Miller says, and Cris makes a
disbelieving noise.

Mina stares at me, her lips thinned. I hadn't told
her about the guns before. "That's bullshit," she
says.

"It was quite frightening," I say. "I almost
whizzed in my pants, actually."

Chris and Miller laugh. I have to tell them what
it was like to be arrested and interrogated, because
they seem to think it's cool somehow.

After that, we all realize we are hot and hungry
for lunch. Miller and Cris head back toward The
Heights, where they both live, and Mina and I go

back to her house. When we turn down her street, a yell comes from one of her neighbors' yards.

"You get away from him, Saramina!"

It is a woman whose name I don't know, bony and sour-faced with long, graying hair. She stomps out to the end of her dog-pitted garden path, her hand on her hip.

"That boy is a rapist and mentally unbalanced." She gestures in my direction with her wiry arms, then glares at me. "You stay away from her and get out of Piedras!"

Mina stops in the middle of the street and faces her, scowling. "You've been listening to lies, Mariah. I was there and saw what happened with Rebekah Esau. She's the one who's mentally unbalanced."

Mariah's lips draw tight over her too-large dentures. She takes a step toward Mina, and I shift on my feet in the gravel, wondering if I should step between them and prevent bad situations from happening. But she stops without getting too close.

"David Esau is a man of God and he and his daughter wouldn't lie," she says. "That boy is more than a little bit off. I've seen him around here. You're going to end up dead or worse if you keep company with him."

"Are you calling me a liar?" Mina demands, tossing her hair out of her face. "I've known you since I was a little girl, and David Esau has been here a few days. I was *there* and I *saw it*."

"You didn't see everything, I'll bet," Mariah says, flinging her hand toward me again. "Clarissa says he stole one of her black cats too. You're too trusting, Mina. The Devil tricks us time and time again."

"Oh for *fuck's sake,*" Mina says.

I tug her arm. "Mina, don't argue. It's no use."

Mina rips her furious eyes from the other woman and looks at me. "Justin, how can you listen to this…?"

"Fighting never makes it better," I say. "It just stirs things up."

She gazes at me for a moment, and her shoulders relax. She whips her head back around to glare at Mariah. "Justin is a better person than any of you." She takes my hand and we start off toward her house, Mina kicking pebbles and sending them skittering over the rough pavement.

"I think the Dark Energy is trying to get me out of Piedras," I say. Mina gives me a worried look.

Chapter 12

My drawing of the interface of the worlds is quite intricate, and I am still working on it when we hear the door open then shut again. "Anybody home?" Eugenio calls in a tired voice.

Mina looks up from her book and we exchange a glance. We get up from her bed and go out to meet him.

"Hi, Dad," Mina says.

"Hello, Mr. Aceves," I say.

Eugenio is hanging his hat on the hook by the door, but stops when he sees us, his eyes searching our faces. "What's wrong with you two?"

Mina stares at her feet. "Justin's mom and that David guy stopped by to see you this morning."

His eyebrows rise. He goes into the kitchen and gets a glass of water from the tap, then leans back on the counter, sipping it. "What'd they want?"

"They wouldn't tell us," she says. "They were acting like total jerks. And they're going around telling everyone lies about Justin. Everyone we've seen today was talking about it, and Mariah yelled at us."

He grimaces and shrugs. "Mariah's a little batshit anyway, but yeah." He sips his water. "That really sucks. Piedras is way too small of a town in some ways. They love to gossip, but sooner or later everyone will figure out what the truth is and things will smooth out."

"You believe us, right, Dad?" Mina says. "I'm worried David just wants to tell you more lies."

"I wouldn't let Justin stay here if I didn't believe you." He gives me a little, kind smile. "I'm still getting used to the idea of you dating my daughter, but I've always liked you. You're a good kid, and I don't believe a word they say."

I smile back at him. I don't get told I'm a good kid that often. "Thank you, Mr. Aceves."

He sighs. "I'd better go talk to them. We need to work this stuff out." He stands there for a moment, giving me a worried look. He runs his hands over his face and heads for the door. "Wish me luck. I'll be back soon."

"Good luck," Mina says in a tiny voice.

My stomach is heavy as I watch him go. I don't know what David and my mom are going to say to Eugenio, but it's not going to be nice.

Mina takes me into her arms and presses her cheek against my chest. We stand there like that, holding each other. "It's going to be all right," Mina says.

"I hope so," I say, but the Dark Energy will move its pawns whichever way it sees fit. There's no way I can win this game if it wants to destroy me.

We go back into Mina's room and stretch out on the bed. I try to draw, but I'm just running my pencil lightly over the lines I've already drawn. Mina stares at her book, hardly ever turning a page. The door opens and we tense up, but then we hear the boisterous voices of Mina's brothers and cousins, back from the pool, and our shoulders slump again.

I wonder what will happen to me if Eugenio kicks me out. Grandma will take me in for a little while, probably, but she doesn't want me there forever. I'm too much for her to deal with, just like with Mom. I only get about eight hundred dollars a month in Social Security, and it's not enough to live on if I live alone. I could get a job, but Mom says no one would hire someone like me. Maybe she's right.

It is almost forty-five minutes before we hear the door open again, and Eugenio's heavy voice. "Justin? Mina?"

She and I exchange a wide-eyed glance and jump up, our feet stumbling over one another as we scramble for the living room.

Eugenio flops in his recliner as we come in. He's rubbing his forehead, and looks very unhappy. Mina and I lower ourselves down onto the couch, watching him.

"What happened?" Mina asks.

"Those two are real pieces of work," he says. He looks at me, his expression sad and worried but not angry. I begin to hope he will not kick me out, but I have to sit there hoping for a long time. Eugenio is silent, gazing at me with a furrowed brow, until

Mina stomps.

"*Dad,* tell us."

He winces. "I'm just not quite sure where to start."

"Well, somewhere," she says. "Did they just try telling you we're lying about Rebekah hitting me?"

He nods. "They did try to tell me you guys are lying to me about what happened with David's daughter, but I told them I believe you. Not only do I trust you guys, but I talked to a guy at the sheriff's office who I went to high school with." He looks from Mina to me, meeting our worried glances with his own. "It's not that I doubted your story. I just wanted the whole scoop. My friend told me in confidence they're considering bringing charges against Rebekah for perjury because they're so pissed off. Her story changed so much and ended up being so ridiculous, they have no doubt she was lying."

"What did she try to say?" Mina asks.

Eugenio shakes his head. "He wouldn't tell me that, because he shouldn't have been talking to me anyway." He shifts in his chair, his expression getting even grimmer. "That's not the worst of it though. The reason your mom and David wanted to talk to me was to try to convince me you're violent and unpredictable, Justin, and Mina and I will be in danger if we let you live here."

"Those horrible shitholes!" Mina yells, pounding on the couch cushions.

"Language, Saramina," Eugenio says, and she snorts.

"Well, they are, and I learned that language from

137

you, Dad."

He rolls his eyes, and massages his forehead.

I feel like my insides are full of biting ants. Everyone keeps thinking I'm violent, and I wish this test would end. I already know that violence is wrong. Is there some other lesson I'm supposed to learn? Am I missing the point?

Tears come into my eyes. "I would never hurt you. I won't fail that test. I know I'm crazy, but not like that."

Eugenio looks up at me sadly. Mina puts her forehead on my shoulder. She sniffs and her tears soak through my shirt.

"I don't like that word, 'crazy,'" Eugenio says. "And if you ask me, that David guy and his daughter Rebekah are the crazy ones. They want to send you to a private mental institution, Justin. They were trying to convince me to help them, to go to the courts and have you committed. They tried to tell me that you'd end up hurting someone and going to jail otherwise, but I don't buy it. You're one of the gentlest people I've ever met."

The Dark Energy hisses around me, jabbing me with knives of fear. Mina squeezes my hand. "Those jerkoffs. They can't do that, can they?" she asks.

"I sure hope not," Eugenio says. "It sounds like it's a horrible place they want to send you to. They do faith healing there, lay hands on people and try to cast the demons out, like Jesus did. They tried to tell me the place has an eighty percent success rate in curing mental illness."

Mina laughs harshly, wiping her red eyes. "They

should go there themselves, then."

"I don't want to go to this place," I say. "It's a trick. I think the people at this place will have the sickness, like Mrs. Talbin did at the school. She wanted me to go into an institution too. I think those places must exist to try to infect you with the sickness."

Mina slips her arms around my waist and puts her head on my shoulder. "You're *not* going there. It's okay, Justin."

"I don't want you to go there, either, Justin," Eugenio says. "You'd be better off just getting on medication and going to therapy. That's what I told David and your mom, and they tried to tell me I'm naïve. They had the nerve to tell me I don't know anything about schizophrenia."

"You know more than I do about schizophrenia, Mr. Aceves," I say.

Eugenio is looking at me with his chin in his hand. "I called your uncle Julio on the walk back over here," he says, quickly looking at Mina. "He says you two can come stay for a week or so, until his new roommate moves in at the beginning of August. That will keep you out of this David guy's clutches, and give people here a chance to calm down. He also says he knows a doctor that might be able to see you right away."

Mina and I look at each other. "That's very nice of him, and of you," I say. I see a tunnel opening in the walls of the trap I'm caught in.

"And then you can meet with the art gallery guy when he gets back from Europe too," Mina says.

"It's really not too much trouble in his life for

me to be there?" I ask.

"He says he's happy to have you," Eugenio says. "He's a big fan of your drawings, and I told him what a great person you are."

"Thank you for telling him that," I say.

"Well, it's true," he says.

The ripples in the Dark Energy have changed. Some of the noisy static has died down.

"I think I'm supposed to get out of Piedras," I say. "I think that's what's meant to happen."

Mina and Eugenio look at me with furrowed brows.

***

Mina wants me to sleep that night so that we can leave early in the morning, but I'm not used to it, and it is very difficult. I lie on the couch for a long while, staring at a stripe of streetlight on the ceiling.

Eventually, though, I realize the light has misty images in it of two women with '50s hairdos having a fight, pelting each other with balls of yarn. It's a movie projected through the front curtains onto the textured ceiling of Mina's house, but I'm not really in Mina's house anymore. I've fallen asleep and slipped into the Other Place.

I sit up on my elbows. The entire floor is a gigantic bed, with rumpled blankets, piles of pillows, and teddy bears with staring eyes and sinister smiles. The girl from the park is lying next to me, her black hair spread out over the sheets, her beautiful brown eyes staring distantly at the ceiling movie.

"Having people to take care of you is good," I say, "but it's better to have someone that you can take care of too."

She blinks at me, her big lips drawing down at the corners. "I can't take care of anyone. I'm too much of a mess."

"If other people are cleaning up the mess, you can keep making it," I say.

The women in the movie are no longer throwing yarn at one another, but they are scowling furiously and having a knitting contest, their needles flashing. One of them finishes and smiles in triumph. She slips her arms through the dragon costume she's knitted and lunges at the other woman, who jumps up and runs, her mouth open in a silent scream.

The girl from the park rolls over and curls against me, and I put my arm around her. It feels good and peaceful to hold her, and I feel a little guilty, thinking of Mina.

I'm jolted awake by a hand on my shoulder.

"Justin," Mina says.

The Other Place drains out of my brain and the Physical World pours in. Mina is sitting on the edge of the couch, and she has a little smile. I smell coffee brewing.

I sit up and rub my eyes. "What time is it?"

"Five. I couldn't sleep."

I smile. "So you wanted to share your gift of sleeplessness."

She shrugs sheepishly. "Sorry."

"It's okay."

We sit cuddled up together, drinking coffee until Eugenio gets up. Mina and I make scrambled eggs while her father grills her with detailed instructions on how to navigate traffic in the Bay Area. I have never been there and he is making it sound like an apocalyptic situation. Mina tries to tell me it is not as bad as he says, but he tells her she's never driven in it so she doesn't really know.

We get dressed. It takes me a long time to find the right clothes for a day like today, because of the complicated nature of events, and the fact that I don't know what is going to happen exactly. I have to try on several different outfits, and by the time I find the right one, Mina is knocking on the bathroom door yelling, very much exasperated about my slowness and how it's threatening to cause us to interface with rush hour traffic.

So I hurry to put all my clothes and toothbrush and hairbrush and my hat and art things in a suitcase. We say goodbye to Eugenio. He gives us both hugs, and we go out into the pink, cool dawn, and climb into the car. We pull out onto empty, quiet Center Street and go past the Heights and the line of eucalyptus and the dead oak tree. Then we are on the highway, with Piedras behind us, and who knows what ahead.

Chapter 13

Mina curses as we drive around and around looking for a place to park. Her hands are tight on the steering wheel, and she is sitting up very straight. She exclaims in triumph as she sees a parked car with its taillights glowing. "That asshole's leaving. I'm gonna take his spot."

We stop and wait for him, and it takes a while. He only has about two inches of space to maneuver out. Mina spits curses at him for his slowness and revs her engine.

I clutch the seat cushions. "You are a wonderful driver," I say.

The car behind her lays on its horn. She scowls in the rearview and tells the person to go and do a bunch of things I'm glad he cannot hear. He would probably get very violent if he could.

The parked car finally pulls out. We pull up to begin the complicated process of parallel parking, and there is a huge upheaval in our lives when the person behind us noses into the spot. Mina is screaming like she is on fire and I sit quietly

143

digging my fingers into the upholstery until the person realizes they don't have enough room to try to parallel park that way. He has to back out, and Mina whips her car into the place with amazing skill. Then she jumps out of the car to run after the person that tried to steal our spot, yelling many words that are probably illegal to say in public. The other driver is certainly a little afraid of Mina, because they rev off up the steep hill like a startled rabbit.

Mina whirls around and stomps back to the car, her face pale and livid. I stand on the sidewalk, clutching my elbows and enjoying being out of the car in the cool, moist air.

"You are a heroic, modern woman," I say. "You are very capable, and know how to conquer life's obstacles with cool bravado."

Her lips twitch, and I am happy to see her break into a smile. "Those fucking dicks."

"Now they have carried their heavy burden of dickery elsewhere, and we wish them Godspeed."

I get out our suitcase and we trudge up the hill, which is lined with narrow, three-story row houses.

I have never been someplace with so many people. The whole city emanates a deep roar which vibrates up through my feet. Mist rolls around us, beading on my eyebrows, the sun breaking through it. It smells much different here than it does in Piedras: like food and exhaust and growing things. Piedras just smells like baking dust. Mina's uncle Julio lives in a tall condo building on top of the hill. We are sweating and panting by the time we get there. Mina has texted him, and he is waiting for us at the locked entrance.

He grins and gives Mina a hug, but his bright, hazel-green eyes are focused on me. He is a fairly young man, very fit and well-proportioned like a magazine model, with short dark brown hair.

"It's so good to see you, Saramina," he says, holding her at arm's length, his eyes sparkling. "I love the haircut."

He shakes my hand. "I'm Julio Morales. You must be Justin, the one who does those wonderful drawings."

"It's nice to meet you," I say. "Thank you very much for letting us come. It's nice to have refuge in times of crisis. You're sort of like a church which gives sanctuary, although you don't look like a church, really."

Julio breaks into a wide smile and laughs. "Happy to have you."

We take the elevator to the top floor. He keeps looking between Mina and me as we go up. Both of them are smirking.

The doors open, and we walk down a marble hallway, lit by a window at the end. Julio takes out his key and opens a door.

We walk into a living room with huge windows and a deck in front. You can see the Bay with mist flowing over it, and the City all around, all those houses stacked together over the hills. "This is very beautiful," I say, wandering over to the windows. "Is that the Golden Gate Bridge?"

"Isn't it gorgeous?" Julio asks. "I love this view. You can go out on the deck. It's even better."

I pull open the glass door and go out. I feel like

145

the scenery is pulling me into it. I leave the door open just a little, and I can hear Mina and her uncle talking.

"It's his first time in San Francisco," she says.

"He's going to love it," Julio says. "Mina, he's very handsome."

Mina snorts. "Hands off, Uncle Julio, he's mine."

"Oh, stop. And he's so talented too. Those drawings are amazing. Stewart is really excited."

"I'm not surprised. You should see them in person. My photos didn't do them justice. But his mom tore up some of the ones I sent you."

"Your dad told me. That's un-fucking-believable."

They fall silent. I feel like I'm flying over the City. The view is all around me. I don't believe I'll ever get tired of looking at it. Julio speaks again, quieter than before, but I can still hear.

"He seems really nice,"

"He's the nicest person I've ever met," Mina says.

"It's so sad that he has so much to deal with. When your mom got sick, I was in medical school, and I hardly knew what was going on. I've always wondered if it could have gone better with her if it had been handled differently."

"My dad did the best he could," Mina says.

"I don't mean to say that. The poor man, he had you and your baby brothers and a job, and no one was helping him at all." He sighs. "Anyway, I called my psychiatrist friend, Doctor Mingle. She's very good, and when I told her the story she made room in her schedule for him tomorrow at one."

"That's awesome," Mina says. "Thank you so much, Uncle Julio."

"No problem, Eenie-Meenie. He seems like someone really special, since you like him so much. Plus, those drawings. Oh, my God. It's like he's pulled every weird dream I've ever had out of my head and rendered it on paper."

She giggles. "Yeah, he sure can draw."

"It seems like the price for artistic talent like that is pretty high, sometimes."

I hear footsteps, and Mina comes out and puts her arms around me. I hold her, the two of us surrounded by the beauty of the view. "Julio got you an appointment with the doctor tomorrow," she says.

"That is very nice of him." I am worried about going to the doctor, but it is hard to have bad feelings right now, in this place, with Mina close to me.

She smiles, then stands on her tiptoes and kisses me, and I feel even better. She takes me by the hand and pulls me back inside.

Julio has to go to work, so he gives us a key to the condo and the door code. "There's food in the fridge," he says, "and there's a really great Salvadoran place down the block, if you're into that sort of thing. I should be back around seven, unless we have an emergency. I'll take you out to dinner." He stops at the door and looks at us. There is a teasing glint in his eyes. "I only have one spare bedroom here, so I guess I'll leave you to fight over it. The loser will have to take the couch. I told your dad I'd guard your virtue with my life." He raises his eyebrows and purses his lips at Mina as he heads out the door.

I stare at my shuffling feet. "I'll take the couch. I don't want to be an imposition or a dark blot in your virtue report."

Mina snorts, then takes my hand and pulls me into the bedroom.

***

It is a wonderful thing to be alone with Mina all day, and to sit drawing in that beautiful, quiet house. Since Mom ripped up my picture of the girl in the park, I draw her again, the way she looked in my dream, staring up at the ceiling movie.

Mina glances at it, and her lips press close together. "You're drawing that girl again."

My pencil stops because of the way she says it. "Why are you angry?"

Her eyes go wide and her nose wrinkles. Her face is telling me I should know the answer to my own question, but I don't, and I have to think about it.

"Are you jealous of the girl from the park?" I finally ask.

She rolls her eyes and crosses her arms to let me know I have guessed correctly, and I put the drawing down and scoot closer to her on the soft couch. She turns her face away from me, and I am a little bit frightened. I sit there for a long while, trying to figure out what to do. I realize that Mina is hiding a smirk because I have been staring at her for too long. I put my arm around her, and she doesn't fling it off or scream.

"Mina," I say, "there's no reason for you to be jealous of anyone. I only like you and besides, girls don't seem to line up for me."

She rolls her eyes. "Justin—"

"I'm very much a lot of trouble for you, having to talk to the police, and stand up for me to everyone, and then you follow me to the City when they drive me out of Piedras. And you bring me to your uncle's house and get me this meeting with the art gallery owner, and a doctor's appointment. Why would I want anyone else when you're so nice to me and also so beautiful and smart?"

"You're worth it," she says. "Justin, you're amazing."

"I'm not amazing. I'm too much. I have problems, is what they say, and they're right, I think."

She cuts me off, pressing her lips to mine. She kisses me for a long time, until my heartbeat slows and I forget what I was talking about. Then she pulls away, smiling.

"No," she says. "You're brilliant and funny and handsome. You maybe think a little bit differently than everyone else, but that's good. And I think medication will help you not, you know...be so scared about things."

I frown. I'm not sure what she thinks I'm scared of, but she avoids my gaze, curling into the crook of my arm. She looks back at my drawing. "Who is she, anyway?" She takes it from me, studying it with a strange look.

I squirm a little. "I only met her once, when I lived with my grandmother. There was nothing ever like that between us. I've only ever had you as a girlfriend, unless you count the girls who used to chase me around the playground as a kid."

She pushes the picture away. "Then why do you keep drawing her?"

I have to think about it. If I draw her, it will bring her into the Physical World, help her not have to live in the Other Place so much, but I don't know how to explain this to Mina.

"I don't know," I say. "Because I keep seeing her in my dreams, and because she's very sad."

"You dream about her?" She suddenly sounds even angrier than before, and it takes me a few moments to say anything. I'm afraid I'm going to say the wrong thing again.

"They're Other Place dreams, not normal dreams," I say. "And they're not sex dreams like the ones I have about you." I feel my cheeks get hot, and I try to smile.

Mina looks at me, and I think maybe some of the anger goes out of her. "She's prettier than I am."

"Mina, no." I brush the hair from her face. "You're beautiful, and you're smart and funny and alive. The girl from the park is very sad, and her soul vibrates like a ghost's. She's partway dead, and I think she's on drugs. I'm very sad for her. That's all."

She keeps looking at me, and her face relaxes. She smiles, and scoots closer, and asks me to tell her about the sex dreams, and I know she isn't mad anymore.

Julio comes home that evening and takes us out for sushi, which I have never had before. I get a vegetable roll and it is very good. I like the way the wasabi burns my nose. Julio is very nice to me, and he tells us funny stories about his friends and suggests all sorts of things we should do while we're in San Francisco.

When we get back to the condo, he asks to see my drawings, so I bring them out. He sits looking at them quietly for a long time. When he gets to the drawing I did today of the girl in the park, his forehead wrinkles. "Who is she? She looks familiar."

I glance at Mina, who is staring out the window with a slight scowl. "She's just some girl I met once," I say. "I don't know her name."

"This drawing makes me want to cry," Julio says. He shoots me a weird look, half-amused, half-distraught. "You're really talented."

"Thank you," I say.

***

Mina insists I take the bed. It is firm and comfortable with clean sheets which aren't even musty. Julio is a rich doctor with a maid who comes to banish the dust and other Physical World detritus once a week. I think I am going to lie awake wondering and worrying about my life and circumstances, but I fall asleep and sleep very well. I am getting better at sleeping at night, and I almost hope Mina is making me into a normal person.

I get up in the morning when I hear Julio

151

banging around in the kitchen. I find him making coffee and cutting up a cantaloupe. On the counter is a plate of huge poppy seed muffins. Mina is eating one, sitting on a stool. Outside the windows, everything is solid grey, because the condo building is wrapped up in a cloud, the first light of dawn shining through. It is a comfortable feeling.

"Good morning," Julio says, smiling. "How did you sleep?"

"Extremely well," I say.

"Good." He pushes a plate with a cantaloupe and muffin in my direction, then slides a slip of paper toward Mina. "I have to go into work, but I've written down instructions on how to get to Dr. Mingle's office."

Mina picks up the slip of paper and gazes at it. "Fanks, Ungle Ooolio," she says through a mouthful, and he laughs.

"Yourff welcomfff," he teases.

I get cold thinking about going to the doctor. I've been to the psychiatrist once before, after I got the sickness, and it was not a pleasant experience. But I don't think that Mina and Julio want me to go to an institution like Mrs. Talbin and my mother did. I don't think they are pawns of the Dark Energy in that way, but I can't be sure.

Julio leaves, and I take some coffee and my drawing pad out to the deck to settle my jitters. The fog kisses my skin with little droplets. It makes the paper wet and the charcoal bleed and smear, but I like it. The odd light created by the sun trying to shine through the clouds makes it look like faces and shapes are trying to emerge from the mist, and I draw them, the lines blotting and feathering into one another. Mina comes out with her coffee and watches me, a blanket wrapped around her.

I'm jolted out of the Other Place a long time later when Mina puts her hand on my shoulder. The fog is starting to fade, and the sun is warm on my face.

"Justin," Mina says, "it's time to go."

This announcement shoots fear through me. I clutch my drawing pad, which is full of fog faces. "I'm not ready to go, Mina. These aren't the right clothes for going to this appointment."

She huffs. "Justin, those clothes are fine. You don't have time to change."

"Bad things will happen if I wear these clothes. They conflict with the vibrations of the situation and I'll definitely get the sickness." I'm sweating and tugging at the sleeve of my black and grey striped shirt. The fabric is like stinging jellyfish against my skin. "I need to change. I need to change right away."

I dart into the bedroom, slam down my drawing pad, tear off the horrible clothes, and start pulling things out of my suitcase. I toss aside my Bugs Bunny shirt and my turquoise shirt, my brown v-neck and my sweater, and it's getting hard for me to breathe, because I'm wondering if the right clothes even exist for what's going to happen to me today. Mina stands with crossed arms in the doorway, very rigid and wide-eyed about how we are going to miss the appointment.

But then I see my banana yellow shirt, and my shoulders relax. The color calls out to me in the correct voice, and when I pick it up and touch it I know it's the one I need to wear.

"It's okay, Mina. I know the right clothes now."

"Hurry! The bus comes in five minutes!"

I very quickly pull on the shirt and my brown corduroy pants, and Mina yanks me by the hand out the door.

The fog is mostly gone, the sun shining through its last, damp tendrils as we run down the hill to the bus stop. The car tires hiss on the wet pavement, and there are lots of people on the sidewalks. The Dark Energy is full of the vibrations of lots of things happening, the ripples created by people's thoughts and emotions. It is good to feel all those people around me, even though our situation is very agitating.

We get to the bus stop just as the bus is coming around the corner. We are breathing hard, covered in sweat and San Francisco humidity as we climb on.

Mina leans against me when we settle into our seats.

"I'm sorry I yelled at you," she says.

I tug at the hem of my yellow shirt and wipe the sweat from the back of my neck. "I'm worried this psychiatrist person is going to try to make me go to the hospital. I'm worried they'll have the sickness."

She brushes the hair from my forehead. "If she has the sickness or wants you to go to the hospital, we'll leave."

"You won't be angry with me?"

"No, Justin."

"Will you come with me into the room when I talk with her?"

Mina hugs me tight. "Yes."

I look out the window as the bus takes us through the neighborhoods, with all the buildings and traffic and people.

"This city is so big," I say. "It goes on and on and on. I think eventually it will take over the whole world. It's like a seed crystal you put into the solution to make it solidify. It's going to do that to the Earth, crystallize the dirt into concrete and skyscrapers and row houses."

Mina wrinkles her nose and laughs. My foot is jittering and I cross my ankles tightly.

We come to our stop and get off. The sun is completely out now, the sky a deep blue, and the air is warm. We walk a few blocks through a busy neighborhood with newer buildings shoved in with old row houses. There is lots of traffic, and the sidewalks are dirty. Every so often a strong urine smell creeps into my nose.

The building where Doctor Mingle's practice is located has a tall skylight in the atrium, with a white marble fountain ringed by live plants sitting in the patch of sun under it. The plants are reaching up toward the sky, and I think they would like to escape and be outside. They want the sun to throw them a rope so they can climb out. "But they don't know it's even worse for them out there," I say. "Too much concrete and tramping feet and urine."

"What did you say, Justin?" Mina asks.

"The plants want to escape," I say. "But there's really nowhere to escape to."

Mina blinks at me and takes my hand.

We take the stairs to the second floor, and then

we're standing in front of the glass door of the psychiatrist's office.

Mina looks at me. She opens the door, and we go in.

My stomach is sick. Mina clasps my hands so I stop twisting them together, and leads me up to the receptionist's desk. She tells her who I am, which is good. I think my voice would squeak if I tried to talk.

The receptionist is a woman with blonde hair and big, hazel eyes. She looks me over, then looks at her computer screen. "Oh yes, you're Dr. Morales' friend. I remember." She rummages around on her desk and hands me a stack of papers on a clipboard, along with a pen. "Fill these out, and Dr. Mingle will be right with you."

We sit down. There is one other woman in the waiting room, older, with short curly grey hair. She's wearing a disconcerting silk blouse with big chunks of different colors which shout at each other with nauseating voices. She gives us a brief glance, then goes back to reading her magazine. Then she gives me another glance, shifting in her seat, and I look away. I wonder if she is thinking I'm crazy because I'm here. Then I remember maybe she is crazy too.

I stare down at the paperwork on my knees, tapping my pen against it. Mina puts her hand on my leg. "Come on, I'll help you."

"The words on the paper are talking but I can't listen to them right now," I say. "My eyes won't stay still."

Mina kisses my cheek and takes the clipboard

156

from me.

She asks me the questions which is easier than the paper asking them. My name and date of birth are easy, but I don't know what my address is. Mina puts down her uncle Julio's. There are questions about my medical history, and Mina puts down what the doctor said about me being schizophrenic, even though I don't think that's right.

I can feel the bad-blouse woman looking at me now, even though she's pretending to read her magazine. I think the Dark Energy might have put her there as a warning or a test. I worry she's going to give me the sickness, that it will be my punishment for wanting to take medication. I can't look at her, and squirm away.

A smiling man comes into the room and fetches her back into the depths of the office. I relax slightly.

A salt water fish tank burbles in the corner, with very bright blue and yellow fish swimming around in it. I watch them as Mina asks me more questions. The fish and I know each other, and I let myself sink into their thoughts. They are happy in their tank. The water is clean and soothing against their scales. They swim and swoop in the currents, surrounded by the hum of the pump motor, which is like Om meditation.

Mina starts asking me yes/no questions about my thoughts and sleep patterns and how I feel about things. I've answered these questions before, but I haven't figured out if it is a test of the Dark Energy or not. The last time I filled it out, things didn't go exactly well for me, but they at least didn't send me to an institution.

I answer the questions: yes, no, yes. My voice sounds like I am barking. Mina has to stop several times and hug me and tell me to calm down. I breathe and try to think about the fish. The receptionist watches us, and asks us if we want water or coffee, but neither of us do. What I want is to run, but I can't leave, because Mina would be extremely angry with me. I press my forehead into my knees while Mina quickly asks me the rest of the questions, her voice shaking a little.

We finish the paperwork finally, and I sit up very straight as Mina takes it up to the receptionist. We wait. I get up and go over to the fish tank so the fish and I can stare at each other.

I hear my name, and look up. Standing there holding a clipboard is a tiny young woman with a dark ponytail and square jaw. She smiles brightly with red-painted lips, but her eyes are shrewd as she looks me over. "Hello, Justin, I'm Julia Mingle."

"Hello, Dr. Mingle," I say. I hold my legs still so they don't run away. Mina gets up with me, and the woman frowns, looking at her.

"I want Mina to come with me," I say.

Dr. Mingle searches my face. She nods slightly and smiles at Mina. "Are you Julio's niece?"

"Yes," Mina says, shaking her hand. "I'm Saramina Aceves."

"Nice to meet you."

Dr. Mingle leads us into the back. She is even shorter than Mina, and her ponytail swings while she walks. I watch it, letting it hypnotize me. I pretend I am a calm fish. Fish can't get the sickness.

158

They can't get put in institutions. They just swim all day in the cool water.

I wonder, if I tried hard enough, would the Energy let me be a fish forever?

We go into a room with a broad, double-paned window looking out onto the street, and Dr. Mingle closes the door behind us. Mina and I sit on the olive green sofa, and Dr. Mingle takes a matching armchair.

The City goes about its business outside, the cars stopping at the light at the intersection, people ducking into the donut shop across the street. There are puffy white clouds in the blue sky above, and pigeons huddled on the roofs of the buildings. It comforts me to be surrounded by people doing things. I like to watch it all happening. It's like watching the fish tank.

"So, Justin," Dr. Mingle says, calling my gaze away from the window, "what brings you to see me today?"

Mina grabs my hand because I am digging my fingernails into the ridge around the couch cushions.

"I'm here because I wanted to try being on medication because Mina thought it would be a good idea," I say. "I'm not sure it's a good idea, and I'm worried right now that the Dark Energy is going to step in and stop it from happening. I think maybe it could give me the sickness, which would be the easiest way."

Dr. Mingle's brow furrows, and she looks at Mina closely, who has her arms wrapped tight around me now. She looks down at my paperwork and flips through it. "You were diagnosed with schizophrenia by a Dr. Paternoster in Paso Robles?"

I nod. "I think that was just part of the plan."

Dr. Mingle squints at me. Her eyes are brown and kind and curious, and there is no trace of the sickness in them. "Can you tell me what led up to you going to see Dr. Paternoster?" Her voice is very soothing. She doesn't act like a lot of people do when I talk about the Dark Energy, which is strange. She must know about it, but isn't good at the social dance, sort of like me.

So I tell her about my social studies teacher, Mrs. Talbin, and how she kept yelling at me because she said she couldn't hear me when I answered questions, and because I didn't like to look at her because she had the sickness. So I had to leave her class and go running to calm the Dark Energy down. She'd cornered me later and yelled at me, and the sickness overflowed from her. I caught it. And it was very bad, how the Dark Energy chewed me up then without giving me any enlightenment and without wanting to forgive me for a long time, because I hadn't been good enough to fight it off. When I came back to the Physical World a long time later, I was in the hospital because my body had collapsed at school and not woken up. Mom and the teacher had said I was dangerous and needed to be in an institution, so Dr. Paternoster came to see me in the hospital."

"But he didn't recommend you go to an institution," Dr. Mingle says.

I'm a lot calmer now. The Dark Energy isn't punishing me yet for saying these things, and the vibrations of my words have soothed it. Maybe

Mina was right, that it wants me on medication, but it's hard to know sometimes.

"No," I say, "he said I wasn't a danger to myself or others. He told me I have schizophrenia and need to be on medication, but I don't hear voices or see things that aren't there, and I don't know if it's right that I take medication. I don't think it would be a good idea to keep myself from getting lessons, even if it also kept me from getting the sickness." Mina grabs my other hand away from my shirt, because I'm twisting it in my fist.

"Do you have thoughts now about harming yourself or others?" Dr. Mingle asks, and I tell her I don't. She asks me a very strange question. "What did your mother do when Dr. Paternoster gave you your diagnosis?"

I roll my shoulders, trying to loosen them up. "She was very angry he didn't put me in an institution. She said he wasn't very good at his job and wondered how he expected her to take care of someone like me alone, because I run around like a scared cat breaking things on accident, or on purpose like she says though I don't know what purpose is if I'm on purpose doing it, and I don't sleep at the correct times, and I'm always cluttering up her personal space with my artwork and fast talking. But then she said at least it was good he called me schizophrenic because it means I can get Social Security money, so she got a lawyer and made that happen."

Dr. Mingle gazes at me for a moment, waggling her pen. "How do you feel about your mother?" she asks.

161

"She's frustrating sometimes," I say. "I don't know how to make her happy. She's always giving me tests, but isn't happy when I pass them. I think she won't love me until I reach enlightenment, but maybe she doesn't even want me to reach enlightenment because of how it's too much trouble to love someone like me."

Dr. Mingle writes some things on her clipboard. "How do you feel about this social studies teacher who you say had the sickness?"

I have to think about this. It makes my stomach hurt. "I feel sorry for her, but she scares me, mostly. I don't like to think about what it would be like to be so used to the sickness that you could just walk around giving it to people like that. I'm very glad the Dark Energy finally brought me back here and cured me of it, and I hope I never turn out like Mrs. Talbin."

"Did you ever have trouble in school before this incident with Mrs. Talbin?" she asks.

"No, I liked school. I was good at it. I liked thinking about things and figuring them out, and my friends were very nice people." I wrap my shirt around my fingers. "I miss my friends sometimes. I haven't really seen them since I got kicked out."

Dr. Mingle asks Mina what happened to make her think I need medication, and Mina ends up telling her the whole story about Rebekah and how the Dark Energy took me and how scared she'd been. She even tells the part about what Rebekah said afterwards, and the cops, and she gets really angry about that part, but then she apologizes and hugs me because I'm clutching my knees very hard.

Dr. Mingle asks me about what happened when I was arrested and I tell her. She asks me how I feel about the police who arrested me and I say I think they were very nice except maybe the guy who yelled at me to lie face down on the ground, but that I think my mom and David probably told him I was dangerous so he felt it was necessary. She asks me how I feel about Rebekah, and this is embarrassing. I can feel Mina being annoyed beside me.

"She is a very strange girl," I say. "The Dark Energy does strange things with her, and I don't know why."

She asks Mina if I ever did anything before the Rebekah incident to make her think I needed medication.

Mina chews on her cheek and looks at me. "Not…really," she says. "He was always different, with the running and how his mind would wander off sometimes. And he'd say weird stuff, but, I don't know, I just thought he was interesting." Her cheeks go pink.

"Little did you know that I'm not interesting at all," I say. "I'm actually a dangerous crazy person."

She winces, and presses her forehead against my shoulder. "No, Justin."

Dr. Mingle sits there looking at us, twiddling her pen, and I'm worried she's going to ask me another question about how I feel about something. But then she looks at the clock on the wall, and jumps a little. "Shit," she whispers, then covers her mouth in embarrassment. "Sorry."

"It's okay," I say. "I don't have any objection to you working blue."

Her lips twitch, and she sighs, leaning back in her chair. "We've gone way over time, but that's okay." She frowns down at her paperwork. "Well, Justin, I have to agree with Dr. Paternoster that you do show signs of schizophrenia. However, it's a very atypical manifestation, and so I won't rule out another form of psychosis. And I'm wondering if you don't have a form of epilepsy. Did you ever have seizures or fainting spells or…episodes where you'd have visions as a child?"

"No," I say. "Nothing like that. The first time the Dark Energy pulled me in was a little bit before I turned eighteen." I feel very strange right now. I don't know what to think, because here is another person telling me I'm crazy. I like Dr. Mingle and don't think she is going to try to put me in an institution, though. She doesn't have the sickness, and if this is a test, I don't know what kind of test it is.

She taps her pen against her teeth. She gets out a prescription pad and writes two prescriptions. She tells me what side-effects to watch for, and she tells me they will help me.

"How will they help me?" I ask. "Will they keep the Dark Energy from giving me lessons?"

She shifts in her chair, and her brow furrows. "I don't know that," she says. "I want you to come back in three weeks, and tell me how you're doing."

I look at Mina, and I know we are both thinking I probably won't be here in three weeks. I don't know where I'll be, but I nod, and thank her, and I make an appointment with the receptionist for a follow-up, just in case I am still here, somehow.

We escape from her office. My shoulders are tense. I'm waiting for my punishment to fall on me, but it still doesn't. On the way back down the stairs, Mina asks me if I'm okay.

"I'm very tired and frightened," I say.

She stops on the landing, and puts her arms around me. "Thank you for doing this, Justin. It's going to be okay."

I hold her quietly for a moment, because it is very peaceful, and the waves in the Dark Energy begin to calm down. The sounds of the fountain in the atrium echo up through the stairwell, along with the voices of two people at the information desk who are arguing about some movie they saw. "You're still going to try taking the medication, right?" she says.

"Yes, Mina," I say. "I said I would and if the Dark Energy hasn't stopped it happening yet, then maybe it won't."

She smiles up at me. "Thank you, Justin. Let's go to the pharmacy, then."

Dr. Mingle told us about a pharmacy three blocks away, so we walk there through the traffic and bustle. We hand in the prescription at the desk, and then wander the aisles waiting for them to fill it, looking at creams and ointments and trial sizes. I find a souvenir dashboard hippie with a beard and round sunglasses which sways when it moves. It says **'I heart San Francisco'** on the base of it. While Mina is looking at the lipstick, I sneak to the counter and buy it for her.

As I swipe my debit card, it occurs to me for the first time that Mom is going to have trouble living without my Social Security money. I suppose she will figure out a way to get David to help her. I'm glad she wasn't successful in getting the money direct-deposited to her account, because it would have been another fight. I'm going to need this money, wherever it is that I end up. I don't want to think about that right now.

They call my name over the intercom, and Mina meets me at the pharmacy counter, where a woman explains to me how to take the pills and what they might do to me. I'm supposed to take one in the morning and the other one at night, but that's all I hear because I'm staring at the little bottles. I was wondering if the Dark Energy would scream about this being a trick once I got the pills, but it's not screaming anything. Everything seems normal.

Mina buys a bottle of water and a bag of spicy cashews, and we head out to the bus stop. While we're waiting, I remember the dashboard hippie, which is wrapped in tissue paper and clutched in my hand. I give it to her.

"I got you a token of my affection and appreciation," I say.

She grins. "That's so sweet of you, Justin." She unwraps it, then glances up at me, smirking. "That's awesome."

"For your car," I say. "Now every time you drive, it's a hippie dance party."

She hugs me. We stand in each other's arms, surrounded by the noise of traffic, the hum of the City vibrating up through the sidewalks. I wonder if there are caverns below our feet, filled with the machinery which runs this place, the gears spinning and exhaust pipes belching steam. Two other guys are waiting for the bus, smoking cigarettes and laughing about something. The bus comes, and Mina and I climb on, rushing to take the last empty pair of seats near the back before the other guys do.

As we start forward, Mina hands me the bottle of daytime pills and the water. "You should take one now, Justin."

I stare at the bottle. It has my name and the long, unpronounceable name of the medication on it. I take the cap off, which requires some effort, sandwiching it between my palms and turning at the same time. I fish out one of the little, oblong pills.

I put it on my tongue and take a gulp of water to send it sliding down my throat before I can worry about it. Nothing happens. The City crawls by outside our windows. The two men from the bus stop have found seats across the aisle from each other, and are talking loudly about some girl they know, how her earrings are huge and jangle like Christmas bells when she gets mad. "Uh oh, here comes the bitchiest reindeer of all," they say, and dissolve into laughter.

Mina holds her dashboard hippie by the base so it dances with the motion of the bus. "Go, hippie, go," she says, and grins at me.

Chapter 14

Julio comes home that night with the news that his friend Stewart, the man with the art gallery, is back in town, and wants to meet with me the next day. "I have a day off so I'll go with you," he says. I'm glad, because Julio is cheerful to be around.

"What time does he want to meet?" Mina asks. She bounces on her heels and smiles.

"At one thirty, at his gallery."

The adrenaline feels like it is a wind blowing through me, swirling in cold currents in the corners of my mind. I'm dizzy, and have a feeling like my life is changing very quickly. It is strange to consider that my drawings might soon be out in the Physical World for people to look at. It feels even stranger I'm here in San Francisco with Mina and her uncle, and I'm taking crazy person medication.

"I hope your friend Stewart likes me," I say.

"He's going to love you," Julio says.

That night we go to an Ethiopian restaurant, where they serve up a huge platter with little piles of food on top of a chewy pancake. There are yellow lentils and spicy cabbage and curried potatoes, and you are supposed to eat it without utensils by scooping it up with bits of pancake. The whole concept seems surreal, as if it were something happening in the Other Place, but everything else seems normal in the restaurant. No one is naked or walking on all fours with goat feet, and the words on the dessert placard aren't morphing into something else, so I know I'm awake and in the Physical World.

I insist on paying for dinner, since I just got my monthly benefits. It seems like I am rich because Mom is not taking her seven hundred and fifty dollars this month. Julio argues with me about it, bouncing in his seat, and trying to grab the check out of my hands.

"You are being very extremely nice to me with all you're doing," I say, holding the bill up out of his reach. "Because of you, I'm not currently a crazy person on the streets. I am a crazy person in a beautiful luxury condominium."

Julio laughs, showing straight, white teeth and the beginnings of crows' feet around his eyes. "You're not a crazy *person* you're a crazy and handsome *artist,* so I'm the envy of all my friends. I should be paying you for the bragging rights."

But he lets me pay the check, which is good, because I am not Andy Warhol and so the novelty of my presence will wear off soon, I think.

When we get home, we sit eating popcorn, and watching a television series about warriors and medieval-type politics and magic. I have never seen it, so Julio has to spend a lot of time explaining it to me.

Mina's phone rings, making a loud buzzing on the thick, wooden coffee table.

She picks it up. "It's my dad." She answers it as Julio pauses the television.

"Hello? Hey, Dad." She listens, and rage sets her eyes on fire. "What? Those fucking bastards! Sorry, but…" Her gaze falls on me, and my heart starts pounding, because I know this has something to do with Mom and David. "Yeah, well did you tell them where he is?"

Julio and I exchange a look. The Dark Energy settles heavily on my chest, making it hard for me to breathe. Mina says a few more things to her father, and then hangs up, cursing loudly enough to make Julio hold up a pillow to shield himself from her.

"Your mom and David sent a psychiatrist out there to evaluate you, trying to get you committed," she says. "My dad told him you didn't live there, and he didn't know where you are, but that he knew you and you weren't at all a danger. The person went away, but he just wanted us to be aware."

"Oh, that's bullshit," Julio says.

I pull my knees up to my chest and press my face into them. "This is very bad," I say.

Mina puts her arm around me. "It's going to be all right, Justin. They can't do this."

The Dark Energy tugs and pushes at me like a riptide. "I can't go back to Piedras," I say, my voice muffled in my knees. "If I do, they're going to catch me, like animal control officers."

Mina holds me tight, but doesn't say anything.

"I'm going to text my lawyer friend and see what she says about this," Julio says.

"I need to run," I say. I pull myself out of Mina's arms and stand up.

"Justin..." she says, looking frightened.

Julio purses his lips, and squints out the windows. "It's dark, and I think it's started raining."

I hide my face in my hands, shifting from foot to foot. "I need to draw, then, drawing will work. I think it has the organizational prowess to sort this out, to sort this out, to...to force it into submission. I need to draw."

I dart into the bedroom, my feet stumbling over each other with their need to move. My pencils and paper are on the bedside table, and I grab them and lie on the bed.

The Dark Energy rises up and sucks me into a terrifying place. A beast opens his toothy jaws to swallow me, his slimy tongue reaching out, and I can smell the rot on his breath. I think there is sickness around me, and I concentrate hard on forming my little bubble and pushing it away.

Mina follows me into the bedroom, but I can't look at her. "Are you okay?" she asks.

"I need to draw," I say, but it's hard to talk.

Eventually, she goes away, and I can hear her and Julio talking in the living room, their voices bleeding through the shadows that separate me from the Physical World.

"Is he all right?" Julio mutters.

"He'll be okay, I think."

"My lawyer friend says they're trying to get him evaluated so that he can be hauled in on a 5150,

171

which is a seventy-two-hour involuntary psych hold," Julio says. "She says that, in theory, it should be hard to have people involuntarily committed but, in practice, it's not. He should get a lawyer if he goes back there, but his best bet is just to stay away. If they can't find him, they'll have a hard time hauling him in."

"But he has nowhere else to go," Mina says. "Goddammit, I *hate* those fucking people."

The tongue of the beast I'm drawing wraps around me like a straightjacket, pinning my arms. I shouldn't struggle. But the fear is horrible, and so I do. I kick and writhe, bathed in the hot stench billowing from the creature's dark throat.

"I wish I didn't have that roommate moving in," Julio says, "but I need the money if I'm going to keep this place. I think I'll talk to him, see if I can work something out. He's a fussy guy but maybe he won't mind someone staying on the couch, at least for a little while."

"That's really nice of you, Uncle Julio," Mina says.

The creature sucks its tongue back down its rotten gullet, and me with it. I cringe and flail and wait for the pain to engulf me, for death to take me.

But it doesn't. Instead, I feel the smooth, warm walls of the monster's membranous throat embracing my skin, pulsing slightly with its heartbeat. It's actually quite comfortable.

"I don't understand why his mom is being like this to him," Julio says in a quieter voice. "He doesn't seem dangerous at all. He doesn't even really seem that crazy. He's different and a little weird, sure, but that just makes him compelling in a strange way."

Mina snorts. "I told you to step off my boyfriend, Uncle Julio."

"Oh, stop."

Once I have been swallowed by the monster, I see that it is not a monster at all. The creature's belly is a safe place, warm, like a womb. It cradles me in light, then births me out into a beautiful place.

I'm lying in a wide, sunny field of grass, surrounded by willow trees. There is a creek here, and a soft breeze blowing. The monster that swallowed me has turned into a small black cat, who is curled up beside me, asleep.

Close by, sitting with her back against the twisted trunk of a willow, her face dappled in moving shadows, is the girl from the park. She glances over at me and smiles slightly, clutching her knees.

"This is a good place," I say.

"Yeah," she says, but her smile fades. She looks away at the mountains in the distance, which are jagged and blue, snow filling their crevices.

"Sometimes when you think things are going to be horrible, they actually turn out better than ever," I say.

I am pulled out of the Other Place, the vision disappearing like a reflection on water when the surface is disturbed. Mina has come in. She sits down beside me, laying a gentle hand on my back. I blink up at her as the Physical World settles back into its place. I smile, because the Energy is much calmer now.

"Mina, I think the Dark Energy is doing horrible things for a good reason," I say.

Mina smiles back, and she is so beautiful. "I hope that's true. And I'm glad you feel better." She looks down at the drawing, and her smile slowly contracts. "How do you draw so well so fast?"

"It's not done yet," I say.

The drawing is of the beast, its mouth open, the beautiful meadow visible deep down past the dark tunnel of its throat.

Mina leans closer to see it, and I notice she has the bottle of nighttime pills in her hand. "Everything you draw is so good. So weird and beautiful and special."

"The world is that way, and the Dark Energy is just teaching me lessons about it."

She scoots closer and gives me a short kiss. "I love you, Justin."

"I love you too," I say.

She turns the bottle of pills over in her hands. It rattles like a baby toy. "You should take your pill."

So I do, swallowing one down with water from the kitchen. Then I brush my teeth and tell Mina and Julio I'm going to go to bed. I'm almost used to sleeping in the nighttime now, and it has been a very long day.

"Are you okay?" Julio asks.

"I'm feeling much better now," I say. "You have been so incredibly nice to me, both of you."

Julio smiles. "It's a pleasure having you here, Justin. You're an amazing person. We'll get this sorted out with your mom, okay?"

I thank him again. I go crawl under the blankets. I hear Mina and Julio talking in quiet voices, and I hear Julio giggle. The door to my room opens, and Mina comes in and slides into bed next to me.

"Mina, what are you doing?" I ask. I'm nervous, but I can't stop my hands from sliding all over her body when she presses close to me.

"Uncle Julio says I can lie here with you until you fall asleep, as long as I keep the door open. He says you probably need company."

"That's very nice of him, and your company is very enjoyable." She puts her head on my chest, which is warm and nice. The Dark Energy is still very calm, and I know I shouldn't be worried, but I am.

"I don't know where I'm going to live," I say.

"Julio is going to talk to the guy moving in and see if you can stay."

"That's not a comfortable solution."

Mina doesn't reply. After a while, I can hear her calm breathing. She has fallen asleep. I think about waking her up so she doesn't get in trouble, but I can't bring myself to because it is too nice having her here.

I lie listening to the sound of car tires swishing over the wet pavement and the rain spattering the window. My bones ache from tiredness, but I can't sleep. I stare at the splash of streetlight on the ceiling and pluck at my covers.

I suddenly feel like someone is pressing a soft pillow into my body. I hear the hiss of white noise in my ears, and a grey veil covers my eyes. And

175

then I am gone, but I don't know where.

***

When I wake up, I'm confused. The sun is up, a beam of it slanting across the bed and into my eyes, and for a moment I think there has been some massive phenomenon which has caused the earth to spin forward too quickly. Maybe Superman gave the planet a push, so night only lasted a few minutes. But then I realize that probably didn't happen.

Mina isn't in bed with me any longer, and I can hear her talking with Julio out in the living room. I sit up, and my body feels heavy and floppy. My legs are numb, and I have to lean against the wall to put on my pants.

I go out into the living room, blinking, and Mina and Julio look up from the couch. "Good morning, how did you sleep?" Julio asks.

"I feel very strange," I say. "What time is it?"

"Eight thirty," Mina says.

I go into the kitchen and pour myself some coffee. I sit down on the couch next to Mina, sipping it with my gummy mouth. My thoughts feel like dry sticks rubbing together.

"I think those nighttime pills are actually for sedating angry bears," I say. Julio laughs.

"Are they really heavy?" Mina asks.

I nod. "I don't like them. I feel like my brain has been scooped out."

Mina watches me with a furrowed brow, but Julio just claps his hands and stands up. "Well, you

176

can still eat breakfast with your brain scooped out, right? Let's go get something to eat. I'm starving and I want some eggs Florentine."

I chug my coffee and brush my teeth. Mina reminds me to take my daytime pill, and I do, though I'm leery of it and it makes my stomach hurt to think about swallowing it.

We go out to breakfast, then come back home and sit on the couch watching TV.

I jolt awake when Mina shakes me. I'm curled up with my head against the armrest and my knees against my chest, but I have no idea how that happened.

"It's time to meet Stewart," Mina says.

I sit up, rubbing my eyes and blinking away the fogginess. My body feels heavy and achy, but my head is clearer. "Those pills are too much," I say.

"That nighttime one really knocked you out," she says, pulling on her bottom lip.

I get up and go to the bathroom to splash water on my face. The bottle of nighttime pills sits on the sink. It has a hard and evil aura around it. I dry my face quickly and leave, so it won't be able to look at me like that.

Stewart's art gallery is walking distance, and I stop and buy a coffee on the way. The satchel Julio has loaned me for my drawing portfolios is slung over my shoulder, and I'm sweating under the strap, even though it's thirty degrees cooler here than in Piedras.

I worry nothing will come of this meeting, like Mom says. Even if Stewart does want to buy some of my drawings, it won't be enough money to pay rent for very long. I wonder if it might not be better to just go to a group home, like Mina's mom. At least then I would have a place to stay.

I jump a little when Mina takes my hand, because it startles me. "Don't be nervous, Justin," she says.

I have my chin pressed tight to my chest, and I think I am walking too fast, so I slow down.

The art gallery is on a busy street, sandwiched between a Burmese restaurant and a clothing boutique. A bell tinkles above the door as we walk in. Sun shines through the big front windows onto a maze of dividing walls, all painted in accent colors and hung with paintings and drawings and collages.

A young couple examines a ceramic sculpture on a pedestal, and they glance at us briefly. I hear two people talking in hushed voices somewhere else in the room.

I am pulled around the place because there is a lot to look at. There are oil paintings, one with big thick strokes in blue and white and grey, looking like houses in the rain. There is a collage made of candy wrappers arranged to look like a cartoon dog. There are lots of other wonderful pieces of art too. Even the walls are nice, how their strange angles cast shadows, the way the paint colors go together from different viewpoints. Julio says my name, and I look up.

He's standing with another man, shorter than him, older, more angular, his hair light brown. He's wearing blocky turquoise glasses, and smiling at me thoughtfully. Mina stands beside them, clutching her elbows, and looking even more punk rock than usual in comparison.

"Justin, this is Stewart Califax," Julio says. "He's the owner of this fine establishment. Stewart, this is Justin Flaherty."

I go and shake his hand. "It is nice to meet you, Mr. Califax. And your fine establishment is very nice."

He examines me closely. "Thank you. Are those your drawings under your arm?"

I fiddle with the strap of the bag. "Yes, these are them. Mina helped arrange them neatly in binders for ease of viewing. She's extremely helpful."

Stewart smiles. "We should go into my office. I'm excited to see them in person."

We go back through the jutting walls, through cubicles where the sun doesn't reach, electric lights taking over and giving a different character to the art.

There is a door in the back wall, painted to blend in. We go through it, down a hallway into a small office. We sit down across the desk from Stewart, in matching chairs of buttery-yellow leather which make me taste pancakes. A little window looks out on the sidewalk, where a group of scruffy teenagers sits goofing around, one of them playing an acoustic guitar.

I open up the satchel and take out my drawings. I am glad Mina took the time to arrange them, because this man seems like a serious and professional person.

I hand him one of the binders, and he carefully spreads it open on his burnished mahogany desktop.

The first drawing is the ants pulling the

179

rickshaw. Mina put it at the very beginning because everyone likes it, and Stewart's lips curl in a faint smile as he examines it. But he doesn't say anything. He silently flips to the next drawing, and then the next, looking at each one for a long time.

I sit with my hands splayed in my lap so I don't fidget. It is not so hard, because those nighttime pills have made the Dark Energy unnaturally calm.

About halfway through the first binder, Stewart finally looks up at me. "These are truly incredible." The binder is currently open to the one of the oak tree grasping the cell phones in its twisted branches. "Your subject matter is really unorthodox, but it's somehow still powerful. You make me relate to these strange images in some way I can't understand. It sort of reminds me of Tetsuya Ishida's stuff, or even Dali or Escher, but I've never really seen anything like it." His eyes glitter as he squints at me. "How old are you?"

"Eighteen," I say.

He blinks. "And you've never gone to art school or anything?"

"No, but I'd like to."

He looks back at the notebook, and turns a page. "Have you ever done any painting?"

Mina takes my hand, which has clenched in my lap. "I've done a little. I like the way oil paints glide and the watercolors bleed. Acrylics are good too. They're chewy and stretchy. But paints and canvas are expensive. It's cheaper to draw."

He glances back up at me, and a crease forms between his eyebrows. "Do you have any of those paintings of yours?"

"No. Mom threw those out."

He scowls, and throws Julio an incredulous glance. "Your *mom* threw them *out*?"

"Don't even get me started," Julio says.

"She ripped up some of his drawings too, a few days ago," Mina adds. "It was unbelievable."

Stewart gazes at me with his mouth hanging open, and there is less stiffness in him now. "I don't mean to say anything bad about your mom, Justin, but you need to get away from that."

"Most things you might say about Mom would be accurate, so I wouldn't argue," I say. "You could even tell yo mama jokes if you wanted. I wouldn't get offended. You could say, 'Oooh, Justin's mama so angry, she sewed his lips to his butthole and then just left the house. He had to roll around looking for the scissors for two hours.'"

I press my lips together. I think too many words have come out of my mouth to be appropriate for the social dance. But then they all bust up laughing, and I let out a breath.

Stewart covers his mouth to stifle his giggles and squints at Julio.

"Seriously, his mom is an uber-snatch," Mina says, squeezing my hand.

"And he can't go back to live with her, anyhow," Julio says. "She's trying to have him sent to some Christian reformatory."

Stewart clutches his heart, his grin disappearing. "Oh, good Lord. That's horrible. That's *horrible*. Stay away from her."

I don't say anything, because I haven't had very much choice in these matters.

We all settle into silence again. Stewart flips another page of the portfolio and stops, his eyebrows shooting up. "Wait…who is this?"

It is the drawing of the girl in the park that I just finished. Mina put it way in the back of the notebook, but she put it in, at least.

"I don't know her name," I say. "It's a girl I met in the park once."

Stewart glances at Julio. "Have you seen this one? She looks exactly like Christina, but with long hair."

Mina shifts in her chair, and crosses her arms.

"Christina?" Julio says, then he smiles, remembering. "Oh yeah, the girl…" He gives Stewart a knowing look.

Stewart turns the drawing around for him to see, and Julio laughs.

"You're right," Julio says. "I was wondering why it looked familiar. Oh, my God, it looks exactly like her. Those big, broody eyes and dick-sucking lips. Except she's not likely to do much of that."

Stewart and Julio giggle.

"Where did you meet this girl?" Stewart asks me.

I pick at the callous on my finger and glance over at Mina, who is staring out the window. "In Paso Robles by my grandmother's house, about a year ago."

"Christina only moved here like six, eight months ago, right?" Julio says. "Wouldn't it be hilarious if this is actually Christina? She's like the most messed-up muse ever."

Stewart smirks and pulls a cell phone out of his tight, chocolate brown jeans. "I'm going to text her right now and have her come over, to see if she's the one."

"You are not," Julio says.

"I am."

Julio rubs his nose and crosses his legs, shooting a look at Mina. "You should have her bring some of her goods."

"Of course," Stewart says, grinning. He puts his phone down and leans back in his chair, giving me a serious look. "Enough of this tomfoolery." He taps his fingers against the wooden armrests of his swivel chair. "Justin, you're the best new artist I've ever seen, and believe me, I'm not just saying that. I'd really like to give you a show here, with an opening and promotion and everything. I'd pay for all of it, as well as the framing of your pieces."

Mina and I blink at each other, and I get a giddy feeling. "I would really like that too," I say.

"Would you be willing to sign an exclusive contract with me for a period of six months?"

I probably look confused, because he explains himself.

"It would mean you couldn't sell your work anywhere else for the period of the contract. I'd have sole rights to it. But I think it would be a good way to get your name out there, and would be beneficial for you because I'd do a lot of promotion. Then, after six months, we could renegotiate."

I don't answer immediately, because all those words are tumbling around in my head, trying to find places to sink in. Mina runs her fingers down my spine, and I can feel her looking at the side of my face. Stewart is watching me too, and after a moment or so he speaks up again.

"I usually have a fifty-fifty contract with artists, meaning each of us gets half of the sales money for their pieces. But if you give me an exclusive contract, I'll do a sixty-forty, the sixty going to you. I really think I can do a good job for you selling your work, and I hope you would consider an ongoing contract with me of some sort after the six months."

I realize I need to say something. I pick at the seam of my pants. "Um, okay, I'll do the exclusive agreement."

Stewart grins. He holds out his hand over the desk, and I shake it.

"This is going to be awesome," he says.

Mina and Julio grin at me. The Dark Energy sings with excitement. We hear the door from the gallery open. "Anyone home?" a woman's voice says.

"Back here, Christina," Stewart calls.

Mina's hand twitches in mine. I look over to find her glowering at her knees. She is worried she is about to meet the girl from the park.

And when Christina appears in the doorway, the Dark Energy swells up inside me, and I know there is going to be trouble with Mina.

Because Christina *is* the girl from the park, the girl from the Other Place. I recognize her big, beautiful brown eyes right away, though now her hair is cut short and dyed very blonde now. Before, it was long and dark.

She smiles in a sleepy sort of way at Stewart. "Hey," she says.

She finally looks at me, and her smile drops off her face.

She blinks. "Justin?"

Stewart and Julio look at each other wide-eyed, and burst out laughing.

"Oh my God, it *is*," Stewart says. "That's *crazy.*"

Christina quirks her lips up at them, then looks back at me, a slight crease between her perfectly-shaped, black eyebrows. Her eyes are very sad, even more so than before, but she smiles a little bit at me now.

"What are you doing here?" she asks, and Stewart and Julio burst out in fresh laughter.

"I'm making deals and signing contracts with Stewart," I say. I smile, and I feel like I'm smiling with my whole self, because the Dark Energy is finally making sense. "Why are you here?" I ask.

She laughs. "The same reason, but I don't think I'll sign any contracts." She smirks at Stewart.

Stewart puts his fist over his mouth, trying to make himself stop laughing. "I always put our transactions on the ledger, Christina. For the tax write-off."

She rolls her beautiful eyes, which then focus back on me. She looks perplexed, which is strange. I know she knows about the Dark Energy, and the synchronicity of this situation is self-evident.

"Justin here drew a picture of you," Stewart says, and he flips the notebook around on the desk so she can see. "When I saw it, I knew it had to be you. That's part of the reason I called."

Christina walks up to the desk. Her eyes go dreamy and wide. "You drew a picture of me.

185

That's amazing." We stare at each other, and other things start to fall into place. It's as if the Dark Energy has done its spring cleaning, hauled all the junk and clutter to the psychic dump, so what's left fits perfectly on the shelves.

"I'm taking us all out to lunch," Stewart says, clapping. "You too, Christina. This is a celebration."

I glance over at Mina, and feel a pang of guilt. She doesn't look like it is a celebration for her at all. Her hand has gone limp in mine.

Chapter 15

Stewart tells Mina and me to go check out the gallery and imagine my drawings on the walls while he, Julio and Christina stay behind. As Mina and I examine the sunlit artwork, she looks over at me with a furrowed brow. "Are they doing a drug deal in there?"

I think about it, though it's hard to think about much else right now besides the things already in my head. "That seems like a reasonable assumption."

Mina frowns at her feet. I stare at the swooping strokes of an oil painting, and I feel my thoughts swooping along with them.

When the other three come back out, Stewart and Julio are glassy-eyed and giggling. Stewart tells a pretty girl with serene green eyes and long dreadlocks to watch the studio while we go out, and she nods and tells us to have a nice lunch.

Christina walks beside me down the sidewalk, her hands in the pockets of her light blue slacks. She chews on her bottom lip, and sends me little quizzical glances.

"How have you been?" she asks.

"I have been well, for the most part. You haven't been well for the most part, however."

Christina winces and gives me a strange, sad look, but doesn't answer. Mina walks on my other side, staring at her feet.

Stewart takes us to a restaurant just down the street. The place has different-colored linen tablecloths, and art on the walls in bold colors. Everyone there is enveloped in an aura of cool, and I am sullying it. We have to stop at two separate tables as the waitress leads us to ours, so that Stewart can say hello to people he knows.

The waitress seats us by the window. I am next to Mina and across from Christina. Mina frowns at her lap.

I press my lips to her neck. "Mina, please don't be angry with me," I say in her ear.

She doesn't respond, just squirms in her seat, her shoulders slouched. Julio catches my eye. He leans over, and says something in Mina's other ear. I can't hear what it is, but Mina sits up a little straighter and stops frowning.

Christina watches me with a faint smile. "I've been having dreams about you, actually," she says.

"Yes," I say.

She sits up straight, and quirks her lips. "What do you mean, 'yes'?"

"We've been in the same dreams," I say.

She wrinkles her nose and gives me a weird look. At first I think this is a strange social dance, but then I realize Christina doesn't know about the

Other Place, maybe, and thinks they are just dreams.

Stewart and Julio look at each other, stifling giggles. Mina squints at me, and chews on her cheek.

"The businessmen in the trees," I say, and Christina's eyes open wide. She looks like I have smacked her in the face with something.

This is not a social dance. She really didn't know.

"The—the movie...on the ceiling?" she mutters, and I grin.

"Yes, and the floor covered in pillows and creepy teddy bears."

Julio and Stewart stop giggling and the table goes very silent. Everyone is staring at me, and it gives me a painful jolt. I've ruined the atmosphere by talking about the Other Place. People usually don't get this upset, though, and I am wondering what especially bad thing I have done this time. I am worried they are all going to get angry, get up, and leave me alone in this restaurant, or that something even more terrible might happen.

But then Christina blinks and lets out a breathy giggle, and Stewart says, "This is crazy." Some of the tension drains out of the Dark Energy. I realize they aren't angry. They are just surprised, I think, because they don't know about the Energy. Either that or this is some sort of test. But I don't think there can be any tests having to do with Christina, because of how special we are to one another. I don't know why the Dark Energy has brought us together, but I know it was meant to be. This is the reason why I was forced out of Piedras.

"You guys have really been having the same dreams?" Julio asks. He rolls his eyes and waves dismissively at us. "No, you're not. This all some elaborate setup you had planned."

"No, it really isn't," Christina says. She is still staring at me with a little open-mouthed smile, and I am happy to see some of the sadness has gone from her eyes. I think she has been very lonely. I think she is glad that we are finally together in the Physical World.

"How about the one in the car?" she asks.

"The convertible," I say, and she twitches. "In the jungle. And that unsettling parrot with the cell phone."

Christina shakes her head as if to clear it. Mina has gone very still. I know she doesn't like hearing about these dreams.

"This is so crazy," Stewart says again. "Look at my new artist. He's some sort of dream psychic. I'm going to use that as part of the advertising."

Julio laughs. "You know who's going to love this story? Michelle."

"Oh my God, she's going to flip out," Stewart agrees. "She's going to run to her medium and ask how she can find the men in her own dreams." He and Julio start giggling again. They are reminding me a little of Miller and Cris at the moment.

"You sold some of your drawings to Stewart?" Christina says, blinking, still looking dazed.

"He's going to put them up in his gallery and try to sell them to other people," I say.

"That's great," Christina says. "Your drawings

190

are really good."

"Justin is probably the most incredibly talented artist I've ever met," Stewart says. "And you know I don't just say that."

My thoughts are being pulled in seven directions, like a pack of dogs is playing tug-of-war with my brain. Mina slouches down in her chair, and I put my arm around her. I do not know what to do about the Mina situation.

Christina smiles at her hesitantly. "You guys are boyfriend and girlfriend?"

"Yes," I say. "Mina is wonderful. She introduced me to her uncle Julio, who introduced me to Stewart, and my life would be very complicated right now if it weren't for her." And this was a good thing to say, apparently. Mina smiles a little bit.

The waitress comes, and we order food. Christina tells me she stopped by my grandma's house last winter, looking for me. "She says you were off with your mom, though. She didn't know where."

"We were in Idaho with Mom's man of the month," I say. "It was not a good situation, and we came back."

"Are you back in Paso now?" Christina asks.

Mina clasps my hand, because I am tensing up. "I am not anywhere right now," I say. "I'm staying with Julio for another few days, but I don't know what will happen after that. Things are getting a bit disordered, actually, but I know it will work out somehow." I know for sure it will work out. Christina is here, and so things are arranging themselves correctly.

191

Christina tugs at her short hair. "It was really nice, what you did for me that night. I don't know what I would have done otherwise."

Mina's head snaps over to look at me. I hadn't told her that part.

Christina sees Mina's bad feelings, and smiles at her, a little flustered. "He fed me casserole, and let me sleep in his bed one night. I mean, I slept while he sat on the floor all night, drawing. I'd just gotten kicked out of where I was, and had no place to stay." She gazes at me sadly. "Then he gave me two hundred and fifty flippin' dollars. Things would have turned out a lot differently for me if he hadn't done that." She looks away, out the window, a shadow passing over her face. She shifts in her seat, and smiles. "It would have turned out a lot worse."

"Though it still didn't turn out exactly well for you," I say. She winces. For a moment she looks like she's going to say something, but she doesn't. Instead, she stares at the table, frowning.

The Dark Energy is strange as our food comes and we eat, because of Christina and me being together and Mina being upset about it. Stewart and Julio do most of the talking. Christina seems to be thinking about something, mostly just poking at her food without eating it. Every so often she struggles to keep her eyelids from drifting closed, and so I know she is still on drugs.

Obviously different ones than what she apparently sold to Julio and Stewart. They are flicking pieces of parsley at each other and arguing about who has the better haircut. Christina takes the Other Place drugs, and they take the Physical World drugs, I think.

As we are leaving the restaurant, Christina turns to me. "Justin," she says, but then just stands there. She lowers her gaze to the pavement, and rubs her nose. She looks up at Mina with a sort of pleading look. "I want to invite you—both of you—to come stay with me. Justin, you saved my ass at one point, and now I'm in the position to return the favor. I have an extra bedroom and...I'd like it if you would come." Her balled-up fists jitter in her tight pants pockets.

A strange vibration goes through me, because this is of course what the Dark Energy wants. It has been the plan all along. But Mina is staring at me with her eyes burning, and I'm suddenly very upset.

"Well, think about it, at least," Christina says. "Stewart has my number."

I want to say thank you, but she turns and walks away down the sidewalk before I can get air in my lungs to propel the words out.

The rest of us turn in the other direction and start back toward the studio. Stewart and Julio stare at me.

"Did Christina just invite you to come live with her?" Stewart asks.

"Yep, that's what just happened," Mina says.

"Oh, Mina, stop it," Julio says, nudging her on the shoulder with his knuckles. "I told you, Christina's the biggest dyke in the City, and that's saying something." He and Stewart burst out in giggles again. Mina's lips twist up, and she hides her face in her hands.

I put my arm around her. "Mina, I really need a

place to live." She clutches her fingers tighter in her hair.

"That's insane that she invited you," Stewart says. "She's very secretive. But she's a great person. I've known her girlfriend Arty for years, since way back in the day." He smirks. "It could be pretty interesting, living with Christina. I think you should do it, and draw some pictures inspired by the experience."

"Oh, my God, yes," Julio says.

Mina takes her hands away from her face. She looks tired and pale. "I don't think my dad would be very happy about me staying there, though," she says.

"Don't tell him," Julio says. "I'll say you're still with me. I can say my roommate decided to come later, or whatever."

"But, living with someone like..." She presses her lips together. She doesn't want to insult her uncle and Stewart by pointing out that living with their drug dealer is not an ideal situation, I think.

"I can't go back to Piedras," I say. "And I think this is what is supposed to happen, so even if it's not the happiest thing it will work out somehow." I am suddenly dizzy with how fast my life is changing.

"Justin," Mina says, and the spinning in my head swirls to a stop. I can hear the hurt in her voice. She doesn't complete the sentence. She doesn't need to.

I take a deep breath and let it out. I know what we are both thinking. We are both thinking about what will need to happen pretty soon if I stay in San Francisco, which is that Mina will have to go home for school, and we will not be together anymore. But I need a place to live, and the Dark Energy has given me one. It might be dangerous to refuse.

"Just ask your dad if you can stay for the rest of the summer," I say. "Then maybe you can ask to stay longer, after that. Maybe your dad will let you finish your high school in the City. I'll bet there are some really good schools here."

Mina doesn't say anything, but I can tell by the look on her face she doesn't think that's very likely.

When we get to the door of the gallery, Mina sighs, and turns toward me. "Okay. We should try living with her for the rest of the summer, and if it's weird, we'll figure something else out."

I let out a breath.

"Yay!" Julio says, throwing his arms up in the air. "Justin's moving to the City!"

Stewart grins at me. "You're going to love it here. And I can help you have a wonderful career too." His eyes shine, and he taps his chin. "I have a feeling you're going to be very big."

As we head across the gallery, I imagine my own drawings on the walls. I imagine being "big," like Stewart says, and picture myself swelling up rounder and rounder as people shove handfuls of money down my gullet. I snort and giggle, but I swallow my laughter down when Mina shoots me a look out of the corner of her eye. She still looks very unhappy.

We go through the back door into the office. "It will be a lot easier having you here close," Stewart says as we sit in our chairs again. "I'll text Christina right now and tell her you're going to accept her

195

offer."

"This is exciting," Julio says.

Mina takes my hand, and puts her head on my shoulder. I wonder what the Dark Energy has in store for Mina and me.

***

When we get back to Julio's condo, Mina calls her dad and asks if she can stay longer in San Francisco. As she listens to his response, her eyes brim with tears, so I know right away that it is not good.

"But, Dad," she says, "school doesn't start for another month almost..." She twists the tassels of a throw pillow in her hand, sniffing, and wiping her eyes. "The boys can take care of themselves, and what about 'Nulfo?"

I realize I'm digging my fingernails into my arms, and I try to stop.

"Dad, there's no reason to be nervous. We're here with Julio..."

She keeps arguing with him for a while, but it's obvious it's no use. Finally, she has to hang up after promising she'll be back home on Monday. She throws her phone down, and spits out bad words and curls into a ball on the couch. I put my arm around her, but I don't know what comfort to offer, because I suddenly feel very empty.

"It's okay, Eenie-Meenie," Julio says sadly. "You can come back and visit every weekend. I'll pay your gas, and I'll beat up your dad if he says no."

"Thanks, Uncle Julio," she says, her voice thick.

"Oh, poor Mina," he murmurs. "This sucks. I'm going to go get some ice cream. Cookies and cream is still your favorite, right?"

"Yeah," she says. "Thanks, that's really nice of you."

He takes his keys and wallet and leaves. I lie down next to Mina on the couch. She begins to cry, and I realize I'm crying too.

"This is not the way it should be at all," I say.

My emotions settle into a sick soup in my stomach. I am angry at Mom and David and Rebekah, because if it weren't for them I could be back in Piedras, living in my house by the park and seeing my beautiful girlfriend every day. I am angry at the Dark Energy, for making them the way they are, and for making all this happen. But I know it is no use being angry. I can't fight against things like these. When the Energy wants something to happen, it's going to happen, whether I want it or not.

Chapter 16

Mina leaves on Monday. She is sullen and sad as I walk her to her car, and I am not feeling much better than her.

I hold her for a long time, standing beside her car. "You'll call me and send me text messages, right?" I say. She has helped me get a phone specifically for this purpose.

"Yes." She presses her face against my chest, and I can feel the dampness of her tears. "Justin..." She looks up at me with red eyes, and I know what it is she wants to say. She wants to tell me not to go live with Christina, since she can't be there. This is the thing she's been wanting to say all weekend. But she won't say it, because she knows it's what the Dark Energy wants and that I have no other choice, really.

"Mina, I love you," I say.

"I love you too, Justin. I'll be back in a couple weeks to visit."

I kiss her. She is tense, and her lips are wet with tears. I let her go, and she gets in her Camry, waves at me one last time as she pulls out and drives away up the hill.

And I am alone.

Later that day, I take the bus back to Stewart's gallery to sign the contract his attorney has written. I have my suitcase and all my things, because Christina is going to meet me, and I'm going to move into her house today.

Julio gave me a present before I left, which was a couple of very nice stretched canvasses, some oil paints and brushes and all sorts of other art things that I'm not even entirely sure how to use. He is an extremely nice person, and I thanked him so much for so long that I think I made him really embarrassed.

I sit in Stewart's office and read through the contract, which is just lines and lines of mixed-up words to me. Stewart sits on the other side of his desk with his hands behind his head. He rolls his eyes when I look up at him.

"Don't ask me what it says. I'm just an art dealer. But, no, what it says is just what we talked about: exclusive agreement for six months, sixty-forty split to you of any sales, I pay for the opening—which will happen in two months—and for any costs of preparing the work for the show. If you break the contract, I get to beat you with a stick, but it can't be bigger around than my thumb."

He holds up his thumb, and I look at it. "That's not that big," I say. "But I think maybe I want that part changed. I think if there are any disputes, they should be settled by a kung-fu battle to the death."

He grins. "Street rules? Do we get to use

weapons? Crowbars and broken bottles?"

"Yes. But no magic."

Stewart laughs. I glance at the paperwork, and shrug. "This contract looks okay to me. All the words seem to be in proper order, forming sentences and everything, with most of the dangling participles modestly covered." I hesitate just a moment with my pen over the signature line. Stewart is a very nice person, but I am still a little nervous. This is obviously a situation the Dark Energy wants, though. I sign it, and slide it over the desk to him.

I hear the door to the gallery open, and Christina appears in the office doorway. She leans on the doorjamb and smiles at me. She looks happier than she did before, probably because we have found each other. I'm glad about that.

"Hey," she says. "Ready for your new home?"

"Yes," I say. "Thank you, Christina."

Stewart smirks at her, and she looks back at him, arching her eyebrows. "What?"

"Nothing," he says. "Nothing."

She snorts and pulls a little baggie of white powder out of her pocket and flicks it at him. He gives me a scared sort of glance, and fumbles for it. It hits him in the face and falls into his lap. A sour note rings in the Dark Energy.

Christina laughs. "Nice lightning reflexes, Batman."

Stewart's eyes are still darting to me nervously. "It's not my fault you throw like a girl, Christina."

She puts a hand on her hip, and squints at him. "Why don't you just admit you're a cokehead? I'm tired of your weird texts where you try to pretend you're not asking me to bring you product."

Stewart's smirk disappears, and he looks at me with wide eyes. "I'm not a cokehead." His gaze swings back to Christina, and he glares at her.

"What?" she asks. "I'm supposed to keep this a secret from him? He's going to be living with me, and you told me he was cool."

"I'm extremely cool," I say quickly. "I'm almost frozen, actually."

They both gaze at me, and I fiddle with one of the buttons on my shirt. I'm not exactly happy about the drug situation, but since the Dark Energy wants me here, I know it must be okay.

Christina blows a raspberry, and flops down in a chair. She raises her chin at me. "Stewart's not really a cokehead. He's really responsible and mature. That baggie actually contains pure vitamin C, to help keep his coat sleek and shiny."

Stewart takes off his glasses and pinches the bridge of his nose. "Shut up." He slides some money over his desk, and Christina pockets it. He looks at me. "I'm really not a cokehead…"

"It's okay, Stewart," I say. "Mom dated a cokehead once, and you aren't like him at all. Your personal hygiene is excellent and you don't live in a trailer behind your aunt's house."

He grins sheepishly, shaking his head. "Gee, thanks."

Christina pummels her feet against the floor. "Are you ready to go, Justin?"

"Yes," I say.

We stand up. "I'll see you back on Thursday to

discuss the show," Stewart says, and we say goodbye.

Christina and I head out, weaving our way through the people on the sunny sidewalks. I roll my suitcase along the uneven pavement, trying to keep it from swerving around like an anxious dog.

Christina carries my canvases under her arm. She leans close to me, and I see how pale she looks in the sunlight, her cheekbones jutting, her pupils tiny pinpricks in deep brown irises. "No one knows where I live," she says, "and I need you to keep it that way, okay?"

"Of course, Christina. Thank you for trusting me, and for taking me in."

"Don't thank me." She studies my face for a long moment. "And my name isn't really Christina. It's Liria. Keep calling me Christina in public but...I just wanted you to know."

She looks away, frowning, and I want to reach out and take her in my arms, because she needs someone to hold her. But I don't. I'm not sure how she would react to that. She's more nervous here in the Physical World than in the Other Place.

She leads me down a quieter street and through an alley, walking quickly and glancing around and behind her a lot. I have to take a deep breath. The back of my neck is prickling, and the Dark Energy is shouting jumpy, wordless warnings.

She stops at a bare steel door flanked by rusty trash bins, leans the canvases against her skinny legs, and gets a key out of her pocket. Her hand tries to be too quick getting it into the lock and so it takes her a couple of tries, but finally she gets it open, and we go inside.

We are in a laundry room, which smells like soap. Washers and driers are lined up opposite each other against the beige walls, like strange chess pieces poised to play. They are all quiet now, and no one is in here.

Christina…Liria…shuts the door, and the strange intensity of the Dark Energy calms down, because we are wrapped up in safe walls.

We don't speak as we go into a lobby. The beveled glass front doors fragment the view of the street like a kaleidoscope. Liria frowns, and taps her foot on the inlaid marble floors as she pushes the button for the elevator.

"Liria is a pretty name," I say when we get in and the door closes.

She gives me a faint smile, and pushes the button for the top floor. "Thanks."

"You're hiding from somebody," I say.

She doesn't answer, but frowns at her feet. We get to our floor, and she takes me down the hallway, unlocks the door at the very end.

We go into a sunny living room. Tall windows look out on a park across the street. There are hanging plants and gauzy curtains with blue and yellow stripes caught up with hooks around the window seats.

"This is a very nice apartment," I say.

"Yeah, it is, I'm really lucky." Her voice is flat, and she doesn't sound like she means it.

She shows me to my bedroom, which has a four-poster bed and a thick Persian rug. Two long, narrow windows look out on the street three stories down.

I put my suitcase by the dresser, and run my fingers over the crimson and white ceramic drawer handles. "This is the best bedroom I've ever had."

Liria smiles, but the smile doesn't last long.

"You're sad again," I say.

She clutches her elbows, and her lips twitch. "You want some coffee?"

"I would like that very much."

She leads me into the kitchen. I sit at a spindle-legged wooden table while she makes coffee. She doesn't talk, and I watch out the window as a man plays Frisbee with his dog in the park. The window glass is old and slightly warped, so the dog seems to move very strangely when it jumps, its body flowing in a twisted arc.

Liria brings me a cup of coffee, and sets a carton of cream, a bowl of sugar, and a white bakery bag on the table. "You want a molasses cookie?" she asks, rummaging in the bag and coming out with one.

"No, thank you." I pour cream into my cup. "Sugar is a thing I don't often eat. It's bad for you."

She shrugs, and sits down across from me. "I eat a lot of sugar."

The sun glints through the wavery glass, splotching her face. She is so pale, and her eyes can barely stay focused. "You do lots of things that are bad for you," I say.

She winces. "Don't go all judgy on me, Justin."

My stomach knots, because I think I've done a wrong step in the social dance again. "That's not my intention."

She crosses her arms. "I just do what I need to do to get by."

"That's all any of us can do." I clutch my cup. "I'm sorry, Liria. Please don't be angry with me."

She glares at me, and slowly her hunched shoulders wilt. Her chin falls, and she picks at the blue polish on her fingernails, her big, soft lips curling down at the edges.

I stay silent, because I don't want to say the wrong thing again. It's harder to get along with her in the Physical World than it is in the Other Place for some reason.

She stands suddenly, and grabs her coffee and the cookies. "Come on, let's go watch cartoons. It's the only thing to do around here."

I get up and follow her into the living room. Liria flops cross-legged in a pile of blue and silver pillows on the harem couch. She puts her cookies and coffee in her lap, turns on the flat screen television, and begins flipping through on-demand choices.

I stretch out next to her, feeling like perfumed royalty with all the pillows piled around me, but like sad and nervous perfumed royalty, because Liria is upset with me.

She settles on Adventure Time and hits play. It is a very good cartoon, but it just seems to make her sadder.

My foot jitters, because the vibrations in here are jumping all over the place. I get up and go into my room, bring out my drawing pad and pencils. Liria's chin has fallen to her chest when I return. I sit, drawing her. It is strange to have her here in the

Physical World with me, and it's not exactly easy, but I am still so glad.

We sit for a long time, the sunbeams creeping across the hardwood floor as episode after episode plays on the TV. Liria's chin jerks up every so often, but then falls again, her eyelids fluttering. She has a hard time staying out of the Other Place, and I think I know why.

The sunbeams have lain themselves across Liria's knees when she finally sits up, wiping her nose and blinking. She looks at me, but has a hard time holding my gaze. She is sadder than ever, and embarrassed.

"You're back," I say.

She shrugs slightly, rubbing her nose again. "What are you drawing?"

I hold it out so she can see, and she scoots over, scattering pillows. "You're drawing me," she says. Her cheeks flush slightly, but then go stark pale as she tugs the drawing from my hands.

"That's Lee Fucking Harvey next to me," she says.

"He's your friend from the Other Place," I say.

She stares at me, licking her lips. Her eyes are glassy, like marbles.

"He died," I say. "But he comes to visit you a lot."

Her eyes fill up with tears, and she hugs herself. "How do you even know that, Justin?"

This is a very strange social dance, but I try to participate. Liria is important to me. "We're in the Other Place together. You know that."

Her tears flow, and she's trembling. She hides

her face in her hands. I sit staring at her, because I'm not sure what to say.

"This is crazy. I've gone crazy," she says between her fingers.

"I think you're not crazy. They call me crazy because I talk about the things that are true."

She wipes away her tears, and stares at me. "What's up with those dreams? You're really...that was really you? And all the stuff you said to me, about love not being the most important thing, if it's not love...?"

"And it being better to have someone to take care of than the other way around. I don't know why I said it. It was just what the Dark Energy gave me to say."

"This is bullshit," she mutters. "This is just fucked up." She tosses my drawing down on the sofa, and gets up and walks out of the room.

I sit tracing the silk embroidery on one of the pillows. It's so difficult to get the social dance right, but I thought it would be easier with Liria.

I can feel her broken heart making waves in the Dark Energy. Finally I can't stand it, and I go find her.

She's in the other bedroom. There's a smell in here, like all the pennies in the world suddenly began to heat up with anger and are coming to get me. It makes my eyes water and my stomach hide behind my liver. Liria is sitting on the unmade bed, clutching a spoon full of brown liquid. The liquid is trembling, sloshing over the edges of the spoon, and she's crying. She twitches when I come in and starts crying harder, but doesn't look up.

I very gently pry the spoon out of her hands and put it on the bedside table, amongst a clutter of cotton bits and syringes and dirty mugs. I sit next to her and put my arms around her, and she leans into me.

"My girlfriend, Arty, stole some money from the mob," she says. "We ran, and stayed in Greece for a while, and in Barbados. I thought we had enough money for...forever, but Arty said it wasn't enough. She sent me back here to work, and I only see her when she brings me shipments. She doesn't like me to go out much, because she's worried her...she's worried someone will recognize me and make the connection and come after us." She shudders and her voice is swallowed by sobs.

"You're lonely, and you feel like she's abandoned you," I say.

She puts her arms around me and presses her face into my shoulder. Her emotions flow through me. They are very painful, by my heart doesn't cringe away from them as if they were my own. My heart absorbs them, and takes some of them away from her so that they can't hurt her as much. She stops crying so hard, and takes a shuddering breath.

I sit holding her, and it feels good. "This is not a good situation for you to be in," I say, and she lets out a noise that is half-laugh, half-crying.

"I shouldn't complain, actually. This is by far the best situation I've ever been in." Her body gets rigid and starts to tremble again, and I run my hand down her back.

"That doesn't mean it's good," I say.

We sit for a long time without saying anything.

After a while, she stops crying. She wipes her eyes, and looks up at me. "You're not like other people, Justin."

"Yes, I'm crazy, like they say."

"You're not crazy. Everyone else is crazy." She looks away slump-shouldered at the walls, her eyes wide and vacant. "I quit dope. I was doing really well. But then I ended up here, by myself, and it's so lonely and boring. Then Arty brought me a fucking shipment of heroin to unload. What did she think was going to happen? It's like she doesn't even fucking care." She wipes her eyes again with a tight fist, smearing her mascara.

"She might not care, but you care," I say. "And I care."

"I want her to care. I love her."

She huddles closer against me. She smells like sandalwood and cloves, and I want to smell just that, and not the drug odor.

"Loving people is good," I say. "But feeling like this isn't."

She is quiet for a long time again. She isn't crying, but she keeps her forehead pressed against me. I'm glad she's not angry with me anymore. It is warm and safe here with Liria. She knows about the Dark Energy, and things make sense with her.

"I feel like I've known you forever," she says.

"I think that's because the Dark Energy wants us to be together," I say, and I feel her tense up. "Not in that way. I have Mina, and you don't like men like that. There are different ways of being important to one another."

The tension goes out of her, but her foot starts

209

jittering. "Lee Harvey and I were important to each other."

I want to ask her how her friend died, but I don't want to upset her again.

"I want to quit dope," she says. "I should never have started again. I want to quit."

"You should."

She sniffs. "It's hard."

I think about it. "It's something I have no experience with, so I don't know. But still, I know you can do it."

"It hurts, and you can't sleep for days and days, and you're so sick. And it's like the whole world has gone dry and bleak. Like it's a sponge, and someone has squeezed all the happiness out of it."

That feeling she is talking about pricks at the edge of my mind, and I squirm away from it. "I think I know what that's like. The sickness was like that, sometimes. And it comes back, every once in a while. Once you have the sickness, I think it never quite goes away."

Liria looks at me, blinking. "What's the sickness?"

So I tell her about Mrs. Talbin, and the school, and the hospital, while she twists her bottom lip between her thumb and forefinger.

"That sounds really horrible," she says.

"It was not pleasant."

She asks me about why I'm homeless, and what happened with my mom and my grandma. So I tell her the whole story about Rebekah and getting arrested. As she listens, I can see a shadow of fear in her. It hurts, because we're in the Other Place together, so she should know I wouldn't do the things Rebekah says I did. But by the time I finish with the story and tell her about the Christian mental institution, the fear has gone away. There is pity and anger in her instead.

"That's bullshit," she says, stomping her foot with a hollow noise against the floorboards. "They can't do that to you. That's bullshit."

"I agree," I say.

She frowns and tugs on her hair. It stays where she tugs it, because it is short and full of styling grease.

"I like your hair like that," I say.

She smiles a little. "Yeah. I did it like this because I wanted to look different. You know, so people wouldn't recognize me. But still, I like it."

I watch her for a moment. Her gaze keeps darting to the spoon full of drugs on the bedside table.

"You should quit those drugs," I say. "If you want to have help sleeping while you do it, you can take my nighttime pills. I don't take them anymore, because they're too much for me." I quit taking them after the first night, but I didn't mention that to Mina.

She raises an eyebrow. "Nighttime pills?"

So I go into my room, dig in my suitcase, and find them. When I bring them back and hand them to her, her mouth drops open.

"Whoa, holy shit. Yeah, this would do it, if you wanted to be put out of action." She stares at them a long time, turning the bottle round and round in her hands, making it rattle like maracas. She clutches it tight in her palm.

"I'm going to quit," she says, and looks at me with fear and hope shining in her eyes.

I smile. "Good. That's a very good decision."

***

That night, I go to sleep before the sun comes up, and I end up in the Other Place with Liria.

She and her friend Lee Harvey have built a huge fort out of the couch cushions, and I wander into it. It has vaulted ceilings hung with colorful embroidered silk and tons of little padded nooks lit by flickering lanterns. There are lots of people in there, sitting in the corners and talking, playing strange musical instruments made out of sour cream containers with living snakes for strings.

Liria and her friend are sitting at a table piled high with little packages. Liria stares at them sourly, and somehow I know they are dream-drugs.

I sit down by Liria, and Lee Harvey smiles. "Here's the new guy."

I don't look at him, because I'm looking at Liria's unhappy face. It makes me angry this dead friend of hers keeps reminding her about the drugs, as if that were an important thing in her life.

I snap my fingers over the table, and the packages writhe and morph into little beetles. They clack and scuttle over each other and down the legs of the table in a glittering black swarm, flowing away into the corners of the room and disappearing under the hangings. Liria looks at me with her brow furrowed, and Lee Harvey sits up straight.

"What did you do that for?" He sniffs, and crawls off his chair onto the floor, nosing around after the beetles, peeking under the floor cushions and the furniture.

"Just because people love us doesn't mean they know what's best," I tell Liria.

She frowns and nods, staring at her knees. She takes my hand, shooting me a little smile. "I don't need him anymore, because I have you."

And this makes me happy.

Chapter 17

When we walk into Stewart's gallery, he's with three customers, gazing at a framed picture on the wall. He breaks into a wide grin, and strides over to us.

"Justin! Here he is, right here!" He gives me a little hug, and then Liria too. "It's so nice to see you. I was just showing these fine folks one of your drawings, Justin."

"You have one of them up already?" I ask.

"I have three of them up, actually. I couldn't wait."

He guides me back toward his friends with his hand on my shoulder. "I have the pleasure of introducing Justin Flaherty, my new artist. Justin, this is Mitch Labelle, Josh Martinez, and Callie Popov."

Stewart doesn't introduce Liria, who slinks off into one of the gallery's quiet corners. Her girlfriend says she isn't supposed to meet new people, but also she is having a bad day because of the fact she's weaning herself off of heroin.

214

Mitch, Josh, and Callie all shake my hand, and look me over as if I were also hanging on the wall.

"It's great to meet you," Mitch says. "Your drawings are absolutely amazing." He has a bushy blonde mustache which is curled up on the ends, and it waggles when he talks. It's hard to look away from it, even though the social dance says I shouldn't stare at people's strange facial hair.

"Yes, incredible," says Callie.

"They certainly are," Josh agrees. "Stewart tells us you haven't been to art school?" He leans back a bit as if to study me at a better angle. His brown eyes remind me of something fresh-baked and still warm.

"I haven't," I say. "I would like to go."

"Do you do any painting?" Josh asks.

"Yes. My friend Julio got me some oil paints. It's goopy and slippery in a way that makes my toes feel weird and sort of excited. I like drawing, but I think I like painting better. Both of them are very organizational, but the colors with the paint are very immediate and pull you in easily."

Mitch, Josh, and Callie laugh, glancing at each other. Stewart makes an "o" with his mouth.

"I want to see your paintings," he says very decisively.

"I'd like to as well," Josh says. He reaches into the pocket of his tight, black jeans and pulls out a wallet. It looks like it's made from the bright green leather of a poisonous frog. He slips a card from it and hands it to me. "I'm a painting instructor at the Art Institute of San Francisco," he says. "You should seriously consider applying."

215

I stare at the card in my hands. I would like to go to art school, but I have no idea what is involved in that sort of thing. Also the Dark Energy gets a little twisty at the mention of school, and I believe art institutes are very expensive. But I smile at Josh, and put the card in my pocket.

"Thank you," I say. "I will seriously consider it."

They all chat with me a bit longer, saying complicated things about my drawings which I don't understand. It seems like they're seeing different things than I am when they look at the pictures, and I wonder if it's a strange social dance, or maybe if the Dark Energy is trying to teach me something about my drawings. But if it is, I don't learn the lesson before Stewart tells them all he has a meeting with me and scoots them out the door.

They all promise to see me again at my opening. "If not sooner," Callie says, looking over her shoulder with a toothpaste-commercial smile on her red-painted lips.

Stewart puffs out a sigh when they're gone. "You're going to be very popular," he says. "Come on, Christina," he hollers at her. "The scary art people are gone now."

Liria shuffles around the jutting wall with hunched shoulders, and we go into Stewart's office.

Stewart is very excited as he shows me all my drawings in frames, the proofs for the invitations to the opening, and the advertisements. Liria slouches in her chair, a distant look on her face. She has picked all her fingernail polish off, but at least I got her to leave the house today.

"Tell me about your painting," Stewart says as

he stacks my drawings away. "What are you working on?"

"I did one of Christina and her struggles," I say, and she shifts in her chair and hunches over more, "but it's not dry yet. And I'm working on another one." I feel myself tense up, thinking about it. "It's different. It's an uncomfortable painting."

Stewart's mouth gets halfway to a smile. "Those can be interesting." A question mark drifts through the statement.

"You have to see it," Liria says. "It's awesome. I can't wait until it's done."

I smile at her, because she is talking. She smiles back slightly, then curls around her knees again, and looks away. I worry she is going to compact herself into such a tiny particle she'll collapse under her own density and form a black hole, which would be a terrifying situation.

Stewart might be thinking the same thing. He gazes at Liria with a frown on his lips and a smile in his eyes. Liria ignores him, and Stewart looks back at me. He sighs. "You'll bring the paintings in when they're dry, right?"

"Of course," I say. "I don't want to invoke the ninja battle clause of our contract."

When we get up to leave, Stewart pulls me aside before I can follow Liria out. "Everything okay at home?" he whispers. "You two getting along?"

"It's wonderful at home," I say. "Christina is just in a wrestling match with her inner drug junkie. She's having a hard time."

He scans my face, and nods, patting my shoulder. "Okay, good. If it ends up not working out, be sure to let me know right away. I don't want you to be homeless."

"Thank you, Stewart. That's very nice of you."

I make an appointment to meet with him again. Liria and I wander back out into the misting rain. She pulls up her hood, and stares at her feet with her hands in her pockets.

"How are your struggles going?" I ask.

Her shoulders twitch under her sweatshirt. "I don't feel great, but it's a lot better than it could be. Those pills help me a lot." She glances up at me. "I'm down to a quarter gram a day."

"I'm proud of you." She smiles up at me. It's like a flower blooming in melting glacier ice, that smile. Color comes into her cheeks, and you can see how truly beautiful she is.

"Thanks, Justin," she says.

She tries to crawl back into her bedroom when we get home, but I slide sideways into her path. "Help me make lunch," I say.

Her eyes have gone dull again. "I'm not hungry."

"But it's lunchtime. And you said that yesterday about all the meals. And I've seen skeletons fatter than you."

She almost smiles. "You hang out with a lot of skeletons, Justin?"

"Yes. After they get done with their long workweeks as medical school models, they like to relax and go dancing with me."

She snorts, and I hook a pocket of her hoodie, pulling her toward the kitchen.

"Come on, we can make beans and rice," I say. "I got the ingredients at the store."

She slouches after me, and I set her to chopping up onions while I cook rice and open cans of beans and tomatoes. "Proper nutrition is important, even for skeletons," I say.

"Sure," Liria says. "If skeletons eat the wrong thing, then it just falls out of their rib cages and the floor gets messy."

"Yes. Skeletons, therefore, need to eat a lot of the large and bulky food groups. Like whole hams and foot-long hoagies."

Liria laughs, which makes me happy. My phone starts to ring from my back pocket. I pull it out and see it's Mina calling. I'm still learning to use it, but I manage to answer without hanging up.

"Hello, Mina," I say.

"Hi, Justin," she says.

I wedge the phone between my ear and shoulder and stir tomatoes into the rice. "You sound very unhappy."

"No, I'm fine." The words heave out of her throat like a sigh. "I just miss you."

"I miss you too, Mina. Very much."

"How's *Christina*?" She says it as if Christina were the name of a disgusting flesh-eating virus.

"She's...okay." I catch Liria smirking at me as she peels garlic. "Can you come down next weekend?" I ask.

Mina makes a little frustration noise. "I told my dad I'm going and that he can't stop me." There's a short silence, and her voice sounds glummer than ever. "He's being weird lately."

The Dark Energy hisses around me, and makes my neck prickle. "What's the nature of his weirdness?"

"People here are still talking about what happened, and more of the real story has gotten out, about how you and I were…together. He heard it, and I think he believes it."

I feel a brassy pang of frustration and fear. "Oh. That's not ideal at all." My knuckles hurt from gripping the spoon as I stir the pot of beans. "Is Eugenio very angry?"

"No. He hasn't said anything about it outright. He's just acting suspicious, and he doesn't want me to come up there."

"I don't think you should come, Mina. I don't want you to get in trouble. Bad things could happen if you come up here, I think."

Mina huffs a blast of air into the receiver. "You don't want me to come?"

"No, Mina, I'm not saying that at all. I want to see you, but sometimes a course of action is actually a path of destruction, and we should take care of ourselves and choose another way—"

"If you don't want me to fucking come, just say so." There are tears in her voice, and my spine goes rigid. Liria stops chopping garlic. I wish I could ask her what I should say right now, but that would just make things worse.

"I really want you to come," I say. "I miss you extremely."

There is nothing but silence on Mina's end, which makes my stomach hurt.

"I want you here with me, Mina. My head is filled up with you all the time. But I don't want to cause problems in your life. I'm trouble. I'm so many problems. Mom is right about me."

"You don't understand what it's like being stuck in Piedras, taking care of my stupid brothers, while you're there having fun with that *girl*." She's crying for real now.

"Mina, no—"

"You're going to forget about me."

"I could never forget about you as long as I live." I listen to her crying, my hand sweating and clutching the phone, and suddenly the world goes white as an idea grips me in its evil fingers. My breath stops, my head goes dizzy, and the Dark Energy pounds with fear.

"Are you a test?" I ask her. "Have you been a test all along?"

She sniffs, and her crying stops. "What?"

"You know about the Dark Energy," I say. My throat is closing up all the way, and I have to gulp air. I wrap my arms around myself and curl up, trying to fend off the terrible certainty that wants to tear me apart. "You were never real. You were part of the trap, along with Rebekah and David and Mom."

"What the fuck do you mean, Justin? You think I'm conspiring with them to get you committed?"

"Is that what you're doing? I don't think people should be like that. I don't think it's fair that people have the channels and pathways for the Dark Energy to use them like that. It's a cruel road to enlightenment." I'm shaking, and I feel Liria's hand on my shoulder, but I shrug it off because it hurts.

"Justin—" Mina says.

"I hope I'm not like that when I'm enlightened,"

I say. "Some things shouldn't be given up to the Dark Energy. I think people should be left with their hearts intact after they're enlightened, and not be heartless."

"Fuck you! I'm not heartless!" I flinch.

Liria turns off the stove. I can smell the beans burning. I've forgotten to stir them. Liria pries the spoon out of my hands, and puts her arms around me. I stand very rigid.

"I need to get out of here," I say, and Liria hugs me tighter.

"No, listen to me, Justin," Mina says. "I'm not conspiring with anybody, and I don't know about the fucking Dark Energy. How can you think those things about me? I thought you loved me?"

She's crying again. The Energy is dangerous and oppressive right now like a cloud of poison gas. "I can't stand this," I say. "I can't handle this. I can't do this lesson."

I can't keep my feet from running anymore. The phone drops from my hand, and I tear myself from Liria's arms.

I'm out the door and down the stairs fast. The Dark Energy clutches at me cruelly. I can hear its mean laughter, and it makes me sick. I'm so tired of being battered around. There's no way I'll ever reach enlightenment if I'm going to have my feelings constantly torn to pieces.

Or is that itself the way to enlightenment? Maybe enlightened people are so heartless because they've had their feelings completely destroyed by the Dark Energy. I push that thought away, because it's too horrible.

I dodge around people on the sidewalks. A car almost hits me as I cross an intersection, and I vaguely hear him honking at me and yelling. I run faster, trying to leave my fear and hurt behind, but they are all around me. The air tastes like them, like unripe bananas and burnt boloney.

I run up a hill so steep, my feet are almost higher than my head. I'm sweating and panting when I reach the top.

It's quieter up here. There's a little park with soft grass and towering trees. I flop down in the middle of it, squinting at the sun slanting over the Bay far below. The Dark Energy is calmer now, but the hurt isn't much better. Tears sting my eyes. I don't want Mina to be a trick.

As my breathing slows, the whiteness clears away from my vision. I start to wonder if maybe she isn't a trick. Maybe she wasn't lying. Maybe she really doesn't know about the Dark Energy.

I sit up on the grass. I hug myself and rock back and forth. I want to believe that, so much. I shake my head, flinging tears from my cheeks.

"I don't want it," I say. "I don't want it." A lady passing by with a dog shies away, because of how I'm struggling against the Dark Energy. I shouldn't struggle so much.

I take a deep breath. I curl up with my arms over my head, and let the Energy beat me up.

It's horrible for a moment, but after a while, the Dark Energy stops hitting so hard, and I can breathe easier.

I'm not as certain as I was before that Mina was a test. I don't know if it's just because I want to believe that, or because it's true.

"Please let her not be a test," I say, and the Dark Energy hisses around me like wind through tree branches.

I realize it doesn't matter if she's a test. The Energy will do what it wants anyway. I take another deep breath.

A cop car drives slowly past the park. The man in the passenger seat is staring at me with suspicious cop eyes.

I jump up and start running again, heading back for Liria's apartment. There is urgency in the Dark Energy. I worry the cops will follow me. Maybe Mom has convinced them to take me to the institution.

But they don't. When I go around a corner, I look back. They're not there.

It takes me a while to find my way back to the apartment, because all the streets look the same. When I knock, Liria opens the door with wide eyes.

She throws her arms around me, which is a little startling. But I realize it feels good. I put my arms around her too, and breathe in her scent of cinnamon and cloves. Liria I know is not a test, because we're in the Other Place together.

"Where did you go?" she asks.

"I went running." I stroke her hair, and it feels like the cashmere sweater Mom keeps in a special box in the closet. I need to take it out and pet it sometimes, and Mom always yells at me if she catches me.

"Why did you go running?" Liria asks. "I was really worried about you. I wanted to go out looking, but I was worried I wouldn't be here if you came back."

She pulls back to look at me. Her brown eyes are just inches from mine. "I had to run," I say. "The Dark Energy was upset because of Mina, but it's better now. I might have hurt her feelings because I was worried about situations that might not be true. But I don't know."

Liria steps back out of my arms, and I feel cold and lonely all of the sudden. "You'd better call her back, Justin. She's not testing you. It sounded like she was just jealous about you living here."

I fidget with the hem of my shirt. "She's really not testing me?"

Liria shakes her head. One corner of her lips curls up, and she brushes a lock of hair from my forehead. "She's really not. And you're right. You probably hurt her feelings by saying that."

A weight lifts off my shoulders. Liria would know these things. She is in the Other Place with me. But I think about how I hurt Mina, and some of the weight comes back.

Liria goes into the kitchen, and comes out with my phone. I take it from her, but I can't bring myself to dial. "I don't know what I'm going to say to her."

"Just call her. She may still be mad, but if she's a good person she'll forgive you. You're just being the way you are, and if she doesn't understand that, then…"

I look at her. Liria knows about these things. "Thank you, Liria. I'm so glad I have someone like you, who gives good advice." She smiles, and I smile back. My fingers feel like I'm wearing big, clumsy gloves as I dial Mina's number.

She answers on the first ring. "Hello?"

There is still crying in her voice, and I stand there with my heart pounding. "Mina, I'm very sorry." It takes all my air to say it.

She blasts out an emotional breath. "Justin, I don't want you to think those things about me, that I'm not real or whatever."

"You are real," I say. "I was wrong. I was just being worried. Just sometimes it's so complicated and so hard to know what's really going on, because of how much the Dark Energy can trick you."

She sniffs, and sounds like she's crying even more. "I thought the medication would make that better."

I pick at a nick in the door frame. "I don't think the medication will give me enlightenment. I think it might be the opposite."

Her breath shudders. "I love you, Justin."

"I love you too. I'm sorry I'm too much trouble in your life."

"I'm going to come up there this weekend," she says.

Liria gently pries my hand away before I pull a long splinter from the door frame. "Okay, Mina. But I don't want your dad to be angry with you."

"I'll talk to him," she says. "It'll be okay."

We say a few more things, and we hang up. Liria comes and puts her arms around me again, and I'm glad for it because I'm very upset.

"I always do the wrong things," I say.

"No. you don't. We all get emotional, and it's

hard to know what's real and what's just our own heads making stuff up. I'm sure Mina does it too. You're a very nice person, and if she can't see that, she's blind."

"Thank you, Liria."

She looks up at me and grins. "Women, am I right?"

I grin back hesitantly. "I'm not very good at the girlfriend social dance."

Her smile disappears. "Me, neither." She looks away out the windows, her fingers twitching as she picks at her fingernail polish behind my back. "You did a good job. You said the right things."

"Sometimes I feel like there aren't any right things to say."

"That's the absolute fucking truth." She backs out of my arms, sighing. "Come on, you didn't eat lunch. I'll heat it up again."

After I eat, Liria puts a band called Beirut on the stereo system, and flops on her belly on the couch to read a Hunter S. Thompson book. I have an easel set up in front of the window, and I work on my painting.

It is a picture of frustrated and wrong-shaped feelings. It is a picture of the Dark Energy knocking and beating against the glass wall the medication is building around me, and seeping through the tiny cracks. When I paint it, the Energy is calm, because I am showing it how to still get through to me.

"I think maybe I should stop taking the medication," I say.

She looks up from her book and pulls on her bottom lip. "Why?"

"Because the Dark Energy seems far away. It can't communicate with me as well. I'm worried I won't be able to learn my lessons."

She squints at me. "But it does scary things to you sometimes, right? Like what you were telling me about, when that Rebekah chick flipped out on you and you had that vision about Hell. Why would you want stuff like that to happen?"

"Because if I don't let the Dark Energy do the scary things, if I don't let it give me lessons, then I won't ever reach enlightenment. And when I'm enlightened, I'll know everything, so I won't have to be tested anymore. The world won't be so scary and uncertain."

She looks at me a long time as my brush slides over the canvas, the rich-smelling oil paint conjuring images from the other world.

"Justin, what's enlightenment?" Liria asks. "What does that mean?"

My brush stops, and I blink at her. "It's when I'm completely in tune with the Dark Energy, so I can't get the sickness, and I don't need to be tested anymore, because I know everything."

"No one ever knows everything," she says.

"Don't you get lessons?" I say.

Her mouth quirks. "No."

"But you're in the Other Place with me."

She hesitates, then nods. "Yeah, I guess I am. But I don't get lessons. Not the way you describe them."

I start painting again. I can feel my brow scrunching up. "Maybe you're already enlightened," I say, and she snorts.

"No fucking way. I'm the least enlightened person on the face of the Earth."

"I don't think that's true. You know about the Dark Energy." I glance at her, wondering. "Maybe your lessons are different. Maybe you're learning them in a different way."

"Maybe." She flips a page on her book, frowning. "Keep taking your medication for now. Give it a chance. If it makes it so you can't paint or something, then you can re-think it, but it seems to me like you're doing really well."

I look at her, and I know that she knows the Dark Energy, even though I don't understand what she means about not getting lessons. But I should probably listen to her.

"Okay, Liria. I'll keep taking it for now."

She smiles, and goes back to her book. I dab my brush into the red paint, feeling very glad that I have Liria around.

***

Liria spends a lot of the next few days sleeping. I think she is taking lots of the nighttime pills. But then I wake up one afternoon and smell onions and garlic cooking, and find her in the kitchen stirring spaghetti sauce with a spoon. She smiles, and it's like rain soaking parched earth and coaxing the seeds to bloom. She is so beautiful.

"I'm clean, Justin," she says. "I haven't had any dope in two days, and I feel really good." She drops the spoon and comes to give me a hug. "Thank you," she says.

I stand there, feeling her in my arms. Our happiness soaks into one another. "Don't thank me. I didn't do anything. You're the one that defeated the bad drug gremlin inside of you."

She laughs and goes back to her sauce. "I wouldn't have done it if you weren't here."

The Dark Energy wraps warm and peaceful around me. It is good to be something besides trouble in someone's life.

"We should go out and celebrate," I say. "My paintings are pretty much dry, so I'm going to take them to Stewart. Then we should go get ice cream or perhaps a whole cake. I'll even eat sugar in honor of the occasion."

Her smile fades a bit, but she forces it back. "Okay, sure."

I know she's thinking about her girlfriend Arty, and how she's not supposed to go out. I overheard her talking on the telephone with her last night. I couldn't hear all of what she was saying, but it sounded like an unhappy conversation with a lot of yelling.

We eat her spaghetti, which is good with lots of garlic and rosemary and olives in it, and it's even better because Liria talks and laughs and tells a bad joke about a gay turtle and a Christian hedgehog.

After we clean up, we take my paintings and go out. I'm glad it's sunny today. My paintings aren't completely dry, and we can't cover them up.

Liria holds her chin high and struts down the sidewalk, her brown eyes shining. People watch her, and they glance at my paintings too. I think we are a spectacle, because Liria is so pretty, and because we are happy and strange, though being strange is not strange in San Francisco, I don't think.

When we get to the art gallery, Stewart has a cluster of people around him again, and they are looking at my drawing of the ants pulling the rickshaw. He throws his arms wide when he sees us. "Justin! And Christina, his beautiful muse. Everyone, this is Justin Flaherty, the one we've been talking about."

The crowd turns to stare at us. Stewart wades through them, his eyes feverish with excitement. They give me warm shivers when they focus on me. He gives Liria and me little hugs, though it is awkward because of the paintings. He grins. "Let me see these. Put them over here."

We lean my paintings against the beige-painted wall, and the crowd wanders over. They all stare at them very silently. Liria and I exchange a nervous glance and move closer to one another for safety, because the vibrations coming off these people are convoluted and intense.

A tall redheaded man in a camel-colored sport coat gestures toward the uncomfortable painting. "I've never seen anyone paint in six dimensions before."

The crowd chuckles. My heart beats a little faster, because someone is finally seeing what I actually painted.

"The two worlds are fighting with each other," I say. "They have to twist up to get in the same space."

He leans down to look at it more closely. "This is truly beautiful and surreal. There's so much detail. I could look at it for hours and not see everything."

"And it looks completely different when you stand back," a woman says, backing up a few paces. She is short and has a narrow and pointy-chinned face, her black hair plastered around it. Her gaze darts to me, her eyes sharp and blue and appraising.

The tall man reaches a finger toward the painting, talking to his neighbor.

"You shouldn't touch it," I say. "It's not quite dry."

He jerks his finger away. "Not even dry yet?"

I shake my head. "Neither of them are really dry, though the one of Christina almost is. Stewart thought it would be safer for them to finish drying here."

"How long does it take you to paint these things?" the black-haired woman asks.

"That one took me three days," I say, nodding at the uncomfortable painting. "The one of Liria took me two."

They all begin staring at me quite intently. Liria reaches up and pries one of my hands off my bicep and holds it. Her calm flows through me. Stewart raises his eyebrows at her, his lips quirking, and one of the other men smiles slightly.

"This other painting is of you, right?" he says, glancing at Liria before stepping over to examine it. "Are you two…?"

Liria blinks at the walls, and I shift on my feet. "We're just very good friends," I say.

"Roommates," Liria says, then she brightens. She puts her arm around me, and lays her cheek on

232

my shoulder. "He's like my brother."

The people start asking me all sorts of questions about my drawings and paintings. The tall man tells me he's an art critic with the newspaper and wants to have an interview with me, so I make an appointment with him for the next day.

Finally, Stewart tells them they'll have to come back to the opening, and shoos them out the door. When they're gone, he puts his hand on my shoulder and steers me toward his office. Liria trails behind, carrying the paintings.

"You're going to be very big, Justin," Stewart says. "I haven't seen people this excited about art…ever, I don't think."

Liria carefully props the paintings up in a corner, and we all sit down.

"I sent off the proofs for the invites," Stewart says. "I moved up the date of your opening to three weeks from now."

Liria scowls. "You what, Stewart?" She glances at me, and seems exasperated I'm not angry. I don't really know what to do with this information, but it doesn't upset me. So she turns her angry face back on Stewart, who sits up rigid. "You're going nutty. You're on one of your little streaks." She flaps her hands in the air. "You're rushing things."

The sparkle goes out of Stewart's eyes, and his mouth gets thin and serious. "It's getting too big. Word about Justin's work is spreading without me even needing to get involved. There's no need to delay it for advertising, and the rest is just catering and all that stuff. My staff has it handled."

Liria purses her lips at him. She tugs a little

baggie out of her jeans and sends it skidding across the desk, and I feel a slight sickness in my stomach.

"I should cut you off," she says.

He shrugs. "Go ahead. I don't need it."

They glare at each other, and the Dark Energy is squirmy.

"I should set Arty on you," Liria says, and Stewart's pressed-together lips spread into a smile.

"You *wouldn't*, you bitch."

Liria snickers, even though I see the pain in her eyes when she mentions Arty. "Seriously, Stewart. Please. Hold it together. This is important to Justin."

A crease forms in his forehead as he looks at the two of us. I get a warm feeling. Liria is standing up for me. I smile at her, and she shoots me a smile back.

"Don't worry about it, Christina," Stewart says, and his tone is much softer. "I've never gone off the deep end. Have you ever seen me do that?"

"No," she says. "But you do get, like, all run-aroundy and slightly manic twisted when you're amped up on some project."

"All just part of the process." He stares vacantly at me for a moment. He slaps the desk with his palm. "This should make you both feel better."

Stewart opens a drawer and pulls out a checkbook and a pen, starts scribbling. He rips off the check and hands it to me.

"This is how confident I am I'm not going to screw up this opening. That's an advance on the money I know we're going to start pulling in."

I look at the check and have to blink a couple of

times, because all those zeroes are blurring together. "This is one thousand dollars."

"Just a drop in the bucket," he says. "I have people trying to bid on your pieces already. Your drawings are going to go for a lot more than drawings usually go for, and you have a zillion of them. The paintings will go for even more. Use that money and go buy some more paint and canvas. You work like a *beast*, so I'm sure you'll have a few more for me by opening day."

"Thank you, Stewart," I say.

He smiles. "Thank you, Justin. I haven't been this excited about anything since Matt Bomer came out of the closet."

Liria snorts, and he raises his eyebrows at her and slides some cash over the desk to her.

"And thank you too, Christina. I promise to be at least somewhat good, now that you're, like, his manager or his soul-sister or whatever."

"Shut up, Stewart," she says, heaving herself up out of her chair.

He laughs. "Just take care of him. Feed him and don't disturb him with your craziness, so he can work. And bring him back here...um...Thursday at one thirty, so we can start planning the layout. And don't forget that damn interview tomorrow with Paul Lagrange. That's big. Huge."

"Of course we won't forget" she says. "Four thirty."

I get up, clutching my check. I thank him again, and I stumble back out through the gallery and onto the sidewalk, Liria beside me.

"He just gave me a thousand dollars for my

drawings," I say. "Is he going to make me pay this back if none of them sell?"

"Aren't you listening?" she asks. "He's going to make a frigging pile off you, Justin. Your stuff is *really* good, and Stewart knows he's hit the jackpot. He should have given you *more* money."

"This is enough money. I have everything I need. And I'm worried about my Social Security. I can't make much more than this this month without losing it, I don't think."

"Don't worry about that right now. After your opening, we can talk to them about how it works. You'll be able to make a living at this, Justin." She tugs at her hair. "As long as you don't let people, you know, take advantage of you." She frowns at the sidewalk, and takes my hand. "Come on. Let's go get you some paints, and then I want to go to the drug store for some stuff."

By the time we make it back to the apartment, our arms are completely full of canvasses and bags, as well as a bakery box containing a whole lemon cream coconut cake.

Liria bought some bright blue hair dye at the drug store, and I help her apply it in the bathroom. She sits on the edge of the tub while I squish and squeeze the foam through her short tresses.

"I've always wanted blue hair," she says.

"Your dreams are finally coming true," I say, wiping some splatters from her forehead with toilet paper.

She giggles. "You're right. I used to have these dreams about these little people with blue hair, and it was all, like, electrical. Sparks would fly off of it.

And their eyes were messed up. They had no white in them. They were dark green, with little, gold rings outlining their black irises and pupils." She opens her eyes and peeks at me. "Do you see those people too, in your dreams?"

"I've never seen them," I say. "You do seem to attract businessmen vultures in the Other Place. I only see them around you."

"Yeah, I know. What the hell is up with that?"

"Sometimes I think there's no telling."

Her eyes crack open again. "Why do you think we have the same dreams?"

I carefully peel off the latex gloves and throw them away. "I don't know why we see each other in the Other Place. It's never happened to me before."

"It's some sort of cosmic, psychic vortex interface."

"It's entirely possible that's true," I say, grinning.

She squints at me thoughtfully. "We were meant to find each other."

"I think that's correct."

She bursts into a beautiful grin, which creeps into my stomach like hot food when I'm hungry, and I realize I want to touch her. I want to slide my arms around her waist, to press my lips to hers. I have to turn away to the sink and wash my hands, because the feeling pulls me toward her. I think it would make her angry if she knew I felt this way, and don't want to make a mistake.

"I'm glad you're here, Justin," Liria says, and I have to force all my confusion away so I can look at her again.

"I'm really glad about that too," I say. I take a deep breath as everything settles back into place. Liria is my friend, and that is important, so I have to remember it.

We wait thirty minutes, which is a little more than two episodes of Adventure Time because that is the measure of time in this apartment, before rinsing the blue goop out of her hair. Then we go into the kitchen and eat cake.

We're standing in front of the window, and I'm running my fingers through her hair, watching how the sunbeams make it glint in blue and golden sparkles, when we hear the door open.

We both freeze, staring at each other with huge eyes. I hear footsteps behind me, and I turn, my heart racing in a painful stampede.

Standing in the doorway is a tall woman with a pale, beautiful face and black hair. Her green eyes burn fiery hot when she sees us.

"I knew it'd be some fucking bullshit like this," she says.

Liria stands stock still, her face pale as spring clouds.

"Arty," she says.

Chapter 18

My ears ring with fear. Arty glares at me like she would like to smash me flat. Then I notice the butt of a very solid-looking pistol sticking from the waistband of her jeans, and the Dark Energy blasts a terrified note.

"Who the fuck is he?" Arty bellows. Her narrow nostrils flare.

"This is Justin," Liria says, staring her girlfriend down with equal intensity.

"What the fuck is he doing here?"

"Staying with me."

"Are you fucking nuts?"

"I've known him longer than I've known you, Arty. He helped me out once—"

"I don't care if he's your goddamn grandma. This is utter bullshit." She stares at me, grinding her teeth. "I should kill both of you."

The Dark Energy gives me a pang, wanting to take me away from this. It tugs at me, but I have walls around me because of the medication. It is a painful feeling.

239

"Oh, yeah, real fucking nice, Arty," Liria says. Tears stream down her face. "Go ahead, kill us. You're just like your dad."

"Keep it down, or the fucking cops will come," Arty says, a little bit quieter.

At the mention of cops I get very dizzy.

"Look what you're doing to him!" Liria says. I feel her arms go around me. "It's okay, Justin," she says.

"I should go," I say, but it's too late to run, I think. The world goes wobbly and I realize my knees have given out. I'm sitting on the kitchen tile.

"What the fuck is wrong with him?" Arty asks.

Liria sits next to me, hugging me tight. "He's different," she says.

"Different?"

"Yeah."

Liria's arms are my last tether to the Physical World, but I can feel the Dark Energy seeping like gas through the cracks in the medication's walls now.

"This apple-cheeked gimp your fucking boyfriend? Is that what this is?"

"*No*, Arty! And what would you care, anyway? You fucking leave me here, and I never see you, and you decide to show up *now*? You don't give a shit about me for the last three months. I'm just another of your hustlers, and suddenly you decide to kick on in in your jack boots and lay down the law?"

Arty yells back at her, but I don't hear it. The Physical World finally lets me go, and evaporates with a *whumph.*

Getting pulled into the Other Place is not the same this time. There is no pain. There is no violence, or smell of death. My mind is a tiny point of blue light in endless, silent blackness. I wonder for a moment if maybe I am dead for real, if maybe Arty shot me, but that notion recedes, along with all other knowledge of the Physical World. I try to cling to my memories, but there is no place for them anymore, and they wriggle away. At first, when the spaces where my memories were linger, I know they are missing, and everything seems strange and panicky, but then I quit struggling. I just am. And it is simple and peaceful.

The Dark Energy is absolutely still.

There is a small ripple, and the wisp of a memory, of pain, of an ache, of loneliness. And then in a tearing, blundering confusion it all comes back. The world claws at me. The voices of the Dark Energy tell me to do a million things, before it's too late. Before I die. I need to always be somewhere else. I need to always be running, to make the Dark Energy happy.

But there is also a beauty that can only bloom in the midst of this chaos. A warmth which can't exist in the void, but can only exist in the Physical World. And, slowly, the veil pulls back from my eyes, and the voices fade from my ears, and I'm wrapped up in that beauty as the Physical World melts back into place, because Liria has her arms around me and her face pressed into my neck. She's crying and saying my name, over and over again. And the harsh voice that I remember is Arty's is yelling, "I'm not calling the fucking ambulance, because the cops will come with them, and fuck that, Liria! Look what you fucking get us into."

I take a breath of air into my just-remembered lungs. "Liria, I'm okay," I say. She gasps, and looks at me.

"Oh thank God, Justin," she breathes.

"Shitfucking Christ," Arty mutters.

I struggle to sit up, and Liria helps me. Her beautiful face swims into focus, chalk white and streaked in tears. "Are you all right?" she asks.

"I'm fine. The Dark Energy just took me."

Her eyebrows pull together. "One of your lessons? That's what it's like?"

"Liria," Arty says, her calm voice hiding a deep menace, "get him the fuck out of here. *Now.*"

Liria's head whips up and she glares poison at Arty. "We'll both go," she says.

Arty looks like someone has just slammed a door shut on her finger. She blinks. The clouds roll in over her face. Her hand twitches toward her gun, and I am extremely scared.

But she doesn't draw her gun. She clenches her hand into a fist at her side instead. "Fine," she spits. "Fucking fine. You'd rather be with this pudding-dicked retard than me? Great. Go. *Get out.*"

Liria helps me to my feet. I'm still a little dizzy. "Come on, Justin," she says quietly. "Let's get our stuff."

My heart feels like it's doing an awkward backstroke in an ocean of muck. Arty sits watching us, trying to cover up her hurt with a vicious look. I stop in front of her, though Liria is pulling at my arm.

"Liria loves you," I say.

Arty scowls. "Fuck off, Adonis."

Liria tugs harder at my arm. "Justin—"

"Liria wants to stay with you, but this is too much hurt for her," I say.

Arty's lips pull back from her teeth, and her thin body goes rigid. She turns and storms into the living room, and I hear the couch frame crack as she throws herself on it.

Liria and I look at each other, and her face is coated in tears. I put my arm around her, and we start getting our stuff together.

It doesn't take long. We don't have much. But it is long enough for a sour emptiness to take over my stomach, because of the vibrations in this house.

We pause at the door, our suitcases and my new, blank canvases in our hands. Liria turns her face toward the living room. "'Bye, Arty," she says.

We go out, then we both flinch as something crashes against the living room wall. But Arty doesn't come after us.

We are glum and silent as we take the elevator down, go out the front doors into the damp San Francisco afternoon, and trudge down the sidewalk.

"Where are we going to go?" I ask.

"There's a hotel down here. We'll stay there until we figure it out."

Her voice is a little unsteady. I watch her. She's not crying any longer, but her eyes let me peek in on a soul which is crushed and bleeding. I want to put my arm around her, but I can't, because they're full.

"It's going to be all right, Liria," I say, and she

winces.

"I know," she mutters, but I can tell that's a lie. She doesn't know.

"Your blue hair is very pretty," I say.

She tries to smile.

The hotel has a very nice lobby with cream-colored couches, and big vases of fresh daylilies on the reception counter, and I worry about the expense of this place. Even with the thousand dollars, I am not a rich person. But Liria shoots me a look when I try to take out my wallet. "I got it," she mumbles.

She hands the clerk a debit card and pays for two weeks in the hotel. She tries to pay for more time, but they say they are all booked up for a conference after that.

The total comes to over three thousand dollars, and I get a ripple of nervousness. As we walk away from the reception desk to the elevators, I clear my throat.

"That's a lot of money," I say.

"Don't worry about it."

We get in the elevator, and she turns to look at me, frightened.

"Arty's going to lock up the account, or drain it, so I wanted to get us situated before that happens," she says. "And she'll also be able to see where we're staying, because of the charge. But I guess there's nothing we can do about that."

I fidget with the handle of my suitcase. "Is she going to come after us?"

Liria's eyes go dull. "I doubt it."

The room is very nice, with two soft queen beds,

244

big windows, and a clean carpet. We toss our stuff in the closet, and Liria immediately turns to me, tearing her fingers through her still-damp blue hair so that it sticks up crazy. "Wait here," she says. "I'm going to run to the bank and see how much money I can withdraw before Arty messes with it."

Before I can even answer, she's gone.

I go to the window and look out. We are twenty-two floors up, and the City twinkles below, the declining sun clashing off the skyscrapers and the windows of the moving cars, the Bay beyond. The pipes of the hotel gurgle and swish around me. There are voices in the hall as people pass, talking about the cost of parking in this goddamn town.

I think about the lesson the Dark Energy has just taught me. I think about how meaninglessness is meaningless, because we can forge beauty and meaning from the void, and I am glad Liria and I found each other in the Other Place, because right now everything is strange and changing too fast. She is the only thing that is real. But that is enough, I think.

I go to the closet and pull out one of my canvasses. I bought some watercolors at the store earlier, and decide to use those. So I am starting a new painting when Liria comes back.

She plops down on the edge of the bed, crossing her arms and blowing a long raspberry. "I squeaked out of there with two grand, but it looks like it was a close thing. They almost didn't let me, because they said they were having problems with the account, or computer problems—they weren't sure which. Arty had already hacked in there, I guess, right when I was withdrawing."

"That's not very nice of her," I say. "Why would she do that?"

Liria shrugs stiffly. "It's her money. She's the one that gave it to me in the first place."

I watch the pain crawl across her face, and I'm not sure what to say.

"Two thousand won't get us far in this town," she says. "I wish I could have gotten more time at this hotel."

"I have a little bit of money too," I say. "We'll figure something out."

She tosses herself onto her back on the bed, and stares at the ceiling. "We'll get by one way or another."

I can feel the vibrations from her, and know she is in that very bad place where she can smell the death rot creeping in around. I promise myself I will figure out a way to take care of her, because I believe the ways she is thinking of to make money are not good ways.

I pick at a dry place on my elbow. "Liria, thank you for staying with me. I don't know what would have happened to me if you hadn't. The world is like a very sickening tornado right now, and you're my safe basement to hide in."

She smiles faintly. "I'm not leaving you. You're the one nice person I've ever met." She curls up, and starts to cry. "I want to get high *so bad*," she says.

I put down my paintbrush, and go lie next to her, taking her into my arms. She huddles close to me, shaking. "It's okay, Liria," I say.

"I don't know what we're going to do," she sobs.

"We have two weeks, and we'll figure it out. I promise."

I don't have any idea what I'm going to do, but I know I have to keep my promise, because she seems to believe it. She stops crying. "I'm so glad I found you, Justin."

A warmth blooms in me, and I smile, brushing the blue hair from her forehead. "I'm glad I found you too."

***

I put off talking to Mina until the next day, because I know it's going to be an angry situation. When I finally do tell her that Arty kicked us out, she gets very much in an uproar.

"I'll talk to my uncle Julio," she says. "He'll let you move back in."

"Don't worry about that right now," I say. "We have two weeks here."

"But, Justin—"

"Julio's house is not a good place for me. He doesn't really have room. I'm hoping I can find something better."

"Two weeks isn't very long," she says.

"I know, but I'm going to talk to Stewart, and see if he knows someplace we can rent. I'll get it figured out."

She is very silent for a long while, and when she speaks again her voice is low and hollow. "You're going to stay living with that girl, aren't you?"

I realize I have twisted my Bugs Bunny t-shirt all

out of shape, and take my hand away. "Mina—"

"I can't stand it," Mina says, and she's crying. "I can't handle it."

The Dark Energy rolls over me like a suffocating avalanche. "Please," I beg. "I'm sorry. Please." I want to promise I won't be so much trouble in her life in the future, but the words won't come. It's a promise I can't make, and the pain of it squeezes the air from my lungs.

She just cries. Liria comes over and puts her arms around me, which barely helps. "Mina, I love you," I choke out. "Please don't cry."

"How can you say…?" Mina takes a huge breath. "I'm still coming up there this weekend. Can I still come up there?"

Her words should make me feel better, but the Dark Energy presses me from all sides. "Of course. I want you to come."

"Okay, Justin. I'll be there on Friday."

I hang up the phone, and the Dark Energy is swallowing me and squeezing me like a snake. I can't feel Liria's arms, even though they are wrapped tight around me.

"I have to run," I say.

"Justin," Liria says. As I'm up and out the door, I hear her say something about being on time for something, but I'm not really listening.

I jog down the hall and down the stairs, my footsteps clattering in the stairwell. The desk clerks stare at me as I fly through the lobby, and then I'm out through the doors, pounding the sidewalks, dodging the people. I jog up and down the hills, past busy stores and restaurants and through quiet neighborhoods, the dense, humid air making me sweat more than usual, even though it's not hot.

The Dark Energy stabs me painfully. I'm too much for Mina. I'm hurting her because I'm staying with Liria. But the Dark Energy wants me with Liria, and I won't abandon her, especially after she left Arty in order to stay with me.

There's no solution. It's just like with Mom. I can't help that I'm nothing but trouble, because that's how the Dark Energy has set it up. It's tumbling me around like laundry in the wash, and it hurts. I want it to stop. Right now I feel like I don't want enlightenment, I just want to have a girlfriend and be happy, but I push that thought out before the Energy hears.

I have been running for a long time before the vibrations settle down. I am still very sad, but my brain isn't all crowded up and I can breathe again.

I'm not angry at the Dark Energy anymore, because I've realized that maybe there is a lesson in this: that if I can become enlightened, then maybe I will see a way to not be so much trouble in people's lives. Then Mina will stay with me. And I think that, if I am able to make enough money with my drawings and paintings, I'll be able to afford a good life. Then Mina could move in with me, after she graduates.

I still don't know what to do about the fact that Mina doesn't like Liria, but I hope that she'll get used to the idea and stop being jealous, because Liria would never be with me in that way, and so she doesn't have to worry.

Then, suddenly, my head clears enough that I

remember the interview with Paul Legrange from the newspaper at four thirty today, and a bolt of panic zings through me.

I have no idea what time it is. I turn back toward the hotel, and run as fast as I can. People watch me as I zoom by.

I'm a long way away from the hotel. By the time I get there, I am completely out of breath, soaked in sweat, my sides aching. The clock in the lobby says it's five minutes to four, and I curse.

It takes the elevator forever to get to our floor, and I realize I'm jogging in place the whole way up, as if that will help me get there faster.

Liria is waiting for me at the door of the hotel room, her eyes wide. She shoves me into the bathroom. "Take a shower, we have to go."

I douse myself in water and soap, buff myself frantically with a towel, then come out of the bathroom and rummage in the closet for clean clothes, hardly caring I'm naked in front of Liria, who is smirking at me.

She pulls me out the door. "Come on, I have an Uber waiting."

She taps her foot, and picks her nails on the way down in the elevator.

"We have ten minutes," I say.

"It'll be fine. No one's ever on time to anything." She sounds nervous.

We sprint to the waiting car. The driver is a pillow-bellied girl with greasy hair who weaves us slowly through traffic, ignoring Liria's huffy noises.

"I'm sorry I went running," I say. "I'm causing a lot of trouble in your life."

Liria drinks me in with big eyes, then scoots over to lean against me. "No, Justin, you're not causing trouble in my life at all. You're making it a million times better than usual."

Having her there makes the waves in the Dark Energy stop crashing against me. I don't say anything. I just hold her, and I'm trembling.

"It's going to be okay," she says, and I realize we are telling each other this a lot lately.

When the car pulls up in front of the café, we're ten minutes late. We dive out of the backseat and into the establishment. The tall redheaded man, Paul Legrange, is sitting at a table in back with a cup of coffee and a tablet computer.

"Mister Flaherty," he says, standing up and shaking my hand.

Liria and I are panting and ruffled. "I'm incredibly sorry I'm late," I say.

"Quite all right. Well within the realm of what counts as 'on time' for artists." He smiles at Liria, and shakes her hand. "And you're the muse."

"Christina Guzman," she says.

"Is it okay if she stays with us?" I ask. "I like having her here."

"Absolutely," Paul says. "Of course."

We all sit down, Paul folding his freckled hands on the table, and examining me through his thick, rimless glasses. He asks me if it's okay if he records the conversation, and I say it is. The waitress comes as he fiddles with the voice recorder on his tablet. Liria and I both order coffees, and I get a water too, because I'm thirsty from running.

"How old are you, Justin?" Paul asks, placing the

tablet between us.

"Eighteen," I say. The little line on the screen jiggles into waves at the sound of my voice, and I watch it in fascination. "I'll be nineteen in January."

His tangled eyebrows arch. "And you've never had any sort of formal art schooling? No classes, or anything like that?"

I tell him I haven't. He goes on to ask me all sorts of questions about my childhood, and how long I've been drawing, and how I met Stewart and ended up in San Francisco. Liria has to hold my hand because it's becoming uncomfortable in here.

Paul notices the discomfort in the Dark Energy. "Do you...excuse me for asking, but do you not get along with your mother?"

Liria squeezes my hand. She's giving me a sort of sly look. "Justin's mom kicked him out," she says. "She tore up a bunch of his drawings, and she's trying to have him involuntarily committed, even though he's not crazy, he's just, you know, he acts like an artist."

Paul laughs. I see the ghost of a smirk on Liria's face. I think I'm staring at her too long because her eyes widen slightly in exasperation, so I turn back to Paul, who is still grinning.

"Yes, if you could be committed for being eccentric, we'd have a crisis on our hands," he says. "The institutions would be packed to the roofs." His smile fades. "In all seriousness, I'm sorry about your mother, Justin. I didn't mean to dredge up uncomfortable subjects. But this could be of interest to our readers and potential fans of your work. Do you...do you mind if I put these details in my piece?"

I fidget, but Liria digs her short-bitten fingernails into my hand, and I know what she wants me to say. "That would be fine to put that in there," I say. "Yes. Do what you want."

He asks me how many pieces I finish in a month, and laughs out loud when I tell him ten or fifteen. "That's incredible," he says.

"It's pretty much all he does," Liria says.

"Where do you get so much inspiration for your work?" he asks.

He is staring at me so closely I can almost feel his eyeballs on my skin, like crawling snails, and I don't know if this is a test of the Dark Energy, trying to get me to talk about it.

"I don't know," I say carefully. "The images just…form under my pencil. I have to pull them into this world or I…I don't feel right. I don't fit into the regular dimensions because my vibrations are wrong."

He blinks. "Amazing."

He is staring at me, and I shift in my seat. He jerks his cleft chin toward Liria. "And I see you've been doing some pieces featuring Christina here. Is she an inspiration for you as well?"

I smile at her. "Yes. Very much."

"How did you two meet?" he asks.

"We met in a park about a year ago," Liria says. "Since then, we've been having dreams about each other, and now we just happened to meet up again in San Francisco. It was meant to happen."

I can't believe Liria is saying these things. She gives me a wicked grin.

Paul asks me a few more questions, and takes my picture. He shakes our hands, and tells us the interview will be out in a few more days.

I thank him for his time, then we go back into the street. My knees are a little wobbly, and I have to heave a big breath of the damp, exhaust-tasting air.

"Why did you want him to know all those things?" I ask. "Why did you talk about the Dark Energy, and about Mom? I think it was a violation of the social dance to say those things."

"People are going to love it," she says. "They like their artists to be a freak show. They like *everything* to be a freak show."

"You're calling me names, I think," I say, and she laughs.

"We're great, glorious freaks, both of us together." She skips a little as she says it. "You're going to be famous, Justin."

"I don't know if that's true."

"It is. You're a genius. Everyone can see it."

I wonder about this statement. I don't feel like a genius. I feel like a man without a home or much money, and a girlfriend who is angry at him. I feel like a man with a problem they call schizophrenia, who can't quite find the right vibrational current in order to fit into this world.

Chapter 19

I sit in front of Dr. Mingle the next day, as she taps her pen on her clipboard, and chews on her cheek. Liria sits next to me on the couch, tugging at her blue hair.

We are all nervous, I think.

"So you had another, sort of, fainting spell, brought on by the stress of getting kicked out of your house," Dr. Mingle says. "I'm sorry that happened to you, Justin. I had no idea your living situation was that unstable. I'll see what resources I can find for you. We have some information at the front desk. I know there are some temporary shelters, but the waiting list for Section Eight is really long…"

"We'll figure it out," I say. I have been in shelters with Mom, and I don't want to go to those places. They are full of dirty vibrations and sickness.

Dr. Mingle gives Liria a quick glance, then frowns at her paperwork. "I want to increase your dosage of the olanzapine. You say you quit taking the Seroquel?"

I squeeze the soft fabric of the armrest. "Yes. It made me feel like my brain cells were glued together."

"I'd like you to try it again. Those effects wear off after a while."

I don't say anything, because I don't want to lie to her and say I'll take it. I am only here because I hope it will show Mina I'm trying to make her happy, and because Liria says I should keep taking the daytime medication for now.

Dr. Mingle scribbles out two more prescriptions on her pad and hands them to me. "I want another appointment with you in six weeks, but call me if you have any more episodes like that."

"Okay," I say.

She squints at me, tapping her pen against her lips. She looks like she's going to say something else, but doesn't. Instead she gets up and walks with us up to the receptionist's desk, where she hands us a bunch of paperwork and information about housing assistance. I thank her and promise her I'll see her again in six weeks.

Liria and I flip through the applications and pamphlets on the Muni ride home, after we go to the pharmacy. It looks like a lot of questions I don't know how to answer, and Liria takes it away because I'm clutching it too hard.

"I'll fill out this stuff from the Housing Authority when we get back to the hotel," she says, "but Stewart says he has that friend with a rental."

"Yes, I hope that works out," I say.

I feel like my insides have floated away.

Everything seems to be falling out from under me again. Liria ruffles my hair, which is very long now, curling down onto my neck and getting in my face a lot. "We're going to figure it out," she says.

"Yes, I know," I say, and I realize she's frowning at me, because I'm staring at my knees too much.

We get out one stop down from our hotel, because there's a bakery there, and Liria wants to replace the lemon coconut cream cake we lost in the uproar with Arty. They don't have the lemon kind, but they have a chocolate mousse cake, so she gets that and they put it in a pink box for us.

We walk through the lunch crowds on the sidewalks, people toting greasy sacks and cups of coffee back to their workplaces. Liria is talking about something to do with some band from the seventies, but I'm not really listening because I'm thinking about the fact that Mina is coming tonight.

Liria stops talking, and halts abruptly in the sidewalk like she's been turned to stone. I follow the direction of her violently disordered glare.

Arty is leaning back against the wall of our hotel, next to the doors. Her arms are crossed, and her green eyes are fixed on us. Their lack of emotion scares me, creating a swirling vortex in the Dark Energy. In the sunlight, I can see the bright red roots of her hair where it is growing out from the black dye.

"Cake, huh?" she says, just loud enough to hear over the traffic. "Having a little party are we, on my dime?"

"Fuck you, Arty," Liria says. "You told me that

money was mine, remember?"

"Yeah, well, that was before you cheated on me with this cheese dick." Her glare shoots through me like bullets.

"Our relationship isn't like that at all," I say. "You're misreading the signs and symbols."

"And what would you even care if it was?" Liria says, stomping up closer to her. "You left me and ran off to goddamn Mexico or some shit for months—"

"I didn't fucking leave you," Arty says. "I had work to do, and it was safer for you here."

We are attracting curious stares from passersby, and I try to look invisible.

"Yeah, you had work to do," Liria says, the cake box crumpling in her grasp. "We could have lived forever on what we had, but you broke your promise. You said you'd give up that bullshit hustle, but you didn't."

"You expected that money to last forever?" Arty asks. "Thought you could just lie around for the rest of your life, eating cake?"

"We could have if you hadn't let yourself get pulled back into that bullshit. If you hadn't fallen for your dad's line of crap."

Arty stares at her for a long time, and I see that her lack of emotion isn't real. It's just a thin shell over her pain and anger.

"If you'd ever worked a day in your life," she finally says very quietly, "you'd know how it was. I'm not going to explain it to you again." She pushes herself up off the wall with a sharp motion of her narrow hips. "Just stopped by to see how you two were getting along, if you'd spent all my money yet and were starving in the streets, but it seems you're not." She glares at me. "I really should have both of you killed. First whispers I hear that you haven't kept your mouths shut, and I will."

She stalks off down the street, and Liria watches her go, her eyes brimming full of pain.

"Come on, Justin," she murmurs, and shoves on through the glass doors of the hotel and across the lobby toward the elevators. I hesitate a moment, my feet wanting to go in seven different directions at once, but eventually I follow her, the housing paperwork crushed to mush in my hands.

Liria doesn't cry or talk on the way up to our room, but she has a lost look and is slightly hunched over, as if someone has just punched her in the guts. I'm not sure what to say to her. I brush her shoulder with my fingertips. She flinches slightly, then winces and runs her hand over her face.

We get off the elevator and go into our room. She tosses the cake down on the table, and flops on the bed, sighing. "Fuck."

I twist the paperwork in my hands. "Arty isn't really going to kill us, is she?"

"No," Liria grumbles. "I don't think so."

This doesn't make me feel much better. "What if she comes back?"

Liria just flops over, and pulls a pillow over her face. I put the wad of paperwork down on the bedside table, and sit down hesitantly next to her.

She lies rigid for a moment, then flips onto her other side, reaching out to me. So I stretch out next to her, and take her in my arms.

259

"Arty is very mean to you," I say. Her lips are very close to mine, but I try not to pay attention to that.

"She wasn't always like that." Her voice is trembling, but she's still not crying.

"She loves you, but it's gotten all tangled up and complicated," I say.

Liria wiggles closer to me. She puts her forehead against my breastbone, and I can feel her breath through my t-shirt. Her big breasts are pressed against my belly, and she slides her fingers up under the hem of my shirt, around my waist to my back, tickling my bare skin. It's only that, but that little touch sends fire through me, and suddenly her smell of sandalwood and cloves engulfs me warm and sensual and dizzying. I want her so bad I have to grit my teeth, and force my mind into blank greyness.

She notices something is wrong with me, I think, and looks up. I can't tell what she's thinking, but she is swirling her fingertips in light circles on my back, and it's driving me crazy. I'm angry with myself, and wish it would stop, but I don't want it to ever stop.

There's a knock on the door.

Fear shoots through me, dissolving my desire in a sick instant. I think it is Arty, with her pistol sticking out of her waistband, come to shoot us both. But Liria frowns, and wiggles away from me. "That's probably Mina," she says.

The fear trickles down into my stomach and congeals into something else. I'm not even sure what it is, because it's just a mash of fermented feelings. I get up and go open the door.

Mina stands there, her hands in fists at her sides. She smiles just a little bit. "Hi, Justin."

And then all those too-many feelings turn to a dull ache. I pull her into my arms. "Mina," I say.

She puts her arms around me too, but she feels tense and shifty, and the Dark Energy vibrates in unsettling ways. "How are you?" she asks.

I stroke the long curtain of hair back from her forehead, tucking it behind her ear. The short side is ruffled and needs cut again. "It has been a difficult day," I say.

Her brow furrows. "What happened?"

I shut the door, and I lead her in to sit on the bed. Liria is propped up on the other bed, hugging a pillow to her chest. "My stupid ex-girlfriend just accosted us at the door of the hotel," Liria says.

"Wait, what?" Mina asks. "That sounds scary."

So I tell her the story while Mina plucks at a seam in the quilt, one corner of her mouth drawing down. "Are you safe here?" she asks.

"Arty's a headcase, but she wouldn't kill us," Liria says. She squeezes the pillow tightly. "She's just worried we're going to do something to get back at her."

"Like what?" Mina asks.

"Like any of a million things I could do to fuck with her or her operation, if that's the type of person I was. But I'm not and she knows it."

Mina frowns at her lap. She looks quickly at Liria, and then at me. She bites her lip. "You guys really are...okay here?"

"Yeah," Liria says. "We are. Arty's being a cunt,

261

but she's not really..." She turns her face to the wall, and doesn't complete the sentence.

"Have you heard back from Stewart yet on that rental?" Mina asks.

"I'm going to talk to him again tomorrow," I say. "And we got some paperwork for housing assistance from Dr. Mingle."

Mina nods, still frowning. "You want to, like, go get coffee, Justin?"

"Sure," I say.

Mina doesn't look up at me. She's staring at her hands. Liria and I exchange a glance. I stand up, and Mina and I go out of the hotel room.

I take her hand as we walk to the elevators. "I've very much missed you, Mina." It's true, but I'm still feeling very guilty. My head is full of Liria.

"I've missed you too," Mina says, but her voice is limp and listless.

"You're still angry at me."

Her gaze darts up to mine. "I'm not angry, Justin."

But I don't think that's exactly true, and it makes my insides even sicker.

The doors open, and we trudge through the lobby, then out onto the sidewalk. I glance around, nervous I'll see Arty, but I don't. There are just young people and homeless people wandering, and people bustling on errands or back from coffee breaks.

We go into a café and get coffees at the counter, then sit down at a table by the window. A man with square glasses squints at his laptop four tables down, but otherwise it's just us, sitting in this café with some folksy girl-singer music playing, and a display of bright, childlike paintings hung up on the grey walls. I wonder if my art will hang in places like this, someday.

Mina wraps her hand around her cup and sits there with her foot jittering. I wait for her to talk, the Dark Energy curdling in my stomach, because suddenly I see the patterns and I think I know what is coming. I think I've known for a while what the Dark Energy wants, but I didn't want to admit it. I don't want to know that I'm too much trouble, that Mom was right. I don't want life to be cruel like this.

"Justin, I love you," she says.

"I love you too, Mina." I'm tearing my drink sleeve to pieces. I want to run but I can't move. Pain is hovering around the edges, but it hasn't bled its poison into my heart yet.

Tears fill up Mina's eyes and fall onto the varnished wood table. "I can't do this," she says, her voice shaking. "You're just not ready for a relationship yet, Justin. It's not fair to you. Maybe after your medication is adjusted—"

"Mina," I say, my voice thick. The pain is trickling in now. "Please don't do this. I'm sorry I'm so much trouble."

"It's not that. It's just that I think I'm making you worse. I'm all messed up over the fact you're all the way here in the City, and with that girl, and my feelings are scary and confusing to you."

I swallow. "You know Liria and I aren't together, and I can't help the way the Dark Energy flows."

"It's not your fault, Justin, I know that. And I know you say that..." She winces. "I just...she...I don't think that things are going to..." She hides her face in her hands, and when she takes them away, her cheeks are smeared with tears. "I just don't want this to end up too complicated. I love you, Justin. And I want...I want you to be okay. You don't deal with stress well, and you've got a lot going on. I want us to be able to stay friends without it turning out bad."

I can feel my throat closing up. The pain is gushing in a torrent. I can't say anything. I lean my forehead against the table, because I can't bear to look.

Mina comes over and sits beside me, and puts her arms around me. "I just...I'm starting school...my senior year...I'd never be able to come see you. My dad's right. It's too much...it's not fair to you..."

"It's not fair, no it's not," I say. I'm so angry at the Dark Energy right now. The pain is unbearable, boiling up from my stomach into my throat, and I'm crying.

"Justin..." She presses her cheek against my shoulder, and I can feel her tears. "Justin I'm sorry."

She kisses my cheek, and then I hear her get up, and she's gone, her presence disappearing from around me like the roots of some beautiful flower that was embedded in my soul, now pulled up, leaving the soil loose and scattered and pointless.

I don't know how long I sit there, because the world doesn't make sense to me right now and I'm not paying attention to it. All I know is that eventually I feel arms go around me again, and I smell sandalwood and cloves.

"Come on, Justin," Liria says.

I take my head off the table, look up at her. "What's happening? How are you here?"

"I knew she was going to pull this bullshit, so I came looking for you after a while." She takes my hand very gently. "Let's go."

We leave the coffee shop, and I stumble after her, down the sidewalk and back to our hotel room. The whole world is in a haze.

When we're there, I crawl up onto the bed and put my face in the pillows. Liria tugs my shoes off, and stretches out beside me, stroking the back of my neck. I roll over, and take her in my arms. It feels so good to have her there.

Liria and I are together in the Other Place, and so we know each other very well. There are no secrets there. Our souls are laid out for inspection as if they were drawn on paper, and so she probably knows she makes my heart feel warm and full and fierce. She probably knows she turns my pain into something beautiful, because of the way it reflects off of her. I can't help I feel this way about her. I just can't. And, even though she'll never be with me in the way Mina was, I know I'm lucky.

"Liria, I'm very glad I have you," I say.

Liria presses her lips to my forehead, and my skin burns where she touched me. "I'm very glad I have you too, Justin," she says.

It's unfair the Dark Energy would take Mina away and then make me fall in love with someone who doesn't want me like that, but I'm powerless against it, and should count the blessings I have.

Chapter 20

We walk into Stewart's gallery the next day to find the place all torn up, the walls moved around, plastic on the floors, the smell of fresh paint zinging our noses. Stewart's voice comes from the back somewhere. "No, not there, you dope, what is this, a craft warehouse? Are we selling glitter paint and cross-stitch patterns?"

Ghana, his green-eyed employee with the dreadlocks, peeks around the edge of one of the walls at us and smiles. "Justin's here."

Stewart stops yelling, and his feet clack over the tile toward us. "Justin, Christina." He's smiling, but his gaze skitters around nervously. "Let's go in my office."

We follow him back. We sit down in front of his desk, and he settles down into his chair, crossing his legs, folding his hands in his lap, and regarding us with a strange grin. Finally, his jumpy glance settles on Liria. "Arty stopped by yesterday afternoon," he says.

"Fuck," Liria breathes.

267

"She had no idea Justin was my new artist." His voice is sly, and Liria drags her hand across her face.

"You *told* her?"

"Well, I didn't know I wasn't supposed to! I knew there had been an incident, but I didn't know…" He raises his eyebrows, plying her with a grin. "How was I supposed to know it was *him* she's all antsy-pantsy about, Christina? You told me you left because you were tired of her, you know, little business."

Liria snorts. "That *was* why I left. And the fact she didn't want Justin there, because she didn't trust him."

He crosses his arms, looking back and forth between us and smirking openly. "So you chose him over her."

Liria stomps both feet on the floor. "Stewart! It's not like that."

My heart squeezes, because I want it to be like that.

Stewart holds up both his hands. "It's okay. You don't have to justify it to me, Christina. He's a genius, and he's very handsome."

My face is burning, and Liria shoots me a commiserative look before swinging her gaze back to Stewart. I just hope she can't see what I'm feeling in the Dark Energy around me.

"Is there a point to this commentary?" she asks.

His grin falls and he sighs, taking his glasses off and pinching the bridge of his nose. Then he looks at us more seriously. "Arty has just been my friend for quite a while—"

"You're not going to let that bitch talk you out of this contract with Justin!"

"No, no way, Christina, calm down." They are locked in a staring contest for a few moments before Liria settles down a bit.

"There's no way I'd back out of this contract," Stewart continues, "so don't worry about it. I just had to do some crowd control. That's all." He uncrosses and crosses his legs the other way.

"I'm sorry I've caused you so much trouble, Stewart," I say.

He looks at me, and his face fills up with a sort of pity. "No, Justin, not at all. I mean, Christ, even if Arty shot up the place with a machine gun you'd still be less trouble than half the artists I've worked with." He winces, as if recalling an uncomfortable situation. "Anyhow, she's all settled down now. She really liked your work, even. I mean, of course she did, everyone does. She made me an offer I couldn't refuse on the painting of you, Christina. So that one will go to her after the show."

Liria presses her fingers to her eyes, and I think about how complicated human relationships are.

"Also," Stewart continues, "just fair warning, she'll be there, at the opening."

Liria brings her hands down in a hard smack on her thighs, and stares, tight-jawed, at Stewart.

A hard jitter runs through me. "I think that's not a good idea," I say.

"Now, we're all adults here," Stewart says. "We can handle a little relationship drama without going off the deep end, right?"

"She keeps threatening to kill us," Liria says.

269

Stewart waves his hand dismissively. "Oh, that's just Arty. She always does that."

We all suddenly burst out laughing, although it isn't exactly funny.

"Really?" Liria asks. "Has she threatened to kill you, Stewart?"

He shifts in his seat. "Yes, once. It's a long story."

Liria and I stare at each other, communicating our fear silently. Liria sighs. "We'll be good if *she* is."

"Excellent," Stewart says. He grins. "Those shenanigans aside, everything is going well here with the show. Also I talked to my friend Terry, and he does have a studio apartment coming available in a couple weeks. I convinced him to let you have it for a fifteen hundred a month on a year contract. It's an absolute steal. The location isn't bad—it's far enough up from Tenderloin you could almost call it Nob Hill. And it's beautiful. I've seen it. He says you can go look at it tomorrow or the next day."

My heart dries up in my chest. "But I don't have fifteen hundred dollars a month," I say. "Only eight hundred from Social Security."

"Oh, you'll be making money," Stewart says. "Just keep painting. And Christina here, I'm sure she'll get some sort of job, right?"

She and I exchange a glance. "Sure," she says, rolling her eyes at him. "My references are excellent. I'll just have them call Arty."

"Use me as a reference," Stewart says. "I'll say you worked here, but I fired you for being too efficient and good-natured. If they know my

270

employees, they'll believe me."

Liria gets a sort of blank look on her face, and clutches her elbows. "Okay. I'll get a job. Tell him we'll take the apartment."

"Christina—" I say.

"Don't worry about it, Justin. I'll get a job. This is our only real option right now."

I know we're both thinking this must be what the Dark Energy wants. I nod. "Okay," I say.

"Super," Stewart says, clapping. "I'll call my friend today."

***

As soon as we get back to the hotel, Liria puts on a dress to go out job hunting. I suggest that maybe we should dye the blue out of her hair first, but she snorts and tells me I don't know about San Francisco. "I'm not going to apply to be the mayor," she says, carefully drawing thick, black lines around her beautiful eyes. "Just at coffee shops and stuff."

She struts out to gather applications, and I'm proud of her because she's told me she's never really had a job before, at least for more than a few days.

I get out my big, new canvas and start painting with watercolors while I wait for her. The Dark Energy smoothes out when I paint, and my pain about Mina doesn't crush me so much.

I like how watercolors soak into the canvas and bleed into one another, although it takes longer to paint with them than it does with oil paints,

271

especially when it's the sort of thing I'm working on now, on a canvas this big. The Dark Energy is showing me a dollop of different-sized soap bubbles all reflecting an image of the City out my window, each image slightly different, and when you stand back, the little bubbles make an image of a big bubble reflecting a grassy landscape with willow trees.

I'm not sure why the Dark Energy is having me paint this. There might be a lesson in it somewhere, only I have to work harder to learn it because of the medication.

I'm not sure how long I'm painting, because I'm pulled into the Other Place and there's no time there. I come back to the Physical World when the door opens and Liria comes back in with a slight grin.

"I got a job," she says.

I blink as everything fades back into existence around me, both my dull sadness because of Mina, and the warm pang I get from being around Liria.

"That was very fast. Most people say it's difficult to get a job."

Her smile goes lopsided. "I know how to talk to people. That's all."

I study her smug, happy face. "What is this job? Is it the mayor job, after all? Or something even better?"

"At a coffee shop down the road from here, the Mean Bean. I start tomorrow."

"That's good," I say. "I'm very proud of you."

She comes over, and puts her arms around me. I have to hold the paintbrush out so I don't accidentally smudge her. Her good smell is all around me, and her cheek is warm against my shoulder.

"Thank you, Justin," she says.

"I don't know why you're thanking me. You're the one getting the job."

She grins, and she is incredibly beautiful. "You make my life so much better, is why."

For a moment, my good emotions are overwhelming. It's like the feeling I got the time Mom took me on a roller coaster, and it plunged downward so fast I felt like I was falling, then I got lifted up in a loop-de-loop. "You also do that for me," I say, though I wish I had the words to say more than that.

***

Liria gets up early the next morning, and spends a long time in the bathroom. I hear the hair dryer going, and when she comes out she looks very nice, with her blue hair sticking up just right and held down with an arrangement of clips. She smiles. I can tell she's excited.

I tell her to have a nice time at her new job, and she skips out the door, her hips swaying in her blue slacks.

A couple hours after she leaves, I get a call from Stewart.

"Have you seen your interview in *The Chronicle* yet?" he asks.

"No," I say. "Is it out?"

He laughs like a kid who has eaten too much

candy. "Yes. Come down here, and I'll show it to you."

So I stow away my paints and brushes and walk to the gallery. Mist billows over me as I walk, and I'm soaked by the time I get there, my hair hanging like a damp rag over my ears and down my neck. I wonder if I should get it cut, but I don't want to waste my money on those sorts of things. It's just hair and it's not going to truly screw up anyone's life by being long, despite what Mom always says.

Ghana is clearing away the plastic from the floor as I walk in, and she smiles. "Hey, Justin."

"Hello," I say.

Stewart comes from around one of the dividing walls. "There you are! Good Lord, you're all wet."

"Yes, it's raining," I say. "I think maybe the Rain God sits over the City, and that's why it's always drenched. Maybe his ex-girlfriend lives here with her new lover and he's spying on them, and trying to punish them."

Ghana laughs, wrinkling her nose. "He's like, 'Take that, bitch! You mess with Rain God, I'm going to make you all wet!'"

I wipe the droplets from the back of my neck. "It'd be hard to forget about a relationship with Rain God when he's always reminding you of it that way."

Stewart smirks at us. "You two." He squeezes my shoulder. "Come on into my office, Justin."

When we get there, he hands me a section of the newspaper.

My fingers leave damp smudges on it as I read. The article is on the front page of the arts section, and there is a picture of me Mr. Lagrange took during the interview, as well as pictures of several of my drawings and the uncomfortable painting.

I sit and read while Stewart twiddles his thumbs and taps his pen. The article is mostly about how I am a boy from horribly sad circumstances who has no education, but who draws and paints what Mr. Lagrange calls "fantastic and bizarre images which combine the ethereal with the gut-wrenchingly corporeal." He calls me "the most promising new artist and most developed natural talent" he's ever seen in his career. It gives the date of my opening at the end, and some information about Stewart's studio.

I put the paper down when I'm done.

"Well? Pretty excellent review, right?" Stewart says. He's almost bouncing in his chair.

"He says some nice things about my pictures," I say. "I don't know how I feel about what he said about my life, though, because it makes me sound pitiful. I don't know why Christina wanted to tell him those things."

Stewart wrinkles his nose. "Oh, that. People love a good story. It will get the old ladies on your side. They'll start baking you casseroles and knitting you sweaters, and they'll buy up all your work and hang it where everyone can see, so they'll have conversation-starters for their book clubs. Besides, it's all true, right?"

I twist my hands in my lap. "In a manner of speaking."

"So don't worry about it." He stands up. "Come into the gallery, and tell me what you think of our color scheme."

We spend the rest of the afternoon deciding where to put all of my pictures. Later, he takes me to see the apartment Liria and I will be renting so I can get a look at it.

It's in the middle of being painted and having the bathroom retiled, but it still has a good feeling to it, because of the hardwood floors and big windows all around. It is very small, only slightly bigger than our hotel room, but I guess that's good because we won't have to buy so much furniture.

By the time I get home, Christina is already there, eating a piece of cake and watching cartoons.

"How was your first day as part of the workforce?" I ask.

She swallows her cake, and shrugs. "I messed up a couple coffees, but it was fun. Were you with Stewart?"

"Yes. We were talking about where to put my paintings, and we went to see the apartment."

She sits up straight and huffs, spitting a few cake crumbs over the bedspread. "You went to see the apartment without me?"

I back off from her slightly. "I didn't know it was of paramount importance to you."

"Of course it is! That's going to be our apartment! And I've never had my own apartment before." She stares at me avidly, as if she could see an image of the place in my brain if she looks hard enough. "What's it like?"

So I tell her about the hardwood floors and the big windows. She seems very excited about it, and asks questions about whether we can have a couch and houseplants, and where we will put them.

"Oh, and also, the art review came out," I say, to get her to stop asking questions about the kitchen appliances. I didn't inspect them closely enough, apparently.

"It did? What did it say?"

I hand her the paper, because Stewart gave me a copy, and she sits reading it. She breaks into a grin, and laughs. "This is awesome, Justin."

"Yes, it's really something," I say.

My phone begins buzzing on top of the desk. Liria gives me a wary look. I'm confused about who would be calling me, but then I pick it up and see that it's Mina. A pain shoots through my heart. I hesitate just a moment before pushing the answer button.

"Hello?" I say.

"Hi, Justin." Mina's voice is quiet and hoarse, and I have to give myself time to let some of my sadness drain out.

"Mina," I say. "How are you?"

I hear Liria snort, and glance at her. She's squinting at me with her arms crossed.

"I'm..." Mina says, then takes a huge breath and lets it out. "Justin, I miss you, and I'm sorry I did that to you. I'm sorry I left you there like that. It was wrong. I was just so messed up..."

I sit on the bed and slouch down very low. "I understand. You were very hurt and unhappy because of the way things were happening."

The Dark Energy sings a sad note. Liria comes over, and puts her arm around my shoulders, and it helps, but I also feel guilty because of how I feel

277

warm inside, and how my skin tingles when she touches me.

"Justin…" Mina says. "Justin, I still love you and want to be with you."

I pluck at the quilt. "Then why did you leave me, Mina?"

"Because I'm just so…I mean, I just can't stand spending all my time thinking about you, and feeling jealous and alone and worried. But it's no better now."

I don't know what to say, so I don't say anything. My emotions swirl around in my stomach. I'm glad but not glad, and very confused.

"Justin, I want to see you again," she says.

I press my hand over my eyes, because it's hard to look at the world. "I want to see you again too." But I'm not entirely sure that's true, actually.

Liria twitches next to me. *"Fuck that,"* she hisses. "Tell her to fuck off, Justin."

I know Mina hears her, because there is a silence. She speaks in a very small voice. "Are you with her now? Is Christina your girlfriend now?"

"No, Mina. We're just friends, like always."

"Then you don't have to listen to her," Mina says. "Justin…I just want to see you, and talk."

I pluck at the quilt some more, the stitching beginning to fray. "When could you come?" It's hard to get the words out through my tight throat.

But then Liria yanks the phone from my hand and brings it to her ear, her brown eyes flashing.

"Stop fucking with him, Mina," she says, and I can feel the heat of her anger as I sit there frozen. "He's the nicest, most amazing person in the world, and I don't blame you for realizing you were a dipshit to throw him away, but he has enough to deal with right now without you jerking him around. You need to figure your own shit out and grow up, but leave him out of it."

I hear Mina's voice yelling, and Liria's eyebrows scrunch together. "You should have *seen* what he was like after you broke up with him. He doesn't need that. He needs to move on. *So fuck off* and leave him alone."

Liria jabs the hang-up button and tosses the phone on the bed. She looks at me as I sit there with my mouth hanging open.

"You don't deserve that bullshit," she says very seriously.

"I don't know," I say. "I don't know what I deserve."

She raises her eyebrows, and throws her hands up in the air. "Justin. She's fucking with you. It's not fair."

I feel very shaky inside, with my emotions shoving around everywhere. I go to my easel and get out my paints.

I think I know now what lesson the Dark Energy is trying to teach me, and it's that seeking enlightenment is much easier than dealing with girls.

Chapter 21

Stewart is wide-eyed and pale, with sweat beading on his forehead. He's ordering his employees around with a voice like an angry Chihuahua, and the Energy around him is very agitated. I'm nervous. It's the day of my opening, and I wish I could go running or paint, but Stewart wants me there. I'm not sure why, though, because I'm mostly just standing here watching him be angry.

Caterers bring in boxes of wine and glasses and plates of finger food. Ghana tries to adjust the lighting while Stewart yells confusing instructions at her. I clutch Liria's hand, watching the chaos spread around me.

"This is bullshit," Liria mutters. "I'd rather be back in our apartment than watching Stewart have an episode."

"Yes, we could sit on the floor and stare at the bare walls," I say. "It would be very peaceful."

She shoots me a little grin, and rolls her eyes.

Terry, Stewart's friend, let us move in early

since we lost our hotel room, but we still have no furniture, so it is just our clothes and my painting stuff and some sleeping bags Stewart loaned us. We've been so busy we haven't even had time to buy air mattresses.

"I'm glad you took the day off of work to be with me," I say.

She grins, and bumps her hip against mine. "Of course I did, Justin. This is really important." Then her smile fades, and she gets a strange look on her face. "This is important to me too, because you're my best friend. You're the best friend I've ever had."

I feel warm when she says this, but I also feel like someone has poured lemon juice on my guts.

"You're the only person that I've ever met in the Other Place," I say. "You're the most important person to me."

She breaks into a big grin, and she is so beautiful.

Then Stewart claps his hands. "Justin! Hello! I'm talking to you!" And so I let go of Liria's hand so I can go help him decide if we need to switch some of the drawings around yet again.

I finished my large watercolor painting a few days ago. It took me a long time, because it is so big and complicated, and because I've been so busy. It is up in the prominent place on the back wall so that everyone will see it as they walk in. Stewart says that it is the most amazing thing he's ever seen, but I believe he is over-excited about most everything lately.

Before too much longer, people start showing

281

up, even though it's early. Paul Lagrange is there with a photographer and some friends.

Stewart isn't barking anymore. His voice has melted into a stream of honey. He is acting very polite and shaking hands, introducing me to everyone, taking them around to see my drawings.

I try to answer all of their questions, but it's difficult. What they say sometimes doesn't make sense to me. They are using words like arrangement and contrast and juxtaposition, and telling me how I did this or that as if I'd put the images together like a puzzle, but they are over-thinking it, because I just drew or painted what the Dark Energy put into my mind. But I don't want to say that, so I do a lot of nodding and smiling.

Every time I hear the door open, both Liria and I jerk our heads in that direction. We are expecting Arty to walk in at any moment. Every time we look and it isn't her, a sizzling blast of adrenaline trickles down into my stomach and fizzes there.

Two o'clock comes, which is the official time the opening is supposed to start, and a lot more people start showing up. There is music playing, and I'm being introduced to so many people I can't remember their names. Their bright-eyed faces swirl around me, laughing and eating little pastries and slices of cheese. They are all very nice and ask me lots of questions, and tell me lots of good things about my pictures.

There is a man there who says he is with the New York Times, who read Paul Lagrange's article and was curious about me. He stands talking to me a long time, going around to all my different pictures. He doesn't tell me what techniques I've used to make the images, like other people do, but instead asks me why I've made them. He listens more than other people do too, and I think he knows about the Dark Energy, because of the deep look he gives me when I tell him about the lessons behind some of the pieces.

After he has seen everything he shakes my hand and goes to talk to Stewart, and I feel strange because he is having thoughts that I can't quite understand, I think.

I'm standing in front of my big watercolor with a woman named Patty, who is making little gaspy noises, her finger hovering an inch from the canvas as she traces the lines I've painted, when I feel an angry ripple in the Dark Energy.

I look over at Liria. She is staring at something behind me with her lips pressed tightly together. I get a jolt of fear, because I know Arty must finally be here.

But when I glance around, it isn't Arty. It's Mina, looking very pretty with her hair freshly cut, in a blue dress that I've never seen before. My heart twangs and aches as she comes over to me, her hands clutching the straps of her backpack.

Her eyes dart around the room. "Hi, Justin."

"Mina, you came." I stare for a moment, the Dark Energy tightening and zinging around me. Liria is glaring at Mina, and Patty is looking confused, and I remember that she is there, and that I have obligations. Stewart has spent a long time preparing me for this social dance.

"Mina," I say, "this is Patty. Patty, this is my

friend, Mina, who originally introduced me to Stewart, turning the first cog in the circumstances machine which brought about this art opening."

Patty shakes Mina's hand, and says some things, but I can't pay attention. Mina's eyes keep finding mine, and they are nervous and sad.

Patty wanders off to another painting, and for a moment Liria, Mina, and I stand in turbulent silence.

"It was very good of you to come, Mina," I say, and Liria fidgets beside me, picking at her fingernails.

"Of course I came," Mina says. "This is a big deal, and I wanted to be here to support you. Although it looks like you drew a crowd, and don't really need my support." She stares around, but she doesn't look like she's really seeing anybody.

"Yes, Stewart did a good job with advertising," I say.

She looks back up at me through her long, black eyelashes. "Would you...would you maybe go out for coffee or something with me when this is over?"

"I think that would be very nice," I say, although my stomach hurts saying it.

I still love Mina. I still want to be with her. I know I really want to be with Liria, but that is not possible because she doesn't like me that way. So I don't know how to feel about anything.

Stewart comes over and introduces more people to me, and Mina wanders off, looking at all my pictures.

There are a lot of people here, and and I'm trying to concentrate, even though my feelings are like angry sharks snapping at my insides. I have just finished talking to a woman and her husband who were telling me how much they like the uncomfortable painting, when Liria grabs my hand.

"I need to talk to you," she mutters.

She glances around to make sure Stewart isn't watching, then pulls me through the back door and into his office. I let her pull me, fear prickling the back of my neck, because I'm certain that she's going to tell me that Arty has arrived, or something else bad.

It is quieter back here, the murmur of voices and music coming through the walls, and I can hear my heart beating. "What's wrong?" I ask.

A crease forms between her eyebrows. "Justin, I don't want you to go out with Mina after this."

This is not exactly what I was expecting. My heart settles down a little bit, but finds a different way to race. "Why not?" I ask.

"She's just going to hurt you again!"

Outside the window it's starting to rain, and people are walking by, some of them laughing with each other, others slouching through the damp with brooding faces. There is so much going on in the world right now all around us. For a moment, I can feel the Dark Energy flowing, all of these people and their lives and thoughts fitting together like an ever-changing puzzle which makes up the world, and me part of it, here at this little art opening, with all these confusing things going on with the women in my life.

"I don't think that's her intention, to hurt me," I say. "She just wants to have coffee."

"Justin, she wants to get back together with you."

"That's not trying to hurt me," I say.

I pause for a moment, twisting the untucked hem of my nice button-down shirt. My words are all jumbled up on my tongue and don't want to come off.

Liria takes my hand to stop me from tearing my shirt apart, and suddenly the feeling of her skin against mine is like sweet fire and I almost want to take my hand away, because I can't stand it. It's too much.

"I don't know if I should get back with her," I say in a hoarse voice. "But…"

I can't complete the sentence. I don't want to make Liria mad, because she seems to have a strong opinion about Mina. I want to at least be Liria's friend. The Dark Energy brought us together, and it might be dangerous to mess it up.

"Justin, she's no good for you," Liria says. She huffs and stomps and then looks up at me, and something about her eyes makes my breath stop, my heart beat against my ribs. "Justin, I don't want you to be with her."

I want to ask her why not, but I don't have the air to get the words out, because Liria steps closer to me. I can feel her body pressed against mine, all her curves fitting perfectly against me. "You're not like other people," she says very quietly.

"Liria," I say. And suddenly I want to tell her everything. I want to tell her I love her, but that doesn't even seem like the right word. It is more than that. It is a feeling which seems to rise up out of the earth and clean away the confusion, and make everything settle into place and make sense. But I don't get a chance to say anything because we hear the door open, and Stewart's voice.

"Justin, are you back here? Oh…" We turn, and he's smirking at us, tapping his fingers against his lips. But behind his smirk his eyes flash with fear, and the Dark Energy sings an unsettling note.

"What, Stewart?" Liria says angrily.

He opens his mouth and takes a breath, then closes it again and winces. "Now, I don't want you guys to freak out." He falls silent and fidgety again.

"Well, if you don't tell us what's up, we're going to," Liria growls.

Stewart's eyes meet mine, and his look gives me a jolt. "The police are here," he says.

"What?" Liria says, going very stiff.

"Why are the police here?" I say, pressing closer to Liria. She puts her arm around me, running a soothing hand along my back. I'm very dizzy. I'm thinking they're here to arrest Liria for selling drugs, or Stewart for taking them, and that there is going to be a huge commotion. I imagine the officers smashing up my paintings with their clubs, looking for hidden cocaine. I wonder if there is a back exit.

"I don't like the police being here," I say. "I don't have anything to do with illegal situations. I don't know why these things keep happening."

Stewart lays a hand on my shoulder. "Don't worry. It's going to be all right."

"But the police being here is the definition of things not being all right," I say. "They have death in them, and hurt and fear and humiliation." The Energy jitters up inside me, and I cover my face with my hands.

Liria wraps her arms around me. "I'm not going to let them hurt you," she says. "I promise, Justin."

I take my hands from my face and look at her, and some of my agitation calms down.

"You okay?" she asks.

"Yes," I say. "I'm okay because you're here, Liria."

She blinks at me and smiles, then turns to Stewart, her smile falling into a frown. "But why are they here? You haven't even told us."

Stewart grimaces. "Because of your goddamn mom, Justin."

The Dark Energy courses through me like electricity and sewage. All of my organs jostle around like they place is on fire and they're looking for the way out.

Liria pounds a foot against the floor. "What the fuck! Why? What did that bitch do now?"

"Is this about Rebekah again?" I ask, and my legs are shaking.

"Now, calm down," Stewart says. "It's going to be okay. We're going to handle this, all right? It's not about any Rebekah, or whoever. They just want to talk to you for a second, and give you some papers. Are you going to be okay with that, Justin?"

He looks at me searchingly, and I know he is worried the Dark Energy will take me. I am very dizzy, but Liria is holding me. That and the medication are keeping me here in the Physical World.

Liria's dark eyes are worried. I wipe the sweat from the back of my neck.

"I'm going to be okay," I say. I look at Liria and Stewart very seriously. "But please don't let them arrest me. That is very extremely unpleasant."

Liria's eyes go wide, and she presses her lips together. "Over my dead body. You haven't done anything wrong."

Stewart raises his eyebrows at me. "They're not going to arrest you. I won't let them."

"I'm glad I have friends like you," I say.

Liria's hand creeps up the back of my shirt as she gazes at me, her fingers brushing my bare skin. Stewart looks away at the walls with a strange expression.

But he smiles and squeezes my shoulder. "Let's get this over with. You ready?"

I nod.

"All right, I'll be right back," he says.

He goes out, leaving Liria and me alone again. We can hear talking and laughing when Stewart opens the door to the gallery, and then it is muffled again as it closes.

Liria looks at me. "Justin...," she says, but doesn't say anything else. She just lays her cheek on my shoulder. I hold her, and I'm almost able to forget about everything, about the police, and Mina, and Arty, until I hear the door to the gallery open again, and footsteps in the hallway.

Liria pulls away from me but keeps holding my hand.

Two uniformed police officers appear in the doorway. One of them is a pudgy man, his mousy hair receding back from his temples. The other is thin woman with an unhealthy-looking brown ponytail.

Both of them watch me closely as they come into the room, sidling around me, as if I'm a growling dog. Behind them, Stewart scuttles in.

Then, after him, walking with slow steps, her hands in her pockets, comes Arty, and my guts freeze.

Her eyes fall on Liria, then on me, and then our clasped hands. She smiles very slightly. It is not a cruel smile, but a thoughtful one.

Liria goes very rigid. I wonder why Arty is here, and what she is thinking, but I don't have time to wonder very much, because the female officer speaks.

"Justin Flaherty?" she asks.

"Yes, that's me," I say.

She has a sheaf of paperwork in her hands, and she holds it out to me. "We're here to serve you with a petition for guardianship. Your mother, Jane Flaherty, has filed a petition with the San Francisco County Superior Court to be named as your legal guardian, and the manager of your personal finances, alleging you lack the capacity to do so yourself."

Liria scowls, and huffs, but I just take the paperwork from the officer. I stare at it but I don't try to read it because all those words are just black marks.

"Your mother has also filed a request that you be evaluated by a mental health professional," the officer says.

"But we both know you can't take him into custody for that," Arty says.

The Dark Energy hisses around me woozily. Both officers' faces jerk over to squint at Arty, and she raises her eyebrows at them. She suddenly looks very formidable, with her little superior smile.

"Ma'am, we could certainly take him into custody if we see fit," the male officer says in his cop voice, but Arty just smiles wider at him, as if he were a little child who had just said something ridiculous.

"Does he appear to be violent or mentally unstable to you?" she asks. "If his mother wishes him to be put away so that she can steal all his money, then she can speak to his lawyer, Patricia Harris at Harris, Castoro, and Miller. But it's not worth your jobs, I'm sure, to take a perfectly peaceful and law-abiding man into custody on an involuntary psych hold, and one who is certainly competent enough to pull off a very popular art opening in San Francisco."

The hard scowls on the officers' faces melt away, and they shift on their feet, looking at me quickly. I stand very still and let this all happen around me, because I'm not entirely sure what's going on.

"You don't seem to be an imminent threat to yourself or others, Mr. Flaherty," the female officer finally says. "We're just going to serve you with this paperwork, and leave it at that for now. Be sure to have your lawyer take a look at it right away, because you need to answer the petition within thirty days."

"I will," I say, clutching the paperwork in my sweaty hands.

The officers nod at me, then they head back out the door, this time skirting around Arty as if she were the barking dog. The voices in the gallery get louder as the door opens to let them out. Then it shuts again, and it's quieter.

Arty looks me over. Stewart frowns and stares at the ground. I just stand there, my heart fluttering in my chest. The Dark Energy is saying a lot of things right now, but it is talking too fast for me to hear it all.

"What the hell is going on here?" Liria says. I realize she is still holding my hand, because Arty's eyes dart to it again, and I wonder if I should let go. But I don't, because it is comforting.

"I just saved Justin's ass," Arty says calmly. "Where's the gratitude?"

"Thank you very much, Arty," I say. "But I'd also like to know what's going on, because it doesn't make sense that you would be taking an interest in these proceedings."

She blinks at me, then shakes her head at Stewart. "You didn't tell me he was such a gentleman."

Stewart runs his hand through his hair and gives her a jerky smile, but doesn't respond.

"Would you all please cut the crap?" Liria begs.

Stewart sighs. He finally looks at me, and his eyes are hard and bitter and pleading. "I didn't want to, Justin," he says. "I would never have...but I think it will be better for you anyway..."

I feel a sharp fear. This a bad thing, whatever it

is.

"What did you do?" Liria says, and I can hear tears in her voice.

"He did something that I think will turn out very well for all of us, *Christina*," Arty says, with a slight emphasis which turns Liria's fake name into a whole freight train full of emotions rumbling over toward us.

Arty focuses on me, her green eyes intent. She looks embarrassed, but I can see in the Dark Energy that she is not really embarrassed. She is something else, sly and hard and deliberate.

"Justin…I really apologize that we got off on the wrong foot," she says. "But I've been talking to Stewart, and I know now that I was wrong about you. You seem like a very nice and well-intentioned person, not to mention an extremely talented artist. Anyway, I'm sorry I was a jealous bitch. I hope we can start over, because I'd like to be friends."

"I'd like that too," I say carefully. Liria shifts on her feet beside me.

"Anyway, I hope that we can have a good working relationship," she says, smiling and showing her white teeth.

I look at Stewart, and he stares back at me like a frightened deer. "I don't know what you mean," I say, and Stewart winces, drawing his hand across his forehead.

"Arty bought your contract," he says in a strange voice. "You're *her* new, amazing artist now."

I go very stiff, because the Dark Energy has turned to concrete around me. Liria and I exchange a very frightened glance.

Arty smiles. "We're going to make a lot of money, you and I," she says.

Acknowledgments

I don't really know where to start with this book…of course I want to thank my lovely editor, Laura Kemmerer; my critique partners Katie and Chaitanya and Joey, Mike and Lillian and Jeannie; as well as my loyal beta readers and friends Faith, Aleena, Keith, and Joy (the latter whom has ended up being a better friend and supporter than I've any right to expect, as well as a great writer who has taught me a lot).

I also want to thank my daughter, Juniper, who, for the first time, read one of my books and became its wholehearted champion. You're my favorite person. You're an awesome kid who is growing into an awesome woman and a great friend, as well as an excellent writer. I'm damned lucky to have you.

This book was more than a technical and artistic challenge for me: it was an emotional challenge. All of you who are still there for me, thank you. I know I'm a piece of work. I guess the whole point of this book is that even those of us who are a piece of work have something to offer the world, and maybe we deserve love and friendship as much as anyone else. Those who offered support, comfort, advice, and even a place to stay when I was living rough in my car…those who kept an eye on my dog and on me (all those listed above, as well as Pastor Ivelisse, Mari, Mom, Dad, Tracy, Van, Tim, Susan, Gary and Naomi…countless others, I'm sure), I owe you my thanks, my life, and an apology. I hope that this book is some sort of recompense. It's what I have to offer, it's my shout into the Darkness, and my attempt at showing the beauty and life that exists for those whom others tend to ignore and avoid; those people in whom society sees very little beauty, to society's detriment.

And, of course, Phoenix. I didn't really know you when I was drafting these novels. You were some amazing dude that I talked to in the park for half an hour, who made me laugh and feel alive, made the world into this immediate place where things were happening and beautiful right now. I couldn't get you out of my head.

Justin is not you, Phoenix, even though you made him come into my mind. Your lives are very different (though, when I got to know you, I discovered the parallels were incredibly eerie). You did help me to know Justin better, though, and to know myself better, and to make this book what it is.

Phoenix: getting to know you has made me believe in God. It has made me believe in scalp-tingling synchronicity. It has made me, for a few incredible hours as well as other passing moments, believe you are a telepathic psychic brain vampire, and that time is non-linear. It has made me question what reality is. It has fucked up my life.

Thank you for fucking up my life, Phoenix. I mean that earnestly. It needed fucking up, and I'm glad it was done. I needed to stop and smell the cinnamon rolls. I've spent my whole life thinking there was something wrong with me, when there's not. I just am a person who spends too much time in the Other Place, and that's cool, especially if I have you for company.

I hope that, because of this book, more people might get to know you and other people with schizophrenia and see them not as objects of pity, fear, or contempt, but as human beings, with as much life and love and intelligence in them as anyone else. Maybe a police officer will read this, and the next time they come across a person dealing with psychosis, they'll think twice before drawing their weapon, or arresting them for no other crime than being alive and being who they are. There is almost always another way, if you have compassion and patience.

And no, the things I wrote into this book will not come true just because I wrote them. At least I don't think so.

So, we're in business. Hey, society: you got your cinnamon rolls?

About the Author

Elizabeth Roderick grew up as a barefoot ruffian on a fruit orchard near Yakima, in the eastern part of Washington State. After weathering the grunge revolution and devolution in Olympia, Washington, Portland, Oregon and Seattle, she recently moved to the (very, very) small town of Shandon, California: a small cluster of houses amidst the vineyards of the Central Coast.

She earned a bachelor's degree in Spanish from The Evergreen State College in Olympia, Washington, and worked for many years as a paralegal and translator. She went on to study chemistry, physics, and higher mathematics, with the goal of becoming a research chemist, but was eventually forced to concede that graduate school would require too much time away from her husband and daughter, and that–despite her good-enough grades –she was perhaps the wrong kind of nerd for such pursuits, being more the type that likes to dress in cloaks and hauberks rather than lab coats and goggles.

She is a musician and songwriter, and has played in many bands. She's rocked pretty much every instrument, including some she doesn't even know the real names for, but mostly guitar, bass and keyboards. She has two albums of her own, which you can listen to at pimentointhehole.com. She writes fiction novels for young adults and adults, as well as short stories, and keeps an active blog at pimentointhehole.com/blog.

Facebook:
https://www.facebook.com/elizabethroderickauthor

Twitter:
https://twitter.com/LidsRodney

Website:
http://talesfrompurgatory.com/

www.ingramcontent.com/pod-product-compliance
Lightning Source LLC
Chambersburg PA
CBHW031555240626
47153CB00002B/511